MURDER BEFORE EVENSONG

A Canon Clement Mystery

MURDER BEFORE EVENSONG

A Canon Clement Mystery

The Reverend
RICHARD COLES

TITAN BOOKS

Murder Before Evensong
Print edition ISBN: 9781803364827
E-book edition ISBN: 9781803364834

Published by Titan Books
A division of Titan Publishing Group Ltd
144 Southwark Street, London SE1 0UP
www.titanbooks.com

First edition: June 2023
10 9 8 7 6 5 4 3 2 1

The Library of Congress Cataloging in Publication Data
is available upon request.

Printed and bound by CPI Group (UK) Ltd, Croydon CR0 4YY.

For Lorna
(who always reads the last page first)

Lighten our darkness we beseech thee, O Lord;
and by thy great mercy defend us from all perils and
dangers of this night.

The Third Collect for Evensong from
the Book of Common Prayer

1

Canon Daniel Clement AKC, Rector of Champton St Mary, stood in his pulpit, looking down on his parishioners. His text was taken from the Book of Numbers, the story of the Israelites turning against Moses for leading them not into the Promised Land but into a wilderness. A resonant story, not only for him but, he felt sure, for all fifty-eight of his predecessors, for flocks, then and now, were apt to turn. Moses averts mutiny by striking a rock, and a cataract of water miraculously pours forth, so his thirsty and restive people may drink; a resourceful tactic that suited Daniel's purposes too.

'Like Moses and the footsore of Israel,' he preached, 'we too must learn to live in hope, to look to the future, and to find in our present circumstances the resources to meet its challenge. As Moses struck the rock of Meribah and lo, a crystal stream poured forth, we too must allow new waters to flow, or rather to flush: my dear people, we need to install a lavatory.'

A frisson went through the congregation, mirroring the reverberation of that last, loaded word. It was as if someone had actually flushed something unmentionable in their midst.

St Mary's, a jewel of English Perpendicular, singled out for architectural merit and pastoral beauty, had managed without a lavatory for four centuries. Numberless Champtonians down the centuries had endured services of far greater length and frequency than today's without mishap; and the clergy, even those who lasted into their leaky nineties, managed too. Daniel suspected he was not the first incumbent of the parish to have discovered the corner between buttress and north wall (not visible from the path) in which a parson, unobserved, might take care of necessities while awaiting an overdue bride.

The frisson had settled by the communion, and Daniel waited at the centre of the altar steps, consecrated host in hand, for his flock to arrive at the rail. This always took longer than necessary. St Mary's, like so many churches, filled up from the back, leaving the front pews for the feeble, so that they could see and hear better (once the whistling of hearing-aid feedback had died down).

'Draw near with faith,' Daniel declaimed, not entirely suppressing a tone of mild exasperation, 'receive the body of Our Lord Jesus Christ which he gave for you, and his blood which he shed for you.'

Those hungry for eternal life would hurry, you might think, to accept so generous an offer. The choir was up in good order to be nourished before a swift return to their stalls to sing the anthem, but on the other side of the chancel arch no one moved until Lord de Floures – patron, landowner, employer, frequent absentee, but here today at Daniel's request – moved. Squeezing out of the family pew at the front, emblazoned with the de Floures circlet of flowers, he led an unsteady way through the chancel arch, wearing his Sunday tweeds (venerable would be a charitable word to describe them, thought Daniel, and wondered if they had strained to contain his father before him). It was the effects of last night's refreshment, rather than Bernard's fifty-seven years, that made him slowish, and he slightly stumbled as he passed the family tombs in the chapel on his left, where his ancestors lay in effigy, awaiting his own arrival.

Falling in behind him was Margaret Porteous, who overtook the other occupant of the de Floures pew, Anthony Bowness, Bernard's cousin and the recently appointed archivist at Champton, looking like Philip Larkin after a particularly bleak day at the library. She scooted past him at the chancel step, in tweeds too, but not so ancient as Bernard's and Anthony's, and with a Liberty headscarf over her shoulders. Margaret was not of the family, nor of the village; she was somewhere between the two, responsible for coordinating the volunteers who showed visitors round Champton House and its treasures on the two months a year his lordship opened it to the public – an arrangement agreed with the Inland Revenue to mitigate death duties (no wonder he seems gloomy, thought Daniel, with his grave on one side, death duties the other). Mrs Porteous, nimble in moccasins, caught up with Bernard at the rail so they arrived side by side, and knelt together. A slow crocodile of the faithful followed and spread and knelt, filling the rail from left to right, like text on a page – a text that told the story of Champton, its hierarchy, its light and shade, those who were in, those who were out, the fortunate, the unfortunate, the saintly and the works in progress.

There was Norman Staveley, county councillor, in cords and a blazer, to whom the world's estimation was important, striding to the rail a little too eagerly. Katrina Gauchet came next, head teacher at the primary school, with her two boys, but not her atheist husband, Hervé, who was at home making brunch (a Bloody Mary, poured when the ding of the sacring bell from the tower gave a fifteen-minute warning of her return). The Misses Sharman, Dora and Kath, twin spinsters, tiny too in stiff Sunday best, squeezed in next to the wriggling Gauchet boys.

Daniel worked his way down the line, doling out their Incarnate Lord.

'The body of Christ...'

'Amen.'

'The body of Christ...'

'Amen.'

'The body of Christ...'

'Thank you...' said Norman politely, as if he had been handed a canapé.

The organist, Jane Thwaite, married to Ned, who always attended but never received communion, struck up with the opening bars of the communion anthem, 'Thou Visitest the Earth', one of Daniel's favourites, the eighteenth-century C of E at its perkiest.

'Thou crooow-nest the yeear, the yeear with thy goo-oo-dness...'

And the year felt good indeed, as the spring sunshine flooded through the clerestory and the motes danced in it, and the queue for communion stretched the length of the nave. Up the people came – knelt, received and departed – most back to their pews, but one or two walked past their places and left, to avoid having to meet their neighbours – or the rector – at the door.

As the final hymn faded and the vestry prayers were said, Daniel went outside to take up his position by the porch. He looked out across the churchyard with its headstones – most now illegible, rearranged in orderly lines to make it easier for the sexton to mow – and beyond, over the ha-ha into the park, made fashionably disorderly by Humphry Repton in the 1790s when the lake was dug and follies built for a de Floures in thrall to the Romantick spirit of the age.

His successor, the present Lord de Floures, was first out, as always. 'Lavatory, Dan? They looked like you'd sworn at them.'

'Yes, odd, wasn't it? Why do you think they flinched like that?'

'Wee-wees and poo-poos. Don't want to think about that in church. We might have a fight on our hands, I fear. Come and see me this afternoon? Tea? Do bring your mother.'

'Thank you.'

Margaret Porteous, faithful follower of the master, was second out. 'Rector,' she said, glancing at him, 'such a lovely service!' as she sped past to catch up with Bernard.

The flower department followed, the formidable Mrs Stella Harper and her sidekick Mrs Anne Dollinger. Like many of their kind they had become flowery almost to the exclusion of everything else and appeared in related – if not quite matching – floral-print Sunday dresses, bought at cost from Mrs Harper's shop. As a badge of rank she had a silk flower corsage pinned wiltingly to the lapel of her jacket. Nature, alas, had not bestowed on either lady the freshness of spring; Mrs Harper was thin and stringy and thistly, described by Daniel's mother once as looking like 'an embittered cardoon'; Mrs Dollinger was bulky and square and slightly slobbery ('a knackerman's dog in drag'). They were stalwarts of the village scene, dutiful attenders at church but not consumed with interest in the items of the Nicene Creed, nor the liturgical proprieties of whatever season the church happened to declare; for them, it was really all about the flowers. There had been tensions in Lent as there were every year when Mrs Dollinger sought to undermine the No Flowers rule for this most austere season. In her view 'the more sombre kind of hyacinth' was not an infringement, and Daniel had been obliged to insist that it was. He sometimes thought they had started to think of the church primarily as a sort of giant flowerpot – the font a convenient oasis, the altar a giant stand for displaying arrangements, the village children walking pedestals for Mayday, carrying hoops wound with blossom and a bouquet for the crowning of the May queen. The Gauchet children, as if in training for the coronation procession, were doing circuits of the churchyard, propelled by energies stored up during the enforced stillness of the service. Stella Harper wrinkled her nose.

'Good morning, Rector,' she said, formal suddenly. 'These … improvements. Any idea of when?'

'Not yet, Stella. It's just a proposal at the moment for the parish church council to consider. What do you think?'

'Quite unnecessary. And the plumbing would be very difficult.'

'I think others would disagree. Many churches have loos now and the plumbing seems to present no difficulty. You have a tap and a sink, after all, for flowers.'

'Yes, but that's *quite* different. The noises, Daniel, the *noises*. No one wants to hear flushing during divine worship.'

'No one,' added Mrs Dollinger, with emphasis.

'No complaints in my last parish when we installed a lavatory there. Quite the opposite. People were glad to have it,' said Daniel.

'*There* is not *here*,' said Mrs Harper.

'Should we follow, like lemmings?' asked Mrs Dollinger.

'And where is it meant to go? In your vestry, perhaps, or the belfry?'

'There's plenty of room, Stella, at the back. We have far more seating than we need. Think of what we could do with that space—'

'I knew it!' said Stella. 'Why do you vicars hate pews so much? I've never met one who didn't want to turn them into matchwood.'

'They are our *heritage*,' added Mrs Dollinger.

'They're Victorian, mostly, so quite recent heritage. People managed without them for hundreds of years.'

'So where did they sit?'

'They didn't. Well, most of them, anyway. They just stood around, as best they could. It's where the expression the weak shall go to the wall comes from. The old and the feeble sat on benches against the walls,' explained Daniel.

'So you will tear out our lovely pews and force us to stand for Evensong?'

'No, just a couple of rows of pews at the back. But, as I said, everything is to be discussed,' said Daniel, flapping his hands in what he thought was an emollient way. 'Won't you stay for coffee?'

Anthony Bowness, on coffee duty that day with the Misses Sharman, was dispensing steaming water from an urn into styrofoam cups given a degree of dignity by dainty plastic holders.

It was not enough to pacify Mrs Harper. 'More discussions? Until you get your way? Your mind is made up, I suppose. Why will *no one* listen to us?'

'I am listening to you, Stella. I'm listening to everyone. It's a proposal. If the people don't want it, we won't do it.'

'You would say that! But you can't just get rid of pews willy-nilly. They're historical artefacts. What do you think English Heritage would have to say?'

'Victorian,' said Ned Thwaite, former headmaster of the junior school, who had spotted Stella from the porch and decided to intervene, 'nothing special, Stella.'

'Thank you, Ned,' she said, without looking at him, 'but I am speaking to the rector.'

Ned, a Boycott-blunt Yorkshireman when it suited him, said, 'I'm on the PCC, Stella, and this is a PCC matter. If you have a problem, stop bothering the rector and raise it with the PCC.'

Ned stuck his chin out and jangled his keys, which hung on a clip on his belt, an accessory so freighted with pouches and clips and penknives and the 'bumbag' a daughter had bought him for a joke in San Francisco that Daniel wondered how it did not pull his many-pocketed trousers down rather than keep them up.

It was enough. 'Oh, I shall, I shall,' said Stella. 'Don't forget, Rector, it's the flower guild AGM tomorrow evening. There's an item on the agenda that might give you pause.' She did not quite harrumph, but her departing look told Daniel that he did not have as much goodwill in the bank as he thought he had. He felt a little spike of anxiety.

'Told you,' said Ned.

'Told me?'

'Told you this would cause a fuss. It's *change*.'

2

It did not seem to matter if Daniel had been away for a week or a quarter of an hour, a loud and dissonant duet of barks was raised by his dachshunds, Cosmo and Hilda, as soon as he turned the keys in the lock. The profession of parson is congenial to dogs. Parsons work from home; country parsons, even in leaner times, have gardens; churches with clergy like Canon Clement for incumbents are dog friendly, the particular embrace of God's creatures indicated by a water bowl outside the south porch. There were darker purposes too: their frantic barking at the approach of callers, which he had decided not to attempt to train them out of, acted sometimes as a useful triage, necessary when you live in a house with a door officially open to all – except it is not, and never could be. Out and about, walking the dogs, they served as both invitation and barrier, and Daniel tried to apply these judiciously. But what he liked most of all about dogs was their innocence of human motives, the self-promoting stratagems and egotism, their affection unstaled by familiarity and reciprocity. This is why the queen surrounds herself with corgis, he sometimes thought: love without deference.

He whistled the fanfare he had started to use to announce his arrival to his mother. Her move into the rectory had obliged a revision of the house rules, but these – like the mysterious sum of laws and principles of the British Constitution – were often more discernible in the breach than the observance. If asked, she would have said she disliked whistling and thought it vulgar, but she had acquired somehow in the course of her life the ability to whistle like a builder, and replied with a piercing variation on his theme. 'I am here,' it sounded out, 'I am here too.'

Audrey Clement was indeed there. Her personality, powerful in her prime, was no less powerful in age, rather rising in proportion to the diminution of her physical strength. She sometimes reminded him of Pope Pius IX, who responded to the loss of sovereign powers over the papal states by making himself infallible.

He stooped to ruffle the dogs' ears, put his keys in the drawer and went into what was once the morning room, now his mother's sitting room. She had always liked the sun, and as she had got older and her eyesight began to fail, she had become greedy for light. Daniel – bachelor in habits, fussy and particular – had spent most of his time in the study, but the arrival of his mother had drawn him away from his desk and her sitting room had become his also, more heatable and more congenial than the drawing room, now reserved for parish business and the social whirl (a misleadingly dynamic phrase).

'Hello, darling,' she said, presenting a cheek to be kissed. 'Scargill. *Desert Island Discs*. On now.'

The sound of a choir singing 'Oh Love That Will Not Let Me Go' came out of the Roberts Radio firmly fixed on what Audrey Clement still called the Home Service.

'It doesn't sound like Arthur Scargill,' he said.

'Well it is. Chapel. From "Oh Love That Will Not Let Me Go" to "The Internationale" is a single step.'

'I suppose so. What else has he had?'

'Piaf. "*Je Ne Regrette Rien*".'

'How defiant. Do you want a coffee?' he said, already on the way to the kitchen, knowing the answer before it was spoken.

His mother had recently discovered decaf, decided it was a guarantee of elusive and uninterrupted sleep, and insisted on it; but Daniel was not prepared to have his morning deprived of its active ingredient. So two cafetières stood beside the kettle, and two Kilner jars, one with his coffee, the other with hers. He sometimes forgot which was which, and neither had noticed any difference, which suggested that both were more matters of the mind than the body.

'And a biscuit!' Audrey shouted.

As the coffees steeped in their pots, Daniel took down the biscuit tin from a shelf. It was round, green, made properly of metal, with a lid that still fitted despite being as dented as a banger car, decorated with a yellow rose that in fifty years had faded rather. Around the sides an accompanying nosegay of yellow roses against a background of green leaves continued the theme. How appropriate, it struck him, for the parson to the de Floures.

It was only a biscuit tin, but it was as precious to him as a reliquary, even if its contents were plain chocolate digestives rather than the withered finger of a discalced Carmelite. It was the biscuit tin of his childhood, salvaged from his parents' bungalow after his father's death, and brought to the rectory.

It had been a wedding present, rather a modest one he thought, but had served for more than half a century, and for that reason contained more than biscuits. It contained promise, reward, satisfaction; and memory too, as sure a key to that lock as Proust's madeleine.

The rattle of the biscuits summoned the dogs and the cartoonish sound of the claws clattering on the stone flags, distantly at first, rose in volume until they burst into the kitchen and skidded to a halt at his feet, Hilda leading Cosmo, tails wagging, nostrils flaring.

Sunday tea at Champton was not quite the splendid affair Audrey Clement had hoped for. A plate of Mr Kipling's French Fancies and a fruit cake that tasted like something baked for British Rail seemed out of place in the library of the splendid house the de Floures had lived in since long before Agincourt. The library was one of the additions of the Georgian era, part of a wing built by a Whiggish peer to provide more congenial living quarters than his predecessors considered necessary. The oldest part of the house, a medieval hall and chapel, was about as cosy as a Cistercian monastery; and that was enclosed by a Tudor house that aspired to be a palace as the de Floures fortunes waxed, full of pomp and state but lacking comfort. A splendid baroque front was added at the end of the seventeenth century, when a conquering peer returned from the wars much enriched for his troubles, but the inhabitants had to wait for the eighteenth century to be comfortable, when the library and the ballroom and a new drawing room were added (and for the nineteenth to be *sportif*, with another wing of bachelor bedrooms built for shooting parties over a suite of smoking room, billiard room and saloon).

The library looked out over the park, one of the best views in England, thought Audrey, admiring, as she always admired, the horse chestnuts and cypresses and oaks, the distant sheep nibbling grass, and more distantly, beside the lake, the deer grazing, brownish dots against silver in the afternoon sun. Her view was slightly impeded by Jove, one of the de Floures' cats, fluffy and white as a cloud, red in tooth and claw, who usually slept on the library steps, but was looking at the deer in the park too, tapping on the windowpane with his paw with an air of nonchalant predation.

'More tea?' asked Bernard, hovering over Audrey with a dribbling stainless-steel pot.

'Thank you,' she said, and tried, in vain, to capture the unpredictable flow in her cup. At least it was a cup, and rather a fine one, though she had not had an opportunity to look under it for a mark. When she and Daniel had arrived at Champton and were invited for the first time to lunch at the house, her first disappointment was the unconcern the family had for the treasures they had inherited. Cups and saucers were just tea things to them, thought Audrey, who knew her Spode from her Derby, and the portraits, thick on the walls, just a fancy album of half-forgotten and long-forgotten relatives – even if the recurring red hair and blue eyes announced them as de Floures as definitively as a toastmaster at a ball. Other disappointments followed. The first time they met, Bernard replied to her courteous use of his title with her Christian name, without offering his own in return, which left her, eight years later, still uncertain of what to call him. So she called him nothing. Her son had no such awkwardness, 'Daniel' to his 'Bernard' from the get-go, confident in this grander world than the one to which she and he belonged. Daniel did not seem to care for rank or title, as she did, which she supposed was a consequence of his calling rather than his character. As a boy he had been just as alert to grades of tone as she was. But then she had put it there.

She had no difficulty Christian-naming the next generation, the fruit of Bernard's second marriage. Honoria, his daughter, came towards her, her top half rippling in a pink cashmere sweater, her bottom tightly encased in what Audrey suspected might be 'designer jeans'.

'Audrey, what do you make of the lavatory drama?'

'I think it is a storm in a teacup' – she rattled hers in its saucer as she said it – 'once it's put in, everyone will be thankful for it and forget all this fuss. Don't you think?'

'Yes, I suppose so,' said Honoria, flicking a strand of hair away from her lovely face (how clever, thought Audrey, to go for pink cashmere with red hair). 'But there's something about lavatory and church that doesn't really go.'

'Wait till you're as old as I am.'

'Do you know, in my great-grandfather's day there were only two bathrooms. Dozens of bedrooms, if you count the attics. One loo between… I don't know, twenty? In the village there was one privy to twelve cottages, Anthony says. Imagine that? I think he said he was reading about it in some minutes from the Champton Charities. The "Privy Council", he called it.'

'I expect they would have washed in a bowl with water from a jug, if they washed at all. I remember doing this when

I was a girl. At school the dormitory windows were kept open whatever the weather, and in winter ice formed on the inside. Try washing with a jug and basin in that. I remember once having to pee in the night and the thought of the freezing cold lavatory was too much so I went in the basin.'

Honoria laughed. 'I can't stand not having enough bathrooms. I mean I can't stand not having my *own* bathroom.'

Honoria lived in London, her allowance supplemented by a job with a grand hotel as an 'executive consultant', a post which had created within her the expectation of en suite facilities.

Her younger brother, Alex, came to sit with them. He was obviously a de Floures too, the reddish-brown hair, the blue eyes, tall and slim like his sister, but with a less fortunate physiognomy – the frog-faced look of an English aristocrat unmistakable, although his outfit was Kings Road rather than Savile Row.

He was technically Honoria's flatmate in London, but since he had left the Courtauld, disillusioned and without a degree, he spent more time at Champton, where there was more room for what he called his 'art practice'. Audrey wondered why he had bothered to go all the way to the Courtauld to look at old pictures when he had so many to look at here, but Alex was not really interested in eighteenth-century portraiture, or portraiture of any period, even if it were of his own ancestors. He had fallen in with Long Pig – a movement that began in the radical fringe of art schools in London's redbrick suburbs – whose anarchic excitements he had found irresistible, and he had wrapped himself in its tattered flags. Today he was wearing a T-shirt Julien Temple created for the vanguard of punk, showing two cowboys greeting each other but naked from the waist down. Audrey, taking it in, noticed that their six-shooters were in fact their genitals.

'Goodness,' she said, 'what entertainments on the High Chaparral!'

In a reversal of the usual social polarity it was Alex who changed the subject, his embarrassment betrayed by the flush of red which went to his face.

'How are the dogs?' he enquired politely. 'Did you bring them?'

'No, they're at home. Unreliable around heritage, I'm afraid.'

She remembered watching Cosmo in the saloon lift his leg to mark a corner of a Persian rug of such antiquity and value even Bernard flinched.

'Heritage *is* terribly vulnerable,' said Alex, 'especially here. God knows how much Ming we've smashed over the years.' He caught Honoria's eye.

Audrey smiled. She could see over his shoulder Daniel talking to Bernard and Anthony Bowness, and sensed that porcelain was their subject too. 'I need to catch up with your father, Alex. Will you excuse me?'

'Of course.'

Audrey weaved her way across the threadbare rug carrying her cup and saucer. 'A refill, Audrey?' said Bernard. 'I'm afraid you'll find it stewed.'

The stainless-steel pot that never poured straight (Why would you do that, design a teapot that cannot pour? thought Audrey), was sitting on a hotplate resting on the lovely sideboard.

'I'm interested in your thoughts,' she said, 'about lavatory matters.'

'We were just talking about that,' said Bernard. 'Weren't you surprised by the reaction?'

'No, not really,' said Audrey. 'There are some things which just can't be spoken from a pulpit. I don't mind people being slain with the jawbones of asses, or Ban the Bomb, it's bodily functions I don't like. Do you remember, Daniel, your sermon on the woman with an issue of blood? That seems all right, somehow, but when you said what it actually was – menstruation – everybody shuddered.'

Daniel sighed. 'I'd forgotten about that. But this is ridiculous. What do you suppose it's really about?'

'I don't know,' said Bernard. 'Putting in a khazi makes perfect sense to me. I'd have written you a cheque today if it hadn't gone down so badly. I rather like the thought of the tenantry thinking kindly of me while they relieve themselves during one of your sermons. But you must sort it out.'

'Daniel,' said Anthony, 'I found a most interesting document in the Champton Charities archive.' There was something of the swotty boy about Anthony, even in middle age, with his slightly crooked glasses that he never fixed, his enthusiasm for arcana, which irritated Audrey.

'Privy Council?' she said.

'Oh,' he said, disappointed. 'You heard.'

'Yes. Honoria mentioned it.'

'Well, it seems ours is not the first lavatory controversy in Champton. One of your predecessors, Old Canon Segrave, caused a terrible hoo-ha in the 1820s.'

Old Canon Segrave, a de Floures cousin, had fathered Young Canon Segrave, his successor. Between them, they were rector for one hundred and one years.

'It was while zeal still burned hard inside him and he decided to put in decent sanitation for the tenantry. Not appreciated by the patron. He thought it an extravagance that would turn his tenants into idlers.'

'And did it?'

'No, it probably saved lives, but it caused a mighty ruction between house and rectory. His lordship wouldn't be crossed, but he couldn't technically get rid of him, and they were cousins anyway, so he tried to make his life unbearable instead. He had all the gates from the rectory to the park nailed shut and threatened the tenants if they went to church. Put in his own man as house chaplain, a terrible fellow, and made them all go there instead. Wouldn't maintain the church. It went on for decades.'

'Thank goodness for the *entente cordiale* of today!' said Audrey, as a clock struck half past five. Evensong followed at six, with its reassuring cadences and Jacobean English, so deeply imprinted in their lives that, unconsciously prompted by the chime, Audrey and Daniel moved to leave simultaneously.

'Thank you *so* much for tea,' said Audrey, as Bernard and Alex escorted them to the great hall. 'You must come to lunch at the vicarage,' an invitation perfunctorily offered and perfunctorily accepted, if rarely realised.

As they left, the sun was slanting through the great window which looked out on to the courtyard, a magnificent medieval account – in glowing stained glass – of prestige, the coats of arms of every de Floures and those who married them from the fifteenth century to the twentieth, set in leaded lozenges. The angle of the slants cast puddles of ruby and amber and sea-green on the flagstones. Audrey said, 'Isn't that lovely. Like a medieval kaleidoscope.'

'Not medieval,' said Alex. 'Twentieth century. The original was a casualty of the war, when the military took over the house. A plane overshot the landing strip and crashed just outside and exploded. The window was completely smashed.'

'But how clever, to put it all back together again.'

'I love the sound of breaking glass!' sang Alex.

I bet you do, thought Audrey.

3

Audrey and Daniel walked across the gravel to his Land Rover, a battered contraption that should have looked out of place in front of the most palatial aspect of Champton House, but did not, the English aristocracy taking a sort of reverse pride in wearing rags and driving bangers. He opened the door for her, but she paused.

'Daniel, it smells of death.'

'What does?'

'The Land Rover. What have you done in it?'

'Nothing, it's just the dogs and… hay bales… and pheasants.'

It had been a gift when he arrived. 'Think of it as a company car,' said Bernard, as the door creaked open to reveal what looked like a rural crime scene. It did not bother Daniel, who preferred old things to new; he thought of the filth that pebble-dashed the interior as patina, unlike his mother who made a show of arranging those sections from the *Sunday Telegraph* that did not interest her over the crusty passenger seat every time she got in. Daniel drove off slowly down the formal drive and then forked onto the smaller road that led through the park to the gates separating house from village. Spring lambs stood dumbly in the way, innocent of kerb drill, until their mothers nudged them off the tarmac. Not that the Land Rover's progress obliged them to move with much haste.

'Alex's T-shirt!' said Audrey. 'What an eye-opener! Do you think Bernard even noticed?'

'I don't think he misses much. But it was very Alex to wear it to tea with the rector.'

'I thought that too. Really, Bernard might have said something.'

'Perhaps he prefers not to fight those fights. Or perhaps he doesn't see what he doesn't want to see. Makes for a quieter life?'

'I wouldn't say diffidence is a paralysing problem for Bernard. On one of those days when they have the public in, I remember an earnest lady asking him what it was like living in a historic house and he said, "It's a – beep – nightmare!" You can fill in the blank yourself.'

They approached the park gates, which opened as if by magic now Bernard had installed an electric motor. There had not been a gatekeeper for years and years, and the lodges had been commandeered by Alex, to live and work in, a little demesne within the demesne.

The gates opened onto the end of Main Street – too obvious a name for the only street – and the little parade of shops opposite, like merchants outside the city's gates of old: the Post Office and General Stores, and The Flowers Tea Shop, the de Floures circlet on its sign, started by the Staveleys and opened only in the season, which began formally with Open Day.

Next to it was the hilariously named Stella: High Class Ladies' Fashion, which Mrs Harper had funded from the proceeds of her divorce – a vanity project that had turned out rather well, for all the better-heeled ladies of the district, including Daniel's mother, bought Tricoville and Jaeger and Country Casuals there.

'I suppose people like Bernard must try and soldier on, but it can't get any easier,' said Audrey. 'You should have seen what it was like after the war when super-tax came in and all the country families went broke, sold up and moved to Putney and let the house fall down, the ones that weren't already falling down. Half of them had been requisitioned and knocked about. It was the war. It changed the way we looked at things, Daniel, when it was over.'

'It didn't seem to affect the de Floures so much. Perhaps they were rich enough to weather those storms.'

'I think it did, actually,' said Audrey. 'It affected all of us. Don't you remember any of it? You were born during the Battle of Britain. It was certainly blood, sweat and tears for me, I can tell you.'

'Not really. I was only five on VE Day. I was more a post-war baby than a war baby, really. I remember bomb sites. And the games we played as children – *Hände hoch, Englische Schweinhund!* A schoolmaster with a wooden leg which he said he'd got at El Alamein. And I remember rationing, of course.'

And he remembered a man he had been to see on his deathbed a few days ago – quiet, sober, his reserve loosened by the approach of death and doses of morphine – telling him about the Normandy landings and the battles to take the villages that lay along the roads to Paris and Rouen, and the day he bayoneted a German soldier to death, a boy younger even than him, and how that death had grown larger to him as the years went by, to the point he would think about it constantly. But he had kept that memory to himself, Daniel discovered, arranging the funeral with his widow and sons, who knew nothing about it. 'He wanted to keep it there,' she said, 'he didn't want to bring it home.'

But we bring everything home, whether we like it or not, thought Daniel.

Evensong encouraged a reflective mood in Daniel, and as the few attenders departed into the dwindling light, he thought how different his present post was from his last, and how it had surprised everyone, including him, when he had made the move.

It was Honoria who had made it happen. She and Daniel had become friends in London when she worked at the Motcombe Hotel, next door to his former church, St Martin's Kinnerton Square, product of the Anglo-Catholic ascendency of the 1850s, looking like a chunk of Manueline Lisbon miraculously deposited in Belgravia. Daniel at first was not sure what she did when she came to see him, wearing a business suit that she managed to make look like couture, with what appeared to be a saddlebag slung over her shoulder, only stuffed with receipts and cuttings and bunches of keys and sachets of face creams and perfume samples, produced by the handful when she was trying to retrieve her Filofax.

She was looking for a match, a smart wedding venue for the smart receptions she organised for her smart clientele, and

St Martin's suited not only aesthetically but logistically. The newly-weds merely had to step out of the flower-bedecked west door and keep going to arrive at the Motcombe's ballroom entrance. Church and hotel constituted a package – to the benefit of both – and when Honoria phoned him up to say they had a reception booked for a Saturday in May and would the church be available for the ceremony, he no longer suggested that it was usually the other way round. Every parish priest, West End or East End, must adapt to circumstances, and his new liberal attitude towards such matters had not only led to a salutary rise in the church's income but also in the numbers of under-forties attending.

There were other benefits. When Daniel resolved to find a way of feeding the homeless who filled his churchyard by night once the Bentleys parked there by day had gone, Honoria was able to provide from the mountain of uneaten canapés and unsold afternoon teas that would otherwise fill the hotel's bins. This meant that the homeless of SW1 grew used to a surprisingly rich diet of smoked salmon and foie gras and even occasionally caviar, until word got round the offices and shops of the parish, and the weak, once again, found themselves pushed to the wall.

Daniel's disenchantment with preaching apostolic poverty in the richest parish in London coincided with a vacancy at Champton Rectory, which Honoria mentioned over coffee one morning. Champton, lovely church next to one of the great houses of England, protected, he imagined, by its rich and noble patron from the straitening economics of a growingly indifferent world; rural rather than urban, middling rather than soaringly high, and – most important – near where he grew up and where his widowed mother still lived. Honoria saw the light in his eye, as she had expected, and, putter-together of packages that she was, made all the arrangements. He went to lunch at Champton and, matching Bernard's consumption of gin and white burgundy and claret without demur or wobble, had passed with merit.

The thought of wine flowing so generously was followed by another, of a flushing lavatory, which dispelled his reflective mood. And then he noticed a figure waiting for him in the church porch. It was Dora Sharman, the more sociable of the sisters, unaccompanied by Kath. He had a feeling she wasn't there to discuss the weather.

'Hello, Dora, how are you?'

'I'm fine, Rector, thank you.'

'No Kath?'

'She had to nip out on the last hymn. Something on telly, Rector. She won't be damned for it, I hope?'

'God is merciful.'

'But I wanted to talk to you about the toilet.'

'Of course. Are you for or against?'

'It's not really about for or against. I wanted to say something about the pews.'

Dora, who spoke with the local accent, pronounced the word 'poos', which made Daniel think of toilets again. 'I wish you would leave them alone, Rector.'

'Can you tell me why?'

'It's where we sit, you see. And I think we should be allowed to keep sitting there.'

'You don't need my permission, or anyone else's, to sit there. But why is that so important, Dora?'

'We've always sat there. It's our place.'

'We're all passing through, Dora. And everyone has a place here.'

'Except Kath and me.'

'You will always have a place here, both of you. It's your church.'

'You say that, but I think you are going to make us move.'

'I am simply asking you to change where you sit.'

'Why don't *you* change where you sit?'

Daniel blinked at this bizarrely impractical suggestion.

'Well… because I sit where the incumbent sits. I have to be there to do my job. You wouldn't expect the organist to sit in the pulpit?'

'So your place is reserved.'

'Not for me, for whoever's rector.'

Dora thought for a moment.

'I know we shouldn't come to church to sit in our favourite places, but we do, and we don't like losing them. Some of us don't have very much, and so what we *do* have we don't want to lose. Do you understand?'

'You wouldn't lose anything, Dora. It would mean moving twenty feet. And you could still have the pew, it would just be in a different place.'

'Yes, I see that, but that's our place, at the back, and we want to keep sitting there.'

'It would still be the back, Dora. It would still be the last pew.'

Dora was perfectly able to see the logic of this but was also determined not to give up.

'Why would the toilet have to go here?'

'Where else would you put it?'

'Couldn't you take out the pews at the side, and put it there?'

'But that would cut the church in half, Dora. You wouldn't be able to see the altar from where you sit now if the...' his mother came to mind '... er... lavatory was there. And it would mean people would come and go in full view of the congregation.'

'Well then: we've managed for centuries without one, why do we need one now?'

'Because we need to make the church more suitable for the community's use. People want to pee, Dora.'

'What's the church for? It's not the pictures, is it?'

Daniel thought of a neighbouring church in London, where the Victorian interior had been overlaid by expensive audio-visual equipment, including a screen lowered by an electric motor on which were projected (to his mind) faintly heretical words to hymns he did not know.

'We must adapt or die, Dora.'

'Sometimes we must stay the same or die, Rector.'

4

Audrey was comfortably set up in front of the television when Daniel got back. The dogs scrambled to greet him as usual, then scrambled quickly back to Audrey's rug-covered knees, where they formed a peaceable yin and yang, curled up nose to tail.

Sunday night was soup-and-sarnie night, a ritual from childhood, when Audrey would have made rounds and rounds of sandwiches from the leftover of the joint – supplemented with pickle or bread sauce, depending – and they would eat these on trays *en famille*, with mugs of tomato soup, listening to *The Glums* on the wireless, the only meal that was eaten without the formality of sitting at the table.

They did not often have Sunday lunch – it seemed too much bother for Audrey, and Daniel's Sundays were usually busy, so nowadays it was a stew or a pie – but the tradition of the soup and the sarnie continued, now in front of the television rather than the glowing radiogram. In the kitchen, rounds of sandwiches awaited, with ham and cheese from Sainsbury's and Moutarde de Meaux – which Audrey liked for the stoneware jar and the cork sealed with red wax – and her own chutney, a rather runny plum. Daniel opened a tin of tomato soup, poured it into a pan and put it on the edge of the Aga plate; it sat there, unmoving, so red, so satisfying, and yet so different from the viney promise of the label. He decided to feed the dogs as the soup warmed through, and as soon as they heard the door open to the cupboard in which their food was kept they jumped out of Audrey's lap, and he heard a little cry of pain as their claws dug in. Hilda led – alpha to Cosmo's beta – and they skidded to a halt, little dinosaur faces upturned, tails wagging, as if it were the most exciting thing that had ever happened in the world. Audrey, in spite of a long litany of rules concerning dogs, broke all of them, including letting them on her lap, on her bed and feeding them morsels from her plate, so the benefits of the rattling kibble he had recently switched to were mitigated.

He commanded them to sit; it was the only command they ever really obeyed, for it was only issued when food was on the way. He placed the bowls in front of them, made them wait and then with a gesture of his finger signalled for them to eat, which they did with a gusto disproportionate to their actual enjoyment of the food. It was wolfed down so quickly, they merely seemed to move their heads over the food before it was gone. This invariably came as a surprise to them, and they pushed their snouts around their empty bowls as if unable to believe that there was nothing left.

His own and his mother's appetite for the soup and sarnies was less keen, but no less present, and they sat eating and sipping and watching television, the dogs properly banished to the floor. There was a film on later, 'a historical drama', as Audrey described it, with Tom Conti playing a pope struggling with his vocation, a proper entertainment for a Sunday evening (although it was preceded by a programme in which luminaries of light entertainment interviewed other luminaries of light entertainment in a show so bland Daniel thought it the cultural equivalent to the milk diet of invalids). It also afforded Audrey an opportunity for judgemental commentary, a chance to offload the resentments which accumulated more frequently, and more readily, as she entered her eighth decade.

'Look at him... I mean, *look* at him: hair like a yeti, and what a *hooter*!... Where *do* they find these people? I mean, fine, if that's what you want at the end of Blackpool Pier, but must we *really* have them on the television?... It's like a nightmare of a nursing home, sitting in a circle with the telly on too loud and nothing but Esther to fret your dying days...'

Daniel thought of his grandmother, who spent her last days in a gentlefolk's retirement home badly adapted from an abandoned manor house, telling him the only things that kept her going were snobbery and *Schadenfreude*. She had a friend, like her the widow of a boot and shoe baron, and they sat near the double doors to the drawing room, ignoring overtures of friendship from people whom they thought not up to their standard, and cackled, like twin tricoteuses, when the 'private ambulance' arrived to take one of those impertinent and lifeless housemates away. Even that ran out, thought Daniel, when he went to see her for the last time, in a side room, horribly bruised after falling out of bed and incapable of speaking. He anointed her and said prayers, and took her hand, as fragile as a moth, and held it but not for long enough, for when he made to go she suddenly squeezed as if to try to hold on. He squeezed back and let go and left. She died later that night, alone, and he had felt guilty ever since.

The film came on, an unpromising scenario that failed to deliver even on that, and as his mother fell asleep during the wretched pontiff's dark night of the soul, Daniel wheeled the trolley through to the kitchen and washed up.

The dogs started barking. He shushed them, but heard the sound of a car door slam outside. No one came calling after Evensong on a Sunday. He went to the front door and saw a car he did not recognise on the drive. It was new: not only brand new, shiny and sleek, but a new design too. It was compact and punchy, like a butcher's dog, a hatchback, or rather a 'hot hatch', a Golf GTI. He had seen an article about it in his mother's *Telegraph*, the motoring correspondent rhapsodic about its modest demeanour and hidden muscle, the size of a runaround but as quick as a Lotus. He guessed whose it was before the dogs turned and ran back to the kitchen; he recognised the pitch and rhythm of the fuss being made over them, and their yapping, in groundhog-day delight, at the visitor.

His brother, Theo, typically unannounced, filled the hall. 'Dan, Dan, what do you think of the new motor?'

They hugged. Theo was the one person Daniel embraced, and only because he left him no choice. It was more like an enveloping hug, a huge vertical half nelson, which was all the more disarming because the younger brother was shorter and slighter than the older. Theo didn't simply hug: he held on to him and patted his back, which as usual made Daniel think he was grappling Kendo Nagasaki rather than saying hello. Perhaps it was because in Theo's world – physical, demonstrative – good manners required it? Perhaps it was a sort of reproach for Daniel's fastidiousness and distance? Perhaps it was because when they were children, Theo's natural affection had been easily received by his brother, ten years older? Now Daniel was greying and approaching venerable, but Theo still seemed the young man he had been when he left drama school.

Daniel extricated himself from his brother's grip as tactfully as he could, stepping back as if to admire him, and saying, 'You look well. You must be doing well?'

'Suckling at the paps of mammon, dear brother.'

'How very generous mammon has been.'

'Sweeties money.'

Theo's voice was still more familiar to the public than his face: it was the voice which recommended the merits of chocolate bars, antiperspirants, holidays in Tunisia, funerals from the Co-op. Daniel did not really understand how it worked, but it evidently did, for his younger brother had bought a little terraced house in Camden and a Golf GTI in the last year. But he seemed sometimes embarrassed by this lucrative enterprise, as he was by a small but recurring part in a television soap opera – *Appletree End* – playing PC Henry Heseltine, the beat copper with a mysterious posh background kept very busy by the unusually high amount of serious crime in his misleadingly tranquil village. That was what had got him some recognition, the part that opened doors, but when Daniel had once complimented him on it, Theo had winced.

'Theo!' said Audrey, appearing from the drawing room with the slightly dishevelled look of the just-awakened. 'What a surprise! Are you hungry?'

They sat at the kitchen table while their mother fussed with a purposefulness which only fell on her, Daniel noticed, when both her sons were home. More sandwiches, more soup and, with his thirsty brother at the table, something to drink.

He went to the fridge and found a bottle of Chardonnay, opened a day ago but still drinkable, the astringency of the oak – typical of New World wines – masking any staleness. He poured two glasses and asked his mother if she wanted one, but she said she'd have a Noilly, her favourite aperitif, drunk by no one else he had ever met (the off licence in Braunstonbury kept a bottle or two in especially for him). He fetched it from the sitting room, where it was kept in the corner cupboard with a bottle of sherry that his father had liked but no one had touched in years. He liked the label on the bottle of Noilly Prat, which made him think of a French café, a rickety zinc table in a sun-drenched street, and the faintly witchy suggestion of bitter herbs.

He poured, they sat, they sipped. Then Theo burst out with the news he had driven from London to announce.

'I'm going to be in a new telly series. It's called *Clerical and Medical* and it's about a vicar and a doctor. You will be alarmed to hear, Daniel, that I'm playing the vicar, the Reverend Stanley Darnley, rough-hewn northern man of God, and she's – yes *she* – is Doctor Shelagh Kennedy, Edinburgh bluestocking. Miss Jean Brodie meets the Vicar of Wakefield.'

'When do you start filming?'

'In a couple of months. Six-parter, ITV.'

Audrey let slip, 'Oh, bad luck.'

'ITV's fine now, Mum. You watched *Brideshead Revisited*.'

'Was that ITV?'

'Yes, it was. All your friends watched it. Do you remember how sumptuous it was?

'Yes, filmed at Castle Howard and with Jeremy Irons who we saw as John the Baptist in *Godspell*. Your father had to ask a vicar who was explaining it to some foreign people not to talk.'

'What sort of drama is it? Will you be solving murders?'

'No, it's what the bloke from Thames calls "gentle comedy".'

'How perfect for you, darling,' said Audrey.

Theo sat back, his arms behind his head, revealing a hole in his jumper (Audrey eyed it like a little Dutch boy a leaking dyke). So different at first sight, he was in some ways very like his older brother. They were both meticulous, only Theo didn't look it, his effusiveness and untidiness disguising his concern with detail and order, which only became evident when he was preparing for a part. He could be single-minded about this, to the point of being offensive: when he was cast as a prisoner of war in *Tenko*, Audrey told him that Bob Achurch had been a prisoner of war of the Japanese and Theo had so pestered him for stories – quite oblivious to the effect of his questioning – until Daniel had to ask him to relent.

And then Theo asked what Daniel had been waiting for. 'Could you bear it if I spent a day or two with you? Following you around, just to get a feel for the warp – and indeed the *weft* – of your life?' Theo made an expansive gesture with his almost empty wine glass.

Daniel refilled it. 'What sort of things are you interested in? I'm not sure how closely my life would resemble the life of a blunt Yorkshire parson married to a GP?'

'Oh, you have to get the details right, what to wear, how you hold something. The letters we get when we do up the wrong buttons, or the bus route is impossible.'

Daniel also noticed such things but had made it a spiritual

discipline not to get worked up about it: he could still remember the terrible solecism on *Barchester* when the psalm chant at Evensong was at least two decades out and he'd been so distracted he'd missed the rest of the episode.

He ruminated for a second.

'Why do film directors always insist on filling every church with lighted candles?'

'It says "church".'

'But it's always wrong. It's not mood lighting, candles *mean* something. And why is the priest always in church when people call in? We're hardly ever in church.'

'We don't make documentaries, Dan. We make things up, we tell stories. I don't think people go to *Romeo and Juliet* and think, ooh she'd never have heard him from that balcony. And why aren't you in church anyway?'

'Because most of what we do doesn't happen there. We're there for services, for flower festivals – which reminds me, I must write the Rector's Welcome for this year's programme – but for most of the day we're out in the parish, we're meeting people, we're doing dreary things with rural deans, and going to see the bereaved, or visiting people in hospital, or taking Holy Communion to the nursing home, or taking assemblies. Actually, most of my time I'm at my desk writing things, or on the phone. That's not something you need to spend a day observing, is it?'

'Writing what? Sermons?'

'Sermons, yes, but mostly letters and references, the diary.'

'That's what I want to see.'

'I don't think you will gain any great insight from watching me write a sermon. I'd like to think you might from hearing me preach one.'

'No, it's the stuff you don't know you're doing that I want to see. That's what's interesting.'

'I see. That might be dull for you – there's a lot of doing nothing.'

'I thought you were supposed to be run off your feet?'

'I don't mean idling. I mean *doing* nothing.'

'I don't understand.'

'It's being, not doing, a lot of the time. And praying – you won't get much out of watching me do that.'

Theo looked thoughtful. 'You know what, Dan, I think it would be better if you just showed me things? And it would be instructive for you too, as well as for me. You would see yourself reflected in me.'

'Perhaps that's what's making me hesitate.'

'Well, it certainly wouldn't be hero worship, if that's what you were worried about.'

Audrey, who had been unusually silent, snorted. 'You *did* hero worship him when you were a little boy. Your brilliant big brother.'

'Still brilliant, still my big brother.'

'Oh, you're not doing so badly, little Theo, are you?' said Audrey, and passed him a glass bowl of cold custard – his favourite – left over from lunch.

'All right,' Daniel said, 'but only what I say you can see. And if I need you to disappear, you must disappear.'

'Understood.'

'I have to go and say Compline now, if you want to see what doing nothing looks like?'

'Yes. Do I need to bring anything?'

'No. It's not an audience participation sort of service.'

They left through the back door, Cosmo and Hilda at their feet, and went through the restored gate from his garden to the north side of the church, where the vestry stood, a sort of neo-Gothic lean-to attached to the transept, with his own door. It was a lovely clear evening, cool and starry, but they did not dawdle lest the dogs, sniffing around the gravestones, found badger droppings, in which they delighted to roll.

'Cosmo! Hilda!' he called from the open door, and they flowed through it, a tiny torrent, into the vestry. The church was dark and empty, and they scampered off between the pews, stopping and sniffing and scampering again, discouraging, he hoped, the mice and bats, faithful attenders of the night offices.

He could not remember the last time he had human company for Compline. It was traditionally the last service of the day in monasteries, said by monks and nuns on their way to bed, and adapted in the highly idiosyncratic prayer book of his theological college to encourage ordinands that it was time for bed. In reality for most it was merely an interruption to the drinks parties held in their rooms, which could last well into the small hours. Daniel had resisted these enticements on the whole, and Compline had become a habit he now found impossible to give up. But then he loved the threshold of night, when he felt closest to his parishioners, and to those in particular need of his prayers, not only the living but the departed also. He went to the altar without bothering to switch on the lights, for he knew the building well enough not to need them.

Theo followed hesitantly. 'Can we have the lights on?'

'It's said in darkness.'

'Oh. Where shall I go?'

Daniel said, 'Why don't you just sit there, in the choir? Try not to make a noise.'

Daniel lit the two candles on the altar.

His brother said, 'See? You *do* light candles and you *are* in church,' but Daniel did not reply. He went to sit in his stall, which was set out with care. On the bookshelf his Book of Common Prayer, his Bible, his Alternative Service Book, his hymn book, and Mowbray's *The Hours of Prayer, from Lauds to Compline*, a copy already old when it was given to him by the widow of the vicar who had prepared him for confirmation when he went to theological college. They were bedecked with ribbons, not for gaiety but to mark his place. Each ribbon terminated in a sort of resinous tear, a blob of clear nail varnish applied to the ends to prevent fraying. To the left were his automatic pencil (plus spare), a rubber (plus spare), a set of tuning forks to pitch the Preces and Versicles for Matins and Evensong, and a block of Post-it notes, which he thought perhaps the most brilliant technical innovation of the age.

He opened his Mowbray's, but he needed no text, for the order was always the same, and he knew it by heart. As an invariable prelude he said silently the Jesus Prayer: *Lord Jesus Christ, son of God, have mercy on me, a sinner.* Each petition was slow, measured, geared to his breathing, and as his mind and body stilled, the lavatory controversy, Stella Harper's hostility, Alex de Floures' T-shirt, they all began to fade from his thoughts. And in that vacated space silence unpacked itself and through the static and hiss, a deeper silence came, like the depths of the sea.

And then the silence was broken by the sound of the dogs gurgling with pleasure as Theo, already bored, tickled their underbellies.

5

St Mary's Champton, like most parish churches of its age and dignity, had always served a double purpose: heaven's and the world's. In the old days there were Ales held in the nave, beery parties to mark Oak Apple Day or Gunpowder Treason Day, and even one to celebrate the delivery from madness of His Majesty King George, for which the then Lord de Floures had erected an obelisk that still stood at the crossroads, puzzling travellers. The Ales had got so rowdy both squire and parson intervened, and in the age of Queen Victoria respectability asserted itself.

The needs of the world, however, continued to be served through the deliberations of the parish church council – a political body whose workings you would think as momentous as those of the Diet of Worms – and perhaps the most taxing meeting of the church's year at Champton, the annual general meeting for the flower guild, which Stella had decreed for Monday evening, normally Daniel's day off. ('That's why she picked it, of course,' said Audrey.)

The ladies of the guild, summoned by Mrs Dollinger and Harper, walked down Church Lane, its steep grassy banks now speckled with primroses, Mothering Sunday time of the year. Champton was at its loveliest, thought Daniel, when the snowdrops and the daffodils, harbingers of spring, delivered on their promise and the fizzy green of new growth was just coming into its strength. Most mornings he walked the dogs down Church Lane on his way to the paper shop to get the news – printed in *The Times*, or confided over the counter – or at least the news people wanted him to know. He had thought, when he was a curate, that he would know everything going on in his parish, but he had found he was often the last to know, and when he finally did discover who was doing what with whom it was usually too late to do anything but deal with the damage. Another reason to maintain vigilance, to look for the indicators of distress; his perceptive powers, which were lively anyway, had become livelier because of it.

Damage limitation was not what he had in mind that evening. The back of the church was full. Anne Dollinger and her helpers had erected a trestle table in the aisle facing the crowds; Anne and Stella Harper sat behind it, with Daniel next to them (*ex officio*) and, as churchwarden and representing Bernard as patron, Anthony Bowness. In the front row, facing them, were Audrey and Theo. Stella had raised an eyebrow at this irregular stiffening of the opposition, but Theo's presence had excited a flurry of interest, a distraction which might suit her, so she had let it pass, smiling graciously to mother and son. To Daniel their presence felt like a double scrutiny so comprehensive he wondered if he had been rash to permit it.

The annual general meeting was the easy part, for it involved only the re-election of officers and nobody was going to oppose that, although Audrey was a little slower than others to raise her hand to show approval. The accounts were presented by Mrs Dollinger, the treasurer, and found to be in order, and then she proposed a vote of thanks to the chairman, Mrs Harper, for all her hard work in ensuring the parish of St Mary's Champton 'continued to praise God not only in song and service but in displaying the beauty of God's creation', a motion Daniel found suitably florid.

Stella Harper rose. 'This year's theme, as you know, is "The Final Frontier", which we have chosen for the exciting opportunities the space age affords for some really splendid displays.' Daniel thought of the space shuttle *Challenger* exploding. 'It is also the Whitsun bank holiday, and as you know at Whitsun we celebrate the Holy Spirit, coming in tongues of fire, or, if you prefer, in the form of a dove' – she nodded at Daniel as if to acknowledge his theological authority – 'and we'll have just had the Ascension too, which, as you can see from our great East Window' – she gesticulated at it – 'has Jesus lifting off from the disciples to go up to heaven, which I think most apt. And thank you, ladies ... and gentleman' – Stella nodded to Anthony, the only man in the village to have volunteered to do a window, and a polite titter rose from the pews – 'for all your ideas and for the willingness with which you have taken on the suggestions of the committee. As you know, all we want is for this year's flower festival to be the best ever.'

Looks were exchanged between a number of the ladies attending who, in the view of the committee, had gone a little too boldly where Champton had not gone before.

'I am delighted by the progress we are making and I would like to remind you that all windows must be *completed* by

Wednesday the eighteenth, because the man from the *Evening Telegraph* is coming on the Friday and the final inspection will need to take place on the Thursday.'

The inspection was known as the Bonfire of the Vanities, and many a poorly placed stock or untidy tendril of ivy had been torn from the ensemble its creator thought finished.

'And now, is there Any Other Business?'

This normally signalled the end was nigh, just the date of the next meeting and the grace to go before people gathered their hats and their handbags and headed for the door. But then Anne Dollinger spoke.

'Yes, Madam Chairman, there is *one* item.'

Everyone put down that which they had gathered up, apart from Dora Sharman, who tutted loudly and sat down in her coat and hat and looked, rather theatrically, at her watch.

'With the growing success, year on year, of the flower festival it is proposed that we develop a plan for extending the flower room and improving its facilities.'

Daniel frowned. This had not been discussed.

Stella stood. 'Yes, ladies. Mrs Dollinger, the committee and I have been concerned for some time that we cannot maintain the high standards you and our many visitors rightly expect from St Mary's with the current facilities. We have limited provision of water, very limited space, and such space as we have we are obliged to share' – a look towards Audrey – 'which can make things very difficult, especially when we have the flower festival to organise and execute. As you know, and as the rector has recently reminded us' – a look towards Daniel – 'we must always be open to change, to embrace the new, and to that end I can announce that the offer of a very generous donation has been made. The committee feels' – Daniel and Anthony, who were on the committee but ignorant of this news, exchanged a glance – 'it provides an opportunity to launch an appeal to seek additional funds to make our vision a reality. So we would like your support formally to approach the PCC for its blessing.'

'All those in favour?' said Mrs Dollinger, jumping in. Nearly everybody raised a hand by reflex, apart from Daniel, Ned, Anthony and Audrey. But it is easier to count a raised hand than an unraised one, and even Audrey's, held in her lap so angrily the atmosphere around her crackled, went unnoticed.

'Carried!'

'Hang on!' shouted Ned.

'Mr Thwaite?' snapped Stella Harper. 'What now?'

'How will this affect other plans to improve the facilities at church, as discussed at the PCC recently?'

'I am sure the flower guild and the PCC are of one mind in wishing to improve facilities at church.'

'I meant specifically putting in a toilet.'

Stella paused and fixed Ned with a stare.

'That is not part of our plan. It is our feeling that there was not much support for that proposal and there are of course lavatory facilities available nearby.' She looked at Audrey. 'At the rectory, for example?'

'Yes, I can see that,' said Ned, 'and I can also see that they have been in demand in the course of this meeting.' At that moment Margaret Porteous emerged from the vestry on her return from one of her frequent and urgent visits to exactly that location and was horrified to see all eyes turned in her direction. 'So I am wondering, if you intend to provide tea and coffee for visitors in church so liberally, doesn't that strengthen the case for installing a lavatory? Or possibly two?'

Audrey smiled. Stella Harper was not the only person who could mobilise opinion in Champton.

'And another thing: won't your plan necessitate the removal of pews?'

'Not at all,' said Stella, 'our explicit aim has always been to preserve the pews, which are among the finest fifteenth-century examples in the entire county.'

'Or just plain old Victorian. We don't know.'

'They don't *look* very Victorian to me, Mr Thwaite, nor to Mr Bowness, who is, as you know, an acknowledged expert in these matters.'

Anthony stood. 'Not quite, Stella. I think they may be Victorian, or some of them at least, but we need to have them surveyed. If they can be moved, we might have room for both schemes?'

Audrey raised her hand. Stella pretended not to see her, so she waved.

'Mrs Clement?'

'If we don't know, Mrs Harper, if the pews are historic or not, then I fail to see how your plan can proceed, even if it were to get passed by the PCC, which is far from certain, of course.'

'Well, then, what would you propose, Audrey?' she snapped, and immediately regretted it.

'Why not use any funds to put in the lavatory, as we intended to do all along?'

'That also would require moving pews.'

'Not necessarily. We could make better use of the existing space. Perhaps by… this is just a thought of course… by reordering the flower room, which takes up so much of it?'

'That is preposterous. The funds I mentioned are very specifically intended to fund the work of the flower guild rather than the disposal of human waste.'

Anne Dollinger stood up abruptly. 'It's time to call this meeting to order. I think we have heard enough for now, and certainly have plenty to take into consideration.' She looked at Stella Harper. 'Perhaps in the first place we should seek advice concerning the pews, because until we are clear about that we can't really do anything.'

Sounds of assent came from the rows.

'In that case we will proceed to ascertain the date and the importance of the pews. Thank you, ladies and gentlemen. Date of next meeting? I suggest a fortnight before the flower festival. Shall we say Monday the ninth of May at seven?'

Handbags were opened, diaries extracted, biros decapped.

'So it remains only for the rector to conclude in prayer.'

Everyone sat still for a moment, in anticipation of the Almighty.

'Let us say together the grace.'

'The grace of Our Lord, Jesus Christ,' they said, in the sing-song way that prayers learned in the nursery are said, 'and the love of God, and the fellowship of the Holy Spirit, be with us all, ever more. Amen.'

Mrs Harper jumped up to leave, but Daniel got to her before she could. 'Stella, might I have a word?'

'Of course, I'll be with you in just a moment, I have to catch someone first.' She rushed to the door, where Mrs Dollinger was waiting to distribute a pile of the St Mary's Champton Flower Guild Guidelines, a set of dogmas so inflexible that grieving widows and weeping brides had been made to pick apart their wreaths and bouquets when the organist had already started the introit.

Daniel began to fold up the chairs to put them away. Anthony came to help. 'News to me, and I think news to you too, Dan?'

'Yes. First I've heard anything about it, although it ties up a few loose ends.'

'Really?'

'Yes, the other night my mother noticed a light on in church and found Stella and Anne there "acting suspiciously". Tidying up, they said, but it didn't look like it: Anne was between pews on her hands and knees, looking for something, she thought.'

'What do you think they were doing?'

'I think I am about to find out.'

Anne Dollinger and Stella Harper approached, Anne carrying a folder.

'I'm off,' said Anthony. 'Let me know, will you? I'm in all evening.'

Audrey had noticed the flower guild's approach and sensed a battle, but Anthony intercepted her and Theo and steered them towards the door.

'Daniel, you wanted to see me?' said Mrs Harper.

'Yes, I was just a little surprised by the announcement this evening.'

'Surprised? Why?'

'You said it had been discussed by the committee. I cannot recall ever having discussed it.'

'Oh. It was the *standing* committee. Didn't I say so?'

'The *standing* committee,' repeated Mrs Dollinger.

'I didn't know there was one.'

'Yes, yes, of course. We've had one for ages, in case something happened that needed our immediate attention or wasn't important enough to take to the committee proper. Before your time, I think.'

'Which applies for drawing up plans for reordering the church: something that needed immediate attention or something unimportant?'

'You make it sound like we've acted improperly.'

'You did say the committee had discussed this matter when it had not. During the AGM. That's not really the right way to go about it.'

'But what can you mean? We wouldn't *dream* of proceeding without taking it to the PCC for approval.'

Daniel knew Stella Harper well enough to be sure she had been drumming up support in the ranks.

'It should have gone to the committee for approval before being presented at the AGM.'

'Well, so you say. I'm sure we will take that into consideration in the future.'

'And for that reason I will have to consider, as chairman of the PCC, whether it should be an agenda item at all. At least until I know what it is all about.'

Stella Harper had not thought of this. She paused. 'What do you want to know?'

'The plan.'

'It's hardly a plan, Daniel, it's just a few ideas, an outline. I'm sure you will find it perfectly suitable.'

She nodded to Mrs Dollinger, who withdrew from the folder a piece of paper.

'May I?' she said, and unfolded it on the trestle table that Daniel had been about to put away.

It was a plan. A detailed plan, with what looked like an architect's drawing of a greatly extended flower room and a kitchen with a counter that took up most of the space at the rear of the church.

'What a bold vision, Stella.'

'It's really just a sketch. But the idea is to extend the flower room, as you can see, and that creates some space here' – she jabbed a finger at the kitchen area – 'to put in a buttery.'

'A kitchen?'

'No, a *buttery,* a serving counter, if you like, not a cooker, just a sink and somewhere to put away cups and saucers, and somewhere to keep things warm.'

'And somewhere to go the loo.'

'I don't think there would be room for that, Rector.'

'But don't you think people will have greater need of one if they are going to be having tea and coffee?'

This was rather a bugbear of Mrs Harper's. 'I don't think so, no. When did we start needing to go to the lavatory every five minutes? I was at County Hall last week...' Daniel wondered what she had been doing there – visiting the planners' office? – 'and in the Victorian building there are two lavatories, for ladies and for gentlemen, on either side of the main hall. That's it. Ample provision for our ancestors. But in the new building there are lavatories on every floor.'

'What have we *become*?' asked Mrs Dollinger, rhetorically.

Daniel started to wonder what people had done in the age of the Ales. He knew what the men had done, because the wall outside the west door of the church was used still as an impromptu gents when the need arose. But what had the women done?

'So you see, Rector,' Mrs Harper had gone formal again, 'I really think there is no need for such a facility in church, which is after all a sacred place, a holy place...'

'... and a florist's shop?' said Daniel.

'Rector, naturally I bow to your expertise in matters of Scripture,' said Mrs Harper, magnificently, 'but I do not recall Our Lord overturning the tables of florists when he cleansed the Temple.'

Daniel was distracted for a moment, wondering what pilgrims to the Temple at Jerusalem, queueing in their thousands to slaughter beasts for sacrifice, would have done when they needed to pee.

'And this donation, Stella. Who is it from?'

'The donor wishes to remain anonymous.'

'That restriction would not apply to me, as rector and incumbent.'

'The donor was most insistent,' she said.

'But *I* must insist in return. It is not from mere curiosity that I wish to know. You will not have forgotten that church and parish are my responsibility, Stella, and I have to be able to account for all sources of funding.'

'We are not money laundering for bank robbers, Rector,' said Mrs Harper, who got more acid, and more forceful, in a corner.

'I would not expect that to be the case, but this is not a

matter for negotiation. We cannot receive funds unless I know where they are coming from.'

An impasse. Anne Dollinger spoke up. 'I wonder if anyone asked for approval for the de Floures to pay for a chapel on the side of the church?'

'That was in 1465, Anne, when the fiduciary responsibilities of the rector were not so sharply defined.'

The de Floures chapel stood next to the north transept, behind an iron grille, a Madame Tussauds of Bernard's ancestors, but memorialised in marble rather than wax, looking out with sightless eyes at the changing world.

'So you see I really cannot, under the terms you describe, allow this as an agenda item at the next PCC, and it cannot therefore go on for approval.'

Stella had learned to get her way by indignation, a tactic she employed so well, she rather overused it. One could always tell when she had worked herself up because little smudges of red would appear on her cheeks.

'We'll have a public meeting!' said Mrs Harper. 'In the village hall!'

'By all means, Stella. I look forward to attending.'

6

Audrey and Theo were waiting for him in the kitchen.

'What's Stella playing at?' Audrey asked. 'You knew nothing about it, did you?'

'I didn't. But they have a plan. Rather an advanced one.'

'For what?'

'To extend the flower room and add what they call a buttery' – Audrey snorted – 'a sort of kitchenette at the back. I quite like the idea of that. But it will only increase the need for a loo, don't you think?'

'Of course it will. But that's what this is about, it's to stop you putting in a loo.'

'Yes, I know.'

'And of course it's not really about that, it's about … all sorts of things.'

'Yes, I know.'

'But that's strategy and we need a tactic. Can you stop them?

'Yes, I think so. I've told her I won't put it on the PCC agenda because it did not come before the committee for consideration. Also, she won't say who this mysterious donation was from.'

'I wondered about that,' said Theo.

'It's from her, and it's probably only twenty measly quid,' said Audrey.

'I cannot accept it if I don't know where it is from.'

'Then you've got her, haven't you?' said Theo.

'But I would rather not have to exercise my powers. Better to reach a common view in the long run.'

Audrey pursed her lips. She found her son's predilection for reconciliation and seeking compromise immensely frustrating. When she challenged him, he responded by saying that he was a priest and pastor not a king or a lord and he had no interest in imposing his will on people. This did not persuade Audrey, who asked once if St Paul compromised with his fractious followers at Corinth, or Rome, or... – she could not remember the other place where they were fractious but thought it might be Galatia, if that's where Galatians come from – and if St Paul was prepared to knock a few heads together to build the Kingdom, then Daniel should be prepared to do the same.

'You will never win over Stella Harper, nor her sidekick, Daniel. They must be brought to heel, can't you see that?'

'She's right, Dan, no point in playing fair with people who aren't going to play fair back.'

'Here's a good example for you, Theo. We *do* actually have to play fair when people aren't playing fair back.'

'Turning the other cheek, and all that? I have to say I've always found that quite daft.'

'There are worse things than looking daft.'

Audrey snorted.

They ate in the kitchen, a Lancashire hotpot, made properly

with kidneys as well as neck. Audrey was distracted, plotting, Daniel assumed, the downfall of the flower guild.

Theo wanted to talk about the meeting. 'She blindsided you, didn't she. Happen a lot?'

'Not, not really, I can't remember it happening before.'

'All about procedure, all very decorous, but it's aggro, just like everything else.'

'I suppose,' said Daniel.

'Aren't Christians supposed to be all Christ-like? Meek and mild?'

'People clash. It's being human. If we weren't, we'd be faking it.'

'So what's the point of you then?'

'To help people work out how to deal with it.'

'I wish you had powers of assassination,' said Audrey, 'that would sort it out.'

Daniel could not help but notice that his mother's relish for a fight was liveliest with those most like her, and that no one had come closer in recent years than Stella Harper. Close in age, comparable in background, both single, and both women whom Daniel thought would have had easier and more fulfilling lives if they had exchanged roles with their husbands. Stella's husband, a bookish and withdrawn town clerk, had retreated in life into the meticulous organisation of affairs, which, among other things, provided a refuge from his wife's restless ambition. Eventually it put him beyond it, because she discovered his distance suited her perfectly well, so she formalised it by divorce. Daniel's father, temperamentally similar, had been obliged to work in the family firm, following his father and grandfather and great-grandfather, men of business and trade and energy and fight, none of which had emerged in his own personality. Audrey had all those qualities, and Daniel wondered if his father had not married his own mother (as men are supposed to do) but in fact his own father, which was more complicated. If he had stayed at home to bring up the boys and keep house and Audrey had gone to work, his father would have been happier and his mother would probably have ended up running ICI or the United Nations. As it happened, her relish and aptitude for power was greater than the opportunities life had afforded for her to exercise it.

Daniel noticed this most vividly when Audrey talked about the war. She had left her Scottish boarding school as the thirties waned, and her womanhood arrived along with hostilities. She had volunteered immediately for the Women's Voluntary Service, making tea and sandwiches for returning servicemen, driving ambulances and staff cars, and preparing for the invasion of Britain – something she enjoyed so much she was almost disappointed when the Wehrmacht failed to appear in landing craft and parachutes on the beaches and in the streets of England. After the war her energies and her drive had gone into her boys; into him, first, and then into Theo.

'Tape measure!' said Audrey. 'Tape measure, that's what she was doing!'

'What tape measure?'

'Anne Dollinger. I caught her and Stella in church last week, I told you. You were at Deanery Synod and I saw a light on and when I came to investigate I found them on their hands and knees. When I – politely – asked them what they were doing, there was a sound like a mousetrap going off, but I bet you it was a tape measure, one of those metal ones the builders use. They were measuring up, hatching their plan. I remember now it made that funny noise when it retracted.'

Daniel gave a little sigh of frustration, not with his mother, but with the flower guild ladies.

'I'm just going to take the dogs down the lane,' he said, but his mother wasn't really listening.

'I'll come,' said Theo.

He took their leads from the hook by the kitchen door, not to tether their wanderings to his, but to summon them from their somnolence beside the Aga; it was not their usual time for a walk, but it was all he needed to do for them to become instantly alert.

He let them out of the back door and onto the path that led to the lychgate, through the gate, past Sexton's Cottage, trim and gingerbread, with its neat thatch and lovely garden, tended by Bob Achurch with the steady care he brought to everything he did. The cherries blossomed on cue every year, then the marigolds, and in summer the roses came, carefully deadheaded so they lasted till the autumn, then the hollyhocks, like thirties film stars, and then the dahlias, like sixties dolly birds, and apples in the autumn. Nothing unusual, nothing out of place. Bob was in his garden turning over some earth with a fork. 'Evening, Rector. Mr Clement.' The dogs barked, but recognised him when he came to the wall, and straightaway resumed their patrol at the edge of Church Lane.

'Evening, Bob. All well with you?'

'Yes, all well. Is that your new runaround?'

'Theo's.'

'A Golf GTI. Stardom brings it rewards, then?'

'Not really stardom.'

'Not yet,' said Daniel. 'But did you see him in *Tenko*?' The moment he said it he wished he hadn't.

'No. It's not really for me.'

'No, of course not.'

Bob was a quiet man, taciturn even, and would no more think of discussing his inner life than walk down Braunstonbury's Market Street naked. But he had an inner life, like everyone else, and his was troubled as a consequence of the war, as Theo had discovered when he'd thoughtlessly blundered into it.

Bob had not forgotten it, and took up the fork again, the commando tattoo blue and blurry on his forearm now, and started to turn the earth. 'Best get on.'

'Good to see you again, Bob,' said Theo, 'and my regards to … the missus. I've never forgotten her scones!'

'I'll tell her that, she'll be glad to hear it.' Daniel imagined her practically forcing the scones down Theo's mouth to shut him up.

The light was falling, almost visibly, degree by degree, and the primroses stood out in greater relief against the darkening grass banks on either side of the path. Daniel and Theo walked to the end, the dogs following in their shifting circuits. At the bottom of the lane, with a view up to the church, Daniel showed his brother where the Staveleys lived, at the Old School House, a Gothic fantasy built by a de Floures with ambitions to improve the lot of his tenants, but which had almost immediately been found to be completely unfit for its purpose. After the new school was built it was sold and used as a Mission Hall. In it the young Norman Staveley had learned the rudiments of the catechism, and how to tie knots, and to sing 'The British Grenadiers'; forty years later, when the estate put it up for sale, he bought it and converted it and would have carried Dot over the threshold had they been twenty years younger. A piece of the Champton estate was now his, and on fine evenings he would spread out on the bench in the front garden with a beer and a panatella to enjoy the view, and his own deep contentment.

He was not there now, Daniel noticed, as they crossed the small bridge over the brook which ran the length of Main Street. They stopped for a moment there.

'You may have seen the bridge in photographs.'

'Yes, I have I think. At Bob's. Was it VE Day?'

'Could be. But Bob wasn't here for VE Day.'

'Must have been his missus ... what's her name?'

'Cynthia.'

'Cynthia. Shocking baker, by the way. I think the French were in the picture too. You could tell just from a glance. Bohemian look. Corduroys.'

Every generation since Queen Victoria had been photographed on the bridge, the most picturesque view of the village: wedding parties in high celluloid collars and hats as big as millstones, boys in rough khaki going off to the Somme, Teddy Boys and girls in hot pants, and even a punk, Alex de Floures, in an ancestor's Guards tunic and bondage trousers.

Daniel liked to walk the beat from time to time, sometimes during the day to see people, to have the kind of conversations you have when you pass in the street; and sometimes just to patrol, like a night watchman. They walked north towards the road which swept down to the gates of the estate. Lights were coming on in cottage windows, like doors opening on advent calendars, and as he passed he told Theo who lived where. Here was the Sharman sisters' cottage, former estate workers, unwed daughters of a head gamekeeper. Their Jack Russell, Scamper, as antisocial a dog as Daniel had ever known, was standing on his front paws on the windowsill looking out in the street. He growled at Cosmo and Hilda, who growled back.

'You should go and see the Sharman sisters. They're avid watchers of *Appletree End*. Or one of them is, I can't remember which one. Kath, I think.'

'Why them?'

'They've been here all their lives. They knew all the parsons before me. And I'm sure they can be persuaded to give you a full account of their lives – not just the official version.'

Next to the Sharmans lived misanthropic Gilbert Drage in a tiny cottage at the end of the row for retired estate workers, Death Row as Audrey called it, and on the other side, Mrs Dollinger, in a cottage that had been sold off, its private state made plain by adornments the estate would not have provided for the cottages still in its care. A larger house, set back from the street, which was once occupied by the factor, was now lived in by Anthony Bowness, employed by the estate but also family; the house had been done up accordingly to reflect the status of its new occupant, but not quite to the standard Anthony would have liked.

'You should go and see Anthony too, if you have time. He can tell you about the church and the estate and how it works. He's shrewd. He notices things.'

'Can't I come with you on a visit? Official business?'

'Depends on what it is.'

'Only I need to observe you. Doing what you do.'

'You've seen me do what I do.'

'I've not *observed* you, though. Think of me as a new curate.'

Daniel was unable to entertain that thought for very long.

'Come up next weekend. It's Open Day. The biggest event in the estate calendar. The house is open, the park, everyone turns out.'

'Oh that would be perfect.'

They came to Ned and Jane Thwaite's house, converted from a barn, little windows punched into a stone wall, a yard with an extension behind it, for the office where Ned worked on local history, his true passion. And then on the other side of the brook, at the very end of the street, standing slightly apart, was 'the new house', Stella Harper's house, built at the end of the seventies by Stella's husband for their retirement, until she retired him first. It looked out of place, at the end of a row of seventeenth-century cottages in stone and thatch, with its steeply pitched tiled roof and dormers, and picture windows on the ground floor through which, behind curtains, the bluish flicker of a television could be seen.

'That's where Stella lives.'

'The Fortress of the Flower Queen.'

'Watching *Wogan*.'

It was now nearer darkness than light, and down by the brook Daniel could make out his dogs only by their movement. He whistled for them and they turned to head back home to the rectory, the darkness of the street part illuminated by shafts of light from the windows behind which his parishioners, in their various degrees and characters and virtues and vices, reposed.

A shape moved across one of the lit windows, the dogs barked and the figure of Anthony Bowness emerged out of the gloom.

'I saw the dogs. I'm not interrupting you, am I?'

'No, not at all.'

'Actually, I was hoping to see you. Have you got a minute?'

'Yes, of course.' He held out the dogs' leads to Theo. 'Would you?'

Theo hesitated. 'Shall I ... push off?'

'I'll see you back at home. You'll need their leads.'

Theo hooked the leads onto their collars. The dogs strained and whimpered as Daniel followed Anthony inside.

Anthony did not really like dogs. Daniel had noticed before that, no matter how compelling the conversation or urgent the business, his eyes would slide away to follow Cosmo or Hilda if they strayed too near a hassock or coffin stool. Once, when Daniel had called and he had invited them in, they had made immediately for the fringe of his ancient rug, followed by the hem of a curtain he had borrowed from the big house and finally the barley twist leg of his late Georgian side table, which had made Anthony squirm in his armchair.

He was not squirming now, partly because he was two drinks into his evening ration, which served to quell most of his anxieties. A third was being prepared alongside a whisky and soda for Daniel. Anthony's choice was gin and ice, both so liberally provided he went to fetch more. The fridge would not be overworked, thought Daniel, for it was as chilly inside as it had been outside and he wondered how Anthony in his old cardigan was not shivering with the cold.

They spoke about Stella Harper's renegade plan and agreed that she would be blocked procedurally, at least temporarily, at the PCC. That matter settled, Anthony leaned back in his armchair, let out a little sigh and stretched his legs so they extended beyond the hem of his cords and exposed two pink bands of flesh. Perhaps he noticed, because he withdrew them suddenly, bending slightly forward, as if he were about to confide something.

'Daniel, how do you think Bernard is doing?'

'Fine, I think. But why do you ask?'

Anthony swirled the gin and ice in his glass awkwardly. 'I've always felt very protective of Bernard. We were like brothers when we were boys.'

Daniel wondered if Bernard had ever felt the need of Anthony's protection.

'My father – he married Bernard's aunt, that's the connection – was killed at Anzio. I hardly remember him, I was only a boy and he was a soldier, career soldier I mean, so always away. Mama didn't fancy widowhood so she married again, in short order, another soldier. Not for him the hearth and home either. He expected her to form her existence around his, rather than around mine, and that was made easier by my dispatch to prep school at eight.'

'Same here. It seems very young now, doesn't it?'

'Oh I loved it, because home was so miserable.' He swirled the diminishing solids in his glass again. 'Bernard thinks I reminded my mother of my father and she couldn't bear it and came to resent me. So school was an escape from that. I remember one half-term waiting for someone to come and collect me, but nobody came. Eventually my housemaster's wife rang my mother to ask what time she was expecting to arrive, but she'd forgotten entirely and they were going skiing. She offered to pay if they would look after me, but she refused, so in the end they sent someone from Champton to come and pick me up. From then on I spent nearly all the holidays here, and it was... home. Bernard and I were the same age – he's two years older – and so we became, as I say, more like brothers than cousins.'

'And yet you are so different.'

'I suppose so. Bernard was always destined for this,' he made a circle in the air with his drinks hand, so the gin slopped dangerously around. 'Literally to the *manor* born ... Are you watching it?'

Daniel nodded. *To the Manor Born*, a comedy about a double-barrelled chatelaine displaced from her ancestral home by a rich parvenu, had been his mother's favourite programme. Indeed, it would be difficult to conceive of a programme more suited to her.

'I, on the other hand, was not,' continued Anthony. 'I wasn't really born to anything. And my place in the world, already indistinct, grew even more so as Bernard became more Bernard, with his destiny and his acres, and I retreated into the library and discovered books. Books were my salvation, actually. And then I went to Oxford, to read history, and surprised everyone by getting a first, and everyone thought I would become a don. But I knew it wasn't for me.'

'Why not?'

'Too obvious. Too comfortable. I didn't want to be discovered dead under a newspaper in the Senior Common Room, unnoticed for a term. Do you see?'

'Yes, I think so,' said Daniel.

'So I went to Grub Street. I started reviewing books for learned journals. And that suited me. And then I started writing for the *TLS* and *The Listener*, to the dismay of my academic peers who rather snarled at my worldly success, such as it was.'

'Was?'

'Yes... I've never really been one for sticking at things.' His voice trailed off and he looked into his glass.

Daniel had been cellarer at his theological college, a most disagreeable post which obliged him not only to keep the drinks cupboard stocked but also to clear up after every Common Room party. It had left him with rather a reduced view of the moral benefit of living life to its fullness, but also with a source of useful intelligence. He knew who drank what and had acquired a publican's practised eye for the signs of alcohol on body and spirit. Not that he really needed it with Anthony, whose patronage of the Royal Oak was steady and faithful and widely commented on.

'I ended up writing articles for the in-flight magazine of a rather unreliable airline that went bust. And so did I. You know why I am here, don't you?'

'You're the archivist, Anthony, and a very excellent one.'

'But you know about my own archive? Kept in a filing cabinet at St Luke's Hospital, where I was dried out. Temporarily.' He got up and went to pour another drink. 'I had to do something called group therapy. There was a woman who loved fuchsias above all things, and a Hong Kong tycoon's son with a heroin habit. And the wife of a rather well-known politician. We had to go trampolining.'

'Oh, were you any good?

'Not really. Balance, you see. One day Bernard's father came on a sort of state visit, he was chairman of the board of governors, and I think the only time I ever saw him flustered was when he saw me bouncing erratically in the gym.'

'Are you finding things difficult now?'

'I always find things difficult, Daniel. Don't you?'

7

Open Day at Champton House fell on the nearest weekend to St George's Day – 23 April, Shakespeare's birthday – which happened to be a Saturday this year, so the flag of St George fluttered correctly over its spiky roof. In the library a rare edition of Shakespeare's plays was lying open in a glass case. ('Rare,' remarked Anthony, 'in the sense that there's only one of them here.') Bernard, however, was not feeling terribly patriotic. He had conceded the invasive and disagreeable inconvenience of Open Day with great reluctance because, in his words, 'If I do, the fucking government might just leave me alone to enjoy my fucking house in peace.' In exchange for a lighter levy of tax the public was permitted to traipse through Champton's great rooms and gardens on bank holidays and when the gardens were at their best in high summer (and Bernard at his house in France). They were guided, supervised and in some cases suspiciously monitored by the tenantry and the village, especially the nosy among them. Margaret Porteous was the coordinator of volunteers, and went about her duties with zeal, a clipboard and a clear idea of who would be suitable for which part of the house.

The volunteers assembled in the great hall at nine in the morning for a briefing.

'Stanilands, to your urns!' They were on duty in the orangery, where teas were served. 'And remember, *ten* slices out of a cake, please!'

'Kath, Dora, would you do the old kitchens? It would be *marvellous* to have people who actually worked in them to explain how it was back then.'

Kath replied, 'It isn't how it was, though. It all got mucked around after the war.'

'I know, I know,' said Mrs Porteous, 'but just give them a flavour. Life above stairs, life below and all that?'

'Stella and Anne,' she continued, looking for the Mrs Harper and Dollinger, 'state drawing room and state dining room. I'll send you helpers to keep an eye on things.'

One year someone had taken a miniature of an eighteenth-century de Floures beauty which hung in a corner. It was later spotted on *Antiques Roadshow*, where it was rather dismayingly undervalued.

'Ned, would you do the library? And again, *no handling of the books*. They won't be interested in them anyway. I need volunteers for the servants' attics. Kath, Dora, perhaps you could split it between you?'

'Just like the old days, Mrs P,' grumbled Kath, 'basement to attic. Stairs stairs stairs. But we ent spring chickens nowadays.'

'I'm sure you'll manage, dear. Now, could we have Dot Staveley in the state bedroom and dressing room, please? And I shall be in the picture gallery as usual. If you need me, you will find me there.'

'Margaret, are the family around to help?' asked Mr Staveley, who was to be one of the greeters in the hall.

'Lord de Floures is not available today,' she said, hoping he had remembered it was an open day and stayed in the private wing of the house. The last time, he had forgotten the public were in and had appeared in his dressing gown in the hall to find a melee of various people wandering through. He had been so rude to the Heritage Society from Harpenden they had written to complain. And worse could happen. 'Alex may make an appearance. If he does, call for Honoria.'

'Which parts are out of bounds?'

'The east range, the loggia, the walled garden, the private bedrooms. And remember: no gossip about the family. If they ask about Lady de Floures, she is travelling on the continent. And keep them *moving*. The more we get through the merrier! Nathan, you are in charge of the old kitchen garden, the old sculleries and the glasshouses.'

Nathan Liversedge, uncomfortable wearing his jeans, flies half undone, and camouflage jacket and boots in the great hall, nodded. He was in his early twenties and had come to the estate in his teens, the grandson of Edgy, the quasi-legitimate gamekeeper; Edgy was from gypsy stock and Nathan had inherited his good looks – good tan, good teeth, nice curly black hair. Edgy, though settled, was never *really* settled, and passed on his way of life and view of the world to his grandson. They had made themselves indispensable, doing the work round the estate that no one else wanted to do now the ranks of gardeners and under gardeners were gone. Bernard had given them the old woodsman's cottage to live in – damp and dark, and probably not fit for human habitation – but Edgy had never complained and Nathan knew no better. There they ran their own enterprise, taking care of the jobs that needed doing, and sidelining in the provision of fancy meats to the restaurant trade, venison mostly, and once a fox that Edgy had skinned and butchered and given to a restaurateur from Leicester with whom he had fallen out. They also cleared drains, laid tarmac, killed vermin, raised game. Nathan had grown skilled in these activities, but he had not followed his grandfather into the rarer specialism of wart-charming. A few old folk would still call round to present their pustules for Edgy's attention, and Ned Thwaite, endlessly curious, had suggested to Margaret Porteous that Edgy do a wart-charming demonstration for Open Day. But Margaret had thought this too risky considering Edgy's language and lack of tact, so it fell to Nathan to front the garden department – and there he stood, looking slightly sick. He, like Bernard, hated Open Day, hated to have his domain invaded by the curious, and found the obligation to be accommodating and friendly so contrary to his nature he churned with anxiety for days before.

'Twenty minutes to opening, everybody, so to your positions – and remember we are *all* ambassadors for the family today.' When she said 'family', she inclined her head to one side in an unconscious act of obeisance.

The Champtonians went to their stations, as their forebears had in livery or aprons, the women carrying coals for the countless fires and the men carrying letters on silver salvers. Today, dressed by Marks and Spencer and C&A and the Grattan catalogue, they carried flasks of tea and coffee, tins of sandwiches and biscuits, and the crib sheets Mrs Porteous had issued:

The big painting over the first fireplace from the library end of the state drawing room is the 23rd Baron, Lord Gilbert de Floures, who was killed in South Africa in the Zulu Wars, and his unfortunate demise meant the 24th Baron succeeded. His portrait is in the billiard room, where he spent most of his time, before the drink took him.

Daniel wondered if Nathan knew his flies were undone. It mattered not only for the poor boy's dignity, but for reasons of clarity too. Daniel had been summoned recently to a conference at Diocesan House on 'Come, Lord Jesus, Look On Daventry!' – as if that unremarkable town might otherwise go unnoticed – and the concluding address had been given by an archdeacon who spoke for forty minutes, unaware that his flies were undone, a spectacle which became the talking point of the day and the only thing anyone remembered.

He caught up with Nathan as he was trying to escape. 'Nathan,' he said, 'forgive the impertinence, but your flies are undone.'

'I know they are, Rector, I'm going to get changed.'

They walked out into the courtyard together. 'Good lad. How's your grandfather?'

'Lying low, the lucky bugger.'

'Indeed so. What are you doing today?

'Tour of the kitchen garden, like. Glasshouses too, potting sheds. They're selling plants next to the car park, so I hope they all bugger off there instead.'

The previous Open Day there had been more complaints about Nathan than anyone else after a visitor had asked him to describe a typical day and Nathan had mentioned drowning kittens in a water butt (a scenario which had reduced several children to tears).

'Try not to swear, Nathan. And perhaps leave out drowning kittens.'

Nathan nodded, but seemed unsure.

At their various stations the people of Champton welcomed the first trickle of the crowds: coach parties with a particular interest in gardens or porcelain or paintings; carloads passing by, looking for tea and a wee; locals curious to tour the great house that had always been at the edge of their lives; and independent travellers with their Pevsners, who knew more about the angle buttresses and the quoins and the solars and the entablatures than the guides.

What was new was the number of people who wanted to see backstage, behind the green baize door, and explore the world which was inhabited by the servants. This was due to the spectacular success of *Upstairs, Downstairs* on the television some years before, a drama which told the entwined stories of an aristocratic family and those who looked after them, and had made the lives of scullery maids and chauffeurs as interesting to people as peers and prelates. This was all rather baffling to Bernard, who had grown up in a world where housemaids and footmen were called by the same name – not their own – to save his grandmother the bother of having to remember their real names. Occasionally the two worlds came into contact in ways that were unpredictable, sometimes alarming, occasionally moving, often improper. When Bernard inherited the estate, he discovered a shortlist of people to whom a sum was paid each year in acknowledgement of their hospitality to children born to housemaids out of wedlock, fathers officially unknown. One name he knew, a boy who had grown up to be a farm labourer in a neighbouring village, a legendary character so tough he had once extracted his own tooth using the penknife with which he castrated piglets. His red hair and blue eyes had also set him apart from the family he grew up in; but not, it was observed, from Bernard's.

Down in the basement, where once the duumvirate of housekeeper and butler ruled, Anthony Bowness had found a set of accounts from the early 1900s, with dozens on the payroll, from dairy maids to clock winders, paid a pittance and crammed, for the most part, into attics as mean and as bare as a workhouse dormitory. How quickly times changed. Two world wars, and the rise of Labour, had drawn down the blinds on that peculiarly charmed existence for the tiny few who enjoyed it.

However, its enchantment had, if anything, grown – now fictionalised, idealised, industrialised, transformed into a commodity which people were beginning to call 'heritage'. But Anthony had the records, the account books, the ledgers, the head counts, the totals, the leases, the evictions, which, if you pieced them together, told a plainer tale of the intersecting lives of the people of Champton. He was looking at a pile of documents now, ledgers from the estate carpentry shop, where a head carpenter, and four under-carpenters, and a boy, then earned their livings, but concentration was made impossible by the shuffling of feet outside. Visitors were being led along the corridor to see the servants' hall with its huge panel of bells on coiled springs to be rung for the morning room, the drawing room, the Duchess of York's bedroom, the ledger room, the state dressing room, the billiard room – an endless tintinnabulation for tea and coal and soda.

His door burst open and a parade of people filed in looking around but not seeing him.

'Can I help you?' he asked, witheringly.

'And *this*,' said Alex de Floures, pushing them in from behind, 'is where the housekeeper ruled over the lives of the female servants, and quite a lot of the male servants too. Disciplines were imposed here. No helping yourself to bits of coal or beef bones, no canoodling with fancy men, and where dismissals were pronounced on those who had, especially if they had canoodled with my ancestors who should have known better. Oh hello, Anthony.'

Anthony stood up.

'This is Mr Bowness, our cousin, new archivist, keeper of secrets, a few of his own too, I should think.'

One of the visitors tittered.

Anthony sighed. 'I'm actually working on the secrets of estate carpentry at the moment, rather detailed, laborious and time-consuming work, as it happens. No dramas, apart from the occasional appearance of death-watch bettle. So… if you would excuse me?'

'Of course, sorry to barge in like this, but I wanted these good people to see the engine room, where the real work was done to keep a place like this going, and the unsentimental reality of life for the below-stairs people, and the superannuated nurses, and the disgraced housemaids…'

'I wonder if that was perhaps the butler's responsibility rather than the housekeeper's?'

'Both, in *living* memory,' said Alex, as he ushered his little group out. Anthony wondered why he was wearing his father's old army beret with its now thinning cockade of red and white.

Anthony decided to retreat, to take a break, and seek the quiet of the back room at the Royal Oak, and a pint of Tolly Cobbold and what they were now calling a ploughman's lunch, which no ploughman had ever eaten, and certainly not with a sachet of Colman's English Mustard, nor with the leisure that he had at his disposal.

The visitors were soon spreading throughout the house, to the basement via the back stairs, to the state rooms on the first floor via the grand staircase from the great hall, and then the lesser staircases which led to the servants' quarters and the attics. Dot Staveley had gathered a cluster around her in the state bedroom.

'It was built in the 1690s for the visit of William and Mary...'

'William and Mary who?'

'King William and Queen Mary, who were on the throne at that time. The then Lord de Floures was a courtier, deputy master of the great wardrobe, and very influential. The king and queen came here in 1692, a great honour, and an expensive one too, because they had to have fitting accommodation, so the very best carpenters and plasterers and what we could call interior designers were brought to Champton, and this is the result.' Her sweeping arm invited them to marvel at the state bedroom, recently restored thanks to a large facility fee which Nicolas Meldrum, Bernard's bean-counting estate manager, had charged a Hollywood producer to film a preposterous period drama. The hangings, left to bleach and fray, were magnificently restored, the pictures cleaned, the plasterwork touched up, and it was now as sumptuous a bedroom as any in England. But what the crowd, after an *ooh* and an *aah*, really wanted to see was the bathroom, installed in Victorian times in what had been a dressing room, a cast-iron bath and a boxy wooden WC.

'Is that where the king went to the toilet?'

'Not King William, the bathroom dates from the reign of Queen Victoria, but her son, Edward VII, would have … known it. He was a friend of the 23rd Lord de Floures and came here often in the 1880s and '90s when he was Prince of Wales.'

'Did he go to the toilet here?'

'He might have done, although there's another room, more comfortable than this, called the Prince of Wales bedroom, named after him. Or was it the one who became Edward VIII? I'm not sure. Perhaps it was both?'

This information was silently digested by the semicircle as they looked at the painted porcelain and polished mahogany throne, imagining, uncomfortably, its royal use.

Dot saw Kath Sharman pass on one of her increasingly resented descents from attic to basement. 'Miss Sharman, do you happen to know if it was Edward VII or Edward VIII who gave the name to the Prince of Wales bedroom?'

'I don't know, Dot. But they both made use of it. Noisy use of it, according to my ma and grandma. Didn't yours ever tell you?'

'Thank you, Miss Sharman.' Dot did not like the Sharman sisters, nor they her, because Dot, or Dorothy as she preferred now to be known, was the daughter of a former ladies' maid and had married up, in the form of Norman, whose father had left service as a chauffeur, started a garage and prospered. Now Dot and Norman lived a middle-class life and socialised with the Porteouses and the Harpers and the Dollingers, but the Sharman sisters could still remember her from the days when her mother wouldn't have been seen in the state bedroom unless she'd been rung for.

Norman Staveley overheard this exchange, or part of it, passing Dora on his way to the state bedroom. 'What was that about?' he asked as Dot's batch of visitors wandered away to look at the picture gallery.

'You know the Sisters Grim, can't let an opportunity to snipe pass. Insulting me about Mother. In front of people.'

Norman shook his head. 'I've come to see if you want to swap.'

'I'd love a break, is it not time?'

'Another hour. But if I take over here you could take ten minutes; Margaret and Daniel are on duty in the hall.'

'OK, thanks, love.'

Dot slipped away, or as near to slip as her build allowed. Her mother had been thin; genes, perhaps, or maybe her unexpressed anger had burned the meagre calories she'd been allotted, but whatever it was, those genes had not come Dot's way, and she had in middle age become plump. Norman had too; a spreading belly had begun to overhang his belt and overhang everything else when he looked at himself naked in the bathroom mirror. He felt more and more uncomfortable with his nakedness, not only because of its pasty wobbliness, but because he only really felt himself when he was dressed up, dinner jacket for a function, in his alderman's robes at council, Sunday best at church. He did not like to be reminded of what he was without them: 'a parvenu', as the last but one Lady de Floures had once described him in a voice too loud for him to suspect she had not meant him to hear. But then he knew their family secrets – and so did Dot: both their parents had served them – although that went both ways. He wondered if Lady de Floures knew his secret, the secret his father had shared with him not long before he died, on his conscience, he supposed, and not something that fitted the official story of his rise from service to business on grit and determination and nous. The thought of Dot discovering that was worse than the thought of her seeing him naked. He did up the button on his sports jacket.

8

Daniel was in the hall. A tall woman approached, with purpose in her step. 'Hello, Daniel, do you remember me?' His mental Rolodex whirred but could not place her. 'I'm Ned and Jane's daughter. Angela.' She thrust her hand at him but looked at him steadily while she shook in a way Daniel felt was more businesslike than cordial. She was dressed a little like Honoria, he thought, in boots and jeans and a sweater under a well-cut jacket, a silk scarf and pearl earrings. Mid to late forties? Hard to tell, thanks to the ministrations of a colourist; her make-up too was not intended to camouflage the years but to present, at best, an estimate.

'Angela. The lawyer?'

'That's right.'

'And you have a sister who … isn't a lawyer?'

'Gillian. No, she followed in our father's footsteps. Teaching. How are you? Dad tells me you're having a battle over pews.'

'Not a battle, exactly. We have yet to form a common mind on the subject.'

'I'm a litigator, Daniel.'

He smiled. 'I hope never to have to speak to you professionally.'

She smiled too, then said, 'Actually, I need to speak to you professionally.' Daniel looked alarmed, but she said, 'Yours, not mine.'

'Oh yes?'

'Can I come and see you? It will have to be soon, I have to be back in London tomorrow.'

'Do you have a moment now?'

'Now? Yes, I suppose so. Aren't you supposed to be on duty?

'I'm a floating presence. Shall we?'

He gestured towards the open doors that led from the hall to the courtyard. As soon as they were outside, she said, 'Have you noticed anything about Dad lately?'

'What sort of thing?'

'Deterioration.'

'No. He limps a bit, but he always has. Ex rugby player, I suppose? If anything, he seems livelier than usual. He's very absorbed in local history.'

'Yes, he told us all about it, and I do mean *all*.' She turned and looked back at the great window. 'I don't mean his body, I mean his mind.'

'How do you mean?'

'I mean he's not as sharp or as vivid or as … he used to be. Sometimes when I'm talking to him I think he's … gone out of focus. If I'm noticing it from phone calls and the occasional visit, I wonder how he looks to the people around him?'

'Have you said anything about this to your mother?'

'God, no. Not yet. It would make her more anxious than she already is.'

'Your sister? Is she here too?'

'Somewhere. In the garden. She's like Mum, a worrier.'

Daniel thought for a moment. 'Honestly, I hadn't noticed, but I haven't been looking. I will now.'

'Thanks.' She reached into her bag and produced a sheaf of business cards, which she looked through before picking one and handing it to Daniel. 'Call me if you need to. My private number's on the back.' There was a pause.

'I'd give you my business card but I'm afraid I don't have one,' said Daniel. 'My telephone number is Champton 431. It's the date of the first Council of Ephesus, if that helps?'

Angela produced an expensive-looking pen. 'Write it down, would you? On the back of this?'

It was a vintage Mont Blanc Meisterstück 146. 'Goodness,' said Daniel, 'what a *treasure*!'

'The pen? Ex-husband's. Like the car and the cottage. Call me sentimental.'

Daniel wrote down his number on the back of another of her business cards. They seemed to come in different editions, some with more telephone numbers than others, the degree of access, he supposed, tailored to the importance of the client. One, he suspected, might be for a mobile phone and he had to restrain an impulse to peer into her bag when she opened it, for he had never actually seen a mobile phone, but she produced a Filofax instead. Something in Daniel quivered, and he felt for a moment not envy, exactly, but disappointment that all he had to boast of was his Parson's Pocketbook, a diary produced for the benefit of clergy, with useful things like Collects and the dates of Ember Days marked in, but no more lambent with the white heat of technology than his bicycle clips.

Angela Thwaite walked off towards the kitchen garden and Daniel returned to the coolness of the hall. 'The family still lives here?' asked a lady with an accent – French, he thought – admiring the great window.

'Yes, still here,' said Daniel, 'it is a family home.'

'And what do they ... *do*?'

'Well, they farm. The estate is very large, fifteen thousand acres, and as you can imagine that requires a lot of looking after.'

'Yes, but what does a lord *do* that is different from a farmer?'

'Lord de Floures sits in parliament, he is a member of the upper chamber, the House of Lords.'

'So they still are in charge of the country?'

'Not in charge, really. That responsibility falls to the elected members of parliament, one of whom is invited to form a government by the queen if he – or she – has the support of a majority of members.'

'So the queen is really in charge?'

'She is the head of state, and without her assent nothing can be done, but she acts on the advice of ministers.'

'A strange way to do things.'

'It seems to work on the whole.'

'In my country we cut off the head of our king.'

'Yes, we did that here too, but after a while we replaced him. The de Floures family played an important part in that, as a matter of fact.'

'Oh yes, we did that too, more than once, but it never ... endured. Perhaps we had no de Floures? Though the name is French. I suppose they come to England in *la conquête normande?* And now milord goes to London and sits with the queen.'

'I'm not sure the present Lord de Floures considers himself particularly close to the centre of affairs,' said Daniel, wondering when Bernard had last addressed his peers in any venue on the parliamentary estate other than a bar. 'But the French connection is strong. This, you probably know, was a Free French hospital during the war. De Gaulle visited.'

'Yes, I know. My uncle was here. I have always wanted to see it. He had strong memories of this place.'

'He was wounded?'

'I think so, but he was not here because he was wounded, he was an ... *instructeur?* He was of the – I don't know how you say it – *Fusiliers marins?*'

'Marines. We have the equivalent.'

'Yes, I know you do, he was very chauvinistic about them. But I know he liked it here. Imagine that, liking the war? Apart from the food. It was so bad they taught the local girls how to make simple French things, *Hachis Parmentier, soupe a l'oignon*, even the *salades* were too difficult for them.'

'I'm afraid their cuisine went with them. It's very ... *rosbif* here now.'

9

It was beginning to get dark when Anthony let himself into the church. It had been open all day for the benefit of visitors, and volunteer stewards had managed, as far as he could tell, to dissuade the thieving among them to take any of its treasures. The grille to the de Floures chapel had been opened and the tombs in their crowded glory had been admired and explained and interpreted, with cheerful inaccuracy, he assumed, by Ned Thwaite, who was a mine of village folklore and a good teller of a tale. Anthony had promised to lock up and was late, very late, having enjoyed his pint and his ploughman's at the Royal Oak, where he had got into conversation with a French lady, who was mystified by the curly-headed king's likeness appearing in a tree on the sign outside. He had attempted to explain, in a more than usually relaxed state, the Stuart Restoration, and the similarities and dissimilarities with the French monarchy. Suddenly the striking of a clock had made him think of the church, open and unattended, and he had hurried from the pub.

The church was empty and he sat at the back, a little breathless, in one of the pews that had been selected for removal should plans be approved. How different the building looked, he thought, from here, all about the backs of people's heads, with their unconscious tells, and beyond them, but obscured, the distant chancel and altar and the holy and important things that happened there. From where he was sitting the bench ends – culminating in poppy heads alternated with roses – looked like the heads of sitting parishioners, silent and unmoving. They looked, if not identical, then very alike, and if some were Victorian and others fifteenth century, it would take someone who knew what he was looking for to tell the difference.

He took a hassock, for some reason emblazoned with a border collie in tapestry stitch, placed it under his knees, and leaned forward in a peculiar attitude of prayer, his forearms flat on the book ledge, his chin resting on the back of the pew in front, his eyes screwed up in concentration.

The Stanilands appeared from the orangery, where they had sweated all day, with the tins gratifyingly full of tea money. The Sharman sisters did a sweep, above and below stairs, and the carpets were straightened, and shutters closed, and runners de-creased, and the house which had been full – as such a house was intended to be – returned to the quiet and emptiness of its daily repose. By a quarter past seven only Daniel, Margaret and Mrs Shorely, the housekeeper, remained to do a final check of the state rooms and switch on the alarms.

'A great success, Rector, don't you think?' asked Mrs Porteous.

'Yes. And more to come.'

It was Sunday tomorrow, and in acknowledgement of the Sabbath the house and grounds would not open until midday.

The church would stay open too, once the liturgical obligations of the morning were done and a steady stream of those visitors who felt up to a quarter-mile walk through the park would come to see its treasures. Daniel had noticed those visits becoming more touristic than pious: each year more needed to be explained about the hope of the Resurrection and life beyond, and the once customary reverence was fading fast. People chatted liberally, sat in the pews with their thermos of tea or a can of Coke, wandered into the sanctuary. One man had put his fag out in the piscina, normally reserved for priestly ablutions. This irritated Anthony Bowness greatly and he could treat such infringements with an unrestrained asperity. Daniel had tried to dissuade him from this, not because he did not share his disappointment at the casual treatment of sacred things, but just because people simply did not know, and if they did not know, then they meant no disrespect. Pulling a face and tutting just made them feel uncomfortable, or insulted, and Daniel was determined that no one should feel either on what could be their first – and perhaps their last – visit to the church.

He said goodbye to Margaret Porteous and walked home through the park to rendezvous with Theo, who had spent the day observing, and would no doubt have questions for him as they had supper (a light collation he hoped, after the pound and a half of date and walnut cake he had felt duty-bound to consume).

Theo, it turned out, was not at home. He had telephoned Audrey to tell her he would get a pie and a pint at the pub, where he'd spent an informative afternoon observing things, and fallen into conversation with Anthony Bowness and a Frenchwoman with fascinating tales to tell about her countrymen's wartime service at the house.

'It sounded like very thorough research indeed to me,' said Audrey. 'I suppose he'll roll in at closing time, smelling of cigarettes and beer. I made a chicken casserole as well, it's in the Aga, but I can't face it, I only want a sandwich. Will you have some?'

'I'm not hungry. Do you mind if I pass?'

'Not at all, it'll be better tomorrow.'

They ate in front of the television, and he left Audrey there with the *Radio Times* and the bone-handled magnifying glass she had started using to read small print (although she could be remarkably sharp-eyed when it suited her). He went to his study to finish his sermon or rather to rewrite it, for Theo's presence – literally looking over his shoulder until he asked him not to – had been so off-putting he felt it necessary to check he had not distractedly recommended a heretical doctrine. Then Cosmo was at his feet, looking up at him, knowing it was time for Daniel to go to church to say his solitary Saturday Evensong. He looked in on his mother, who had fallen asleep in front of *Cagney and Lacey*; the excitements of the Open Day – complete with Bernard's demand that his son disarm the visitors, which she had been fortunate to witness – had tired her, and with another Open Day to follow, her body, if not her mind, had chosen to close down after supper.

He let himself out of the kitchen door, Cosmo and Hilda following, and went into the night. The dogs sniffed round the gravestones as they usually did, and Daniel gave them grace time in which to void, which they did at the churchyard's edges where the ivy falling down the walls met the long grass untouched by mower or scythe. When they were done, he opened the door to the vestry and they followed him in.

The church was in darkness and the dogs ran off to sniff their way round the pews, richer in scents this evening with the crowds (and other dogs) passing through for Open Day. He went to sit at his stall and slowly said the Jesus Prayer, calling to mind the occasions that day when he had been less than patient, less than kind, less than generous, especially when he had been absorbed in his thoughts about the machinations of the Flower Guild and the motivations of Stella Harper, and his mother's combativeness.

And then he felt, faintly, that something was not quite right: something was very slightly disrupting the rhythm of his prayer, pressing at the edge of his consciousness, calling him from the mystery of God and back into the world. He sat silently for a moment, listening, and then realised what it was.

The dogs were quiet.

Normally there was sniffing and scratching as background noise to his prayer, and the quiet percussion of their claws on the flags, but not now. Instead there was a sound he could not quite identify at first. He knew it was the dogs, but they were making a different kind of noise, of licking, almost of lapping. He called them. Nothing. He called them again, sharply, and they ran towards him from one of the pews at the back, and he could just make out behind them what looked like some kind of mark left by wet paws across the flagstones.

'Cossy! Hildy! What is it?'

As they got nearer he saw it was a trail, wet and shining where the slanting moonlight fell across it. It looked like they had run through paint, or varnish? Could a visitor have spilled something?

He followed the trail back to where it led, feeling more anxious with every step.

Lying open on the floor was a pair of secateurs – how careless of the Flower Guild to leave them there – and then he saw a body, crumpled into the gap between bench and kneelers. A body in a tweed jacket with patched elbows. Anthony Bowness's body – and from his neck there spread a pool of blood, thick and dark and shiny, sticky on the paws of his dogs, who now stood beside him, straining to return to their find, their tails wagging with excitement.

10

Blue lights flashed outside the rectory windows as the church of St Mary Champton was turned into a crime scene. Police officers had taped off the entrances, the vestry door and the lychgate, and a forensic team were standing around, half in and half out of their white boiler suits (and what looked to Daniel like his grandfather's galoshes).

Audrey was in the bathroom with the dogs, rinsing from their paws and muzzles Anthony Bowness's drying blood. In the kitchen a kettle, filled and refilled, stood at the side of the Aga, next to the teapot from which Daniel had provided refreshment for the two constables from town who had arrived a few minutes after his call to 999 and had immediately asked for the clothes he was wearing. They had been followed by the ambulance, and the CID, and the doctor, who had ascertained that the churchyard would, in due course, receive another resident.

PC Scott was sitting at the kitchen table with an over-sweetened mug of tea.

'It's a horrible thing to happen, sir.'

'It is. Quite shocking. I don't suppose you are called out to very many scenes like this, Constable?'

'Not in Champton, sir. I don't know when we last had an incident like this here. It's human nature, though: sooner or later something horrible is bound to happen. Even in a place like Champton. But you would know all about that.'

'Yes. It's different, though, when it comes so close to you, and so unexpectedly.'

PC Scott nodded and sipped his tea.

'What happens now?'

'The SOCOs, scene of crime officers, take over. They need to get all the forensic they can and start a full investigation. Because of the deceased's connection to Lord de Floures, the top brass will be interested too, I dare say. And the press. I know you won't talk to anyone out of turn, sir. We'll need to talk to you formally, an interview; tomorrow, I expect. You're not planning to go anywhere?'

Daniel shook his head.

'Are you on your own, sir?'

'No. My mother's here. She's taking care of the dogs. And my brother's staying but he's not back from the pub yet.'

Bernard de Floures knocked on the open back door. 'Am I interrupting, Dan?' He was carrying a bottle of whisky. Twelve-year-old Macallan. What a good soul, thought Daniel.

The policeman stood up, almost as if he were standing to attention. 'Sir!'

'Constable Scott, you know, I assume, Lord de Floures, Mr Bowness's cousin?' said Daniel. 'You will want to speak to him?'

'We are acquainted, sir.'

'Oh it's you, Scott. That's good. Any ideas yet? About this awful thing?'

'Nothing to report just yet, m'lord.'

Daniel pulled out a chair. 'Tea, Bernard?'

'Not likely. Will you join us, Scott?' Bernard plonked the bottle of whisky firmly on the table.

'No thank you.'

Daniel went to get two tumblers and the soda siphon from the drawing room.

When he returned, Bernard was talking to PC Scott, not in the patrician way he normally talked to people, enquiring after their children or the health of a dog, but with businesslike purpose.

'And we will have to make sure the press don't come swarming all over the estate – do you think I should speak to the chief constable about that?'

'I would.'

'And I don't want people all over the village too, but I don't suppose I can do much about that…'

'We'll do what we can, m'lord.'

'Thank you, Scott, that will be all,' said Bernard, forgetting that he was not the host.

PC Scott stood. 'Good evening. If anything should crop up, or if you hear something, you know where to find me.'

As Daniel saw him out, Bernard poured two large tumblers of whisky. 'Bruise of water, Dan? And I know it's barbaric, but don't forget I like ice in mine.'

Daniel shook ice cubes from the plastic tray in the freezer, filled a little jug with water from the tap, and they settled at the kitchen table, side by side, so they did not have to look at each other, a configuration Daniel found more conducive to difficult conversations.

'You know, he wouldn't have been here if it hadn't been for me. I wanted to get our records into order and Anthony was at a loose end.'

'Why now?'

'He lived an unsettled life. A vagabond life, almost. I thought that coming to Champton might help him to settle.'

'What sort of a vagabond life?'

Bernard again looked uncomfortable. 'Oh, I don't know. Anthony never really had a role, unlike me. And the roles we play in life can anchor us, don't you think?'

'They can imprison us too,' said Daniel. 'Do you know if he had made any enemies on his travels? Was he in trouble of any kind? Debt? Can you think of any reason why someone would want to do him harm?'

'No, none at all,' said Bernard. 'But you never really know anyone, do you? He was a drinker, but I'm sure you knew that. He got in a terrible mess with it for a while. Couldn't work, couldn't look after himself. Kept passing out, once conspicuously enough – a memorial service – to be noticed by that awful Dempster who wrote about it in the *Daily Mail* and shamed him. And one day he nearly drank himself to death, rather spectacularly; it ended in a fight with a member of staff at the London Library, who tried to rouse him from his armchair by banging a gong over his head. I got to hear of it, so he went to St Luke's to dry out, and then came here. Archivist at Champton, suits him, don't you think?'

Daniel wondered if it did indeed suit him, collating the achievements of his ancestors, measuring them against his own. The daily reminder of his dependency on the generosity of his cousin.

Bernard paused, and poured another drink, and they sat drinking in silence for a while. 'Poor Anthony,' he said, 'poor fellow.'

A policeman knocked at the door. 'Reverend, your brother is here.'

'Yes, let him in, please.'

Theo almost stumbled in; Daniel couldn't tell if it was haste or Guinness. 'Dan, what the hell's going on? I almost had to give a blood sample to get past those coppers.'

'I just discovered Anthony's body in church.'

'Oh my God! What happened?'

'I'm probably not meant to tell you, but you'll find out soon enough. He was murdered.'

'Jesus Christ!'

Bernard poured another whisky.

11

In the morning, not fully awake, Daniel opened the back door to let the dogs out as he always did, and they immediately burst into furious barking. The police, dark strangers, were trespassing on their territory, the church and its yard temporarily theirs; Daniel called them back in and for a moment they were confused, caught between instinct and obedience. Eventually they returned and he let them out of the front door instead; they went about their business on the tranquil lawn in front of the rectory, the excitement of the previous minute entirely forgotten.

The conscientiousness of Daniel's species, even more unusually developed in him, was preoccupied with the thought of being interviewed, a conversation he had tried not to rehearse in his head, but nevertheless had. After Bernard had left the previous night, he had made some notes as an aide-memoire, for experience had taught him that memory was very often a function of the imagination and he wanted, above all, to be tidy when answering the investigator's questions, to respond with cool reason to the chaos of a violent and unexpected act.

And then he became aware of being watched from the end of the drive. It was Margaret Porteous who caught his eye and waved. Daniel, in his pyjamas and dressing gown, waved back hesitantly, and regretted it immediately because she took that as an invitation to advance and came briskly up the drive with a look of business about her. Daniel retreated into the hall and vaguely considered putting on his heavy black woollen funeral cloak but in the end just fastened his dressing gown more tightly and body-blocked Mrs Porteous on the steps.

'Rector!' she said, formally. 'I'm sorry to disturb you so early, but I wondered if I might be able to help in some way. Such terrible news!'

Champton did not think of itself as a gossipy place, but Daniel had often noticed – and had reason to regret – that information flowed through its houses and cottages like current through a circuit. The circuit had flickered into life, with the first sighting of a flashing blue light last night, and within a few minutes of Daniel telephoning Bernard with the news of his cousin's death, Alex de Floures, sworn to secrecy, was swearing the housekeeper to secrecy too and soon the circuit was buzzing with energy.

'Would you forgive me, Margaret? I'm not fit for company.'

The dogs flowed past them into the hall and Daniel made to follow them.

'Rector. What are we to do?'

'About what?'

'About church. I presume services today are cancelled?'

'No, they are not. We will have an evening service in the house chapel at six. Perhaps you could help spread the word?' he asked, unnecessarily.

'Yes, of course. And the Open Day?'

'Bernard thought it not proper to open today, so that's off. I hope people won't be disappointed.'

'I'm sure they'll understand. And I suppose the police will want to speak to us.'

'Yes, I suppose so.'

'We might have witnessed something. We might have seen the murderer!'

'We don't know much yet, Margaret.'

'All that blood! Dreadful! Are the funeral arrangements underway?'

'I couldn't possibly say. Perhaps it would be better if we just held all those concerned in our prayers for now?'

Mrs Porteous looked chastened, for a second. 'Quite so. Poor, poor Anthony. Who could possibly want to do such a thing? And poor *Bernard*. They were close, you know.'

Daniel had been inching backwards. 'I really must go. Goodbye.'

As she bustled back down the drive, no doubt deciding whom to telephone first, Daniel went to the kitchen to make some coffee and toast and wondered what the day would bring. People would want to know what had happened, visitors arriving for Open Day would have to be turned away, the police would have questions. The funeral would have to be arranged, but they would have to wait until the coroner released the body, which could be some time, and who knew what would stir beneath the surface in the meantime? Deaths go off like depth charges, an explosion, and then the slow surfacing of – who knows what? – as the community comes together and confronts the reality of a terrible deed.

It was not Daniel's first brutal death. In his first parish there had been a murder in his first week, and in the years since several had followed, some brought to book, others unproven, perhaps many that had gone unnoticed? More than once he had buried someone whose murderer he was sure was among the pall-bearers. And then there were the murders by neglect, or abandonment; and the long-fuse murders, the most wicked of all, not visited upon the victim in a moment's rage, but slowly, inexorably, undetectably, killing first joy, then feeling, then leaving a life so emptied out the victim would fade away, or drink themselves away, or just give up.

Who would murder Anthony? Daniel had not known him for long, but he was an unlikely candidate, he thought, for this fate. Was it connected with his past, an enemy made in his indistinct life in town? Or did the cause lie closer, perhaps in the parish for which Daniel had the cure of souls?

By the time he was dressed he had begun mentally to tweak his sermon. His mother appeared for the kitchen passage, a slice of toast in hand.

'I just saw Margaret Porteous practically running down the drive, looking full of news. What did you tell her?'

'Nothing. I was rather hoping the sight of me in my dressing gown would fend her off, but she did not seem to notice.'

A shred of marmalade plopped onto the floor from her tilting slice. 'I think a morning stroll to see the primroses. And to hear what people are saying.'

'Must you, Mum? Better to say nothing.'

'I'm not stupid, darling. I will say nothing, and discover *everything*.' It was the kind of challenge Audrey enjoyed, and she crunched her toast noisily in anticipation.

The doorbell rang loudly, pulled with more muscle than usual.

'I wonder what she wants now?' said Audrey, as Daniel went to answer it. But it wasn't Margaret Porteous; it was a young man with a tape recorder and a photographer, who took a picture of Daniel standing half in and half out in his dressing gown and pyjamas.

'Reverend Clement? *Daily Express*, can you tell us about the murder last night?'

'I can't say anything at the moment,' said Daniel, closing the door. The doorbell rang again, and through the hall window he saw more reporters coming down the drive and a man with a television camera and another with one of those fluffy grey tubular microphones that made him think of Dougal from the *Magic Roundabout* grown silvery with age.

There was the sound of groaning from the stairs and Theo appeared, wearing Daniel's second-best dressing gown open over a shirt and boxer shorts.

'Good morning, darling,' said Audrey.

'Morning. Who was that at this ridiculous hour?'

'The *Daily Express*.'

'Oh good Lord, I'd better make myself decent.'

'It's not a photo call, darling – well, not for you. Why don't you both come and have breakfast?'

They sat at the kitchen table, and Audrey, on the principle that a strenuous day needs heavy stoking, produced bacon and eggs and mushrooms and tomatoes and sausages from Dennis the butcher in Braunstonbury with whom she had a rather flirtatious relationship, like a wartime housewife on coupons using all her charms for an ox heart. It was a breakfast that

Theo, hungover, particularly welcomed, not only for its curative properties but because he had dropped off after two of Bernard's whiskies last night and had an incomplete picture of the horror that had happened.

Daniel went through it, rehearsing, in a way, for the police statement.

'Poor you,' said Theo, 'glad I missed it,' though he must have sounded a little disappointed, because Audrey said, 'Oh, the police will want to talk to you too, Theo. To all of us. To establish where we were. Where were you yesterday? I hardly saw you during Open Day.'

'I was recceing the parish, Dan's suggestion.' A look of anxiety crossed his brother's face. 'You did say, Daniel, didn't you? I talked to people, about you. About your vicaring. They adore you!'

'I'm not up for an award, Theo.'

'I know. Just to say their reports were favourable, very favourable. Not just the posh people.'

'Whom do you mean?'

'Once I'd done the house I did the garden, and got talking to that young gardener – Nathan, is it? He said how much you'd done for him and for his family, so I went to see his grandfather.'

'You saw Edgy?'

'Yes.'

'He let you in?'

'Couldn't have been nicer. After a while. I sat with him in that extraordinary kitchen, like something from a documentary about peasant life in the Balkans. And he gave me his homemade plum gin, more like a wine than gin.'

'Plum jerkum,' said Audrey. '*Very* traditional.'

'And *very* powerful. So we got pissed – well, I did – and he gave me his baccy and papers and I rolled fags, and we talked. What a fascinating man. He started out as a gypsy prize fighter. Paid for it, though, a right mess it made of him. Face like cheese and hands like hooves.'

'A great character, Edgy. And always good for a pheasant or a hare. And he's been good for Nathan. And Nathan good for him,' said Audrey.

'It's one of the things I like about this sort of place,' said Daniel. 'It functions, it perpetuates itself. The generations coming take over from the generations going. Skills are preserved, the old and feeble are taken care of, the young are brought up. Nathan, without having intended to, will inherit from Edgy, like Bernard from his father and grandfather. When the old order passed, the gamekeepers, and the under gardeners, and warreners…'

'What's a warrener?'

'He was the man who kept the rabbits. When they faded away it was people like Edgy who took over.'

'Resourceful?'

'Very.'

'Likes you, by the way. Respects you. Quite old-fashioned.'

'Respects the calling. Gypsies are very religious. It's not always orthodox belief, but they believe. What did you do after Edgy's?'

'Only one thing I could do, I went to the pub.' He was quiet for a second. 'Anthony was there, talking to some Frenchwoman. I must have been one of the last people to see him alive.'

'Write down everything you remember, Theo. The police will want to talk to you as well as to me. And to you, Mum. I must get ready…'

12

Daniel was sitting in his study, a little awkwardly, for this time it was him being interviewed rather than the other way round. His interviewer was a man in his thirties, blond, blue-eyed, big (too big for indoors, almost out of scale – Daniel imagined him playing rugby or dispersing crowds). He was wearing an off-the-peg suit that did not really fit and made him look uncomfortable. He was Detective Sergeant Vanloo from Braunstonbury CID. Vanloo, thought Daniel, Dutch? South African? But the accent was from the north-west, Manchester or thereabouts.

He had declined Audrey's offer of refreshments, and asked if there were somewhere he could ask 'the vicar' a few questions?

He sat in the chair opposite Daniel, looking like a growth-spurted child in a primary-school classroom, but there was nothing childlike about his eyes, which took everything in. He produced a lined A4 spiral-bound notebook and a plastic automatic pencil. It was a Pentel SP 0.9 mm, and Daniel felt a pulse of affinity.

'Forgive me for asking the obvious, but would you state your name, your address and your occupation, please, Reverend?'

Daniel winced at the solecism of being addressed as 'Reverend'. 'I am the Reverend Canon Daniel Clement, and I am Rector of Champton. I live here at the rectory.'

'And now long have you been living here, sir?'

'For eight years now.'

'Anyone else resident at that address?'

'Yes. My mother, Mrs Audrey Clement.'

'Eight years there also, sir?'

'No, four. She moved in after the death of my father. My brother, Theo, is staying with us at the moment, he lives in London normally.'

'Thank you. I need to account for everyone's movements yesterday.'

'My mother's?'

'Hers, and your brother's. But if you could tell me yours, sir?'

'I was busy all day with Open Day at the house, and we had a lot of visitors to church too – it's a big event in our calendar, Sergeant. We saw off the last of our visitors at a little after half past five and I got home at about half past six, I think. Yes, the news was just ending. My mother and I had something to eat, just a tray, and then I went to church to say Evensong.'

'What time was that?'

'About nine, I think.'

DS Vanloo made a note. 'And your brother?'

'Theo? He got back later, after the police arrived.'

The telephone rang. 'Do you need to answer that?'

'My mother will.'

They sat in awkward silence, waiting for the ringing to stop.

'Do you know where your brother was between six and eight?'

'In the pub. He got back about half past ten, closing time.'

'And at what time did you discover the body?'

'It was shortly after nine. Actually, I can be sure of that because *Cagney and Lacey* had just come on.'

'Is that why you went to church?'

'I go to say Evensong and ...' Daniel realised the policeman had made a witticism. 'It's not really my thing. My mother likes it. She rather enjoys police dramas.'

'So why did you go then?'

'We'd both had rather a tiring day and she had nodded off. An opportune moment.'

'Was there a light on in church?'

'No. It was in darkness.'

'So you put the lights on?'

'No.'

'Why not?'

'I don't need to.'

The detective sergeant looked up from his notepad. 'A lot of people would find that quite ... unusual.'

'Oh, there's nothing to be afraid of.' Daniel faltered. 'Not normally. I have a little light in my stall – that's my seat in the chancel – for my prayer book, but I actually prefer the church to be in darkness. I know my way around. So I went to my stall and began to say my prayers ...'

'And you took the dogs?'

'They usually come with me to church. And it's their wee-wee time before bed.' What a ridiculous phrase, he thought. How would that sound read out in court? 'And they like to sniff

for mice. If they're lucky, maybe they'll find half a biscuit...
and I thought they would be particularly enthusiastic this
evening because we had had a lot of visitors come through
church on Open Day and some of them bring dogs. Lots to
sniff. And that's what I noticed. Or rather didn't notice: they
didn't sound enthusiastic. They were barely making a noise, and
that's what made me think something was out of the ordinary.
I called them, they didn't come. And so I called them again.
Eventually they did and I saw that they had left paw marks
all along the nave.'

'In the dark?'

'In the moonlight. I saw they'd left a trail and it was shiny.
So I went to see what they had found. And I saw it was
Anthony.'

'Did you recognise him in the dark?'

'I recognised his jacket – leather patches at the elbows –
and I went to him.'

'Did you think he was alive? Passed out?'

'I knew he was dead.'

'How?'

'From the way the body was lying. Like a rag doll. You know
what dead bodies look like?'

The policeman nodded. 'So why did you approach him?
You know you should not disturb a body?'

'The thought did not occur to me, I'm afraid. Not at first.
I went to pray a blessing over him. But there was a lot of
blood and it was messy and the dogs were excited... so I took
them home, called 999, and went to wake my mother – well,
the dogs woke my mother – and then I realised that I was
covered in blood too. It gets everywhere, doesn't it?'

'Why would Mr Bowness be in church at that time?'

'Anthony was a churchwarden, so he had a key and could come and go as he pleased. He was on the rota to lock up, I think, after Open Day, but he came to church quite often. He seemed to like it there. Sometimes he would join me for prayers in the morning or the evening, sometimes he would come and pray on his own. I suppose that's what he was doing when he met his end.'

'Why do you say that?'

'Because of where I found him. Because of the position of the body.'

'How do you mean?'

'He had fallen into the gap between the seat and the back of the pew in front and he had been kneeling.'

'How do you know?'

'He had used a hassock, a kneeler. To preserve knees from the hard floor. We hang them on hooks on the back of the pews for people to use when they pray. I've seen him do it many times. The hassocks were made for us by the trefoil guild for the Silver Jubilee. They worked so hard on them.'

Daniel recalled, with horrible clarity, the slick of blood, now tacky, that had spread like a flow of magma from the body, and had spilled over the edge of the wooden platform the pew rested on, and pooled on the stone flags of the nave aisle. He had knelt on the hassock next to the body to bless him and even in the darkness he saw blood oozing out, as black and sluggish as oil. When he put the lights on he saw it had jetted and spattered too, across the aisle and the pews on the south side.

'Sergeant, wouldn't the person responsible for this be covered in blood? I had it all over my trousers and my hands and my shoes just from when I discovered the body. Surely the murderer would have been sprayed with blood from head to toe? And he must have stabbed him with tremendous force. Secateurs hardly an obvious weapon?'

DS Vanloo shrugged his shoulders and said, 'The forensic report will give us an idea about that, sir.'

'And footprints …?'

'… in the report, sir.' There was something else. 'Can you think why Mr Bowness would have a pocket torch with him?'

'Yes. You might need a torch when the church is in darkness, to unlock and to get to the choir vestry, which is where the light switches are.'

'You don't need a torch.'

'Well, no. Not necessary.'

'Do you think Mr Bowness arrived in darkness?'

'He may have. It would make sense of the torch. But perhaps he always carried one.'

'The lights weren't on when you arrived.'

'No, they weren't.'

'Are you sure about that?'

'Yes, quite sure.'

'Would that not suggest to you that Mr Bowness had no need to switch on the lights when he arrived because it was still daylight?'

'I suppose so. Which would mean he got to the church before … eight? Or they could have been switched off by someone else.' Perhaps a laudable impulse for thrift had caused the murderer to put the light out?

'What was your relationship to Mr Bowness, sir?'

'Professional. Anthony was a churchwarden here at St Mary's and he's also the archivist for the Champton estate. Our lives overlapped quite often.'

'And personally? Would you describe yourself as a friend?'

'Yes. I think so. He had not been living here very long, but I knew him a little before he took up the post. He's a cousin of Lord de Floures and Champton has always been part of his life.'

'He lived here?'

'In an estate house, here in the village, but he works at the big house. And, as I said, he was a churchwarden here… You know… the bishop's representative among the laity…'

Shock, thought Daniel, is making me talk like this. He had another go.

'It's a layman – or woman – who takes on responsibility for running the church – the building and organisation and day-to-day running, and being a representative of the clergy to the people and the people to the clergy.'

'Did Mr Bowness have any enemies you are aware of?'

'No, none. But as I say, I did not know him well. You would need to speak to the family.'

DS Vanloo made a note. 'I will need to speak also to your mother and your brother, sir.'

It was not only the police who conducted interviews that morning. The journalists and the television news reporters had been up and down Main Street and into the post office, without much luck, because Anthony was a de Floures and a proper discretion was observed by those connected with the estate. No such obligation fell on Stella Harper, who had graciously granted an interview to the young man from the *Express* who had been standing outside her shop when she opened up. Audrey had seen her having her photograph taken with the church in the background, looking solemn and wearing mourning black.

Later Audrey put on the television – almost unheard of in hours of daylight unless it was Wimbledon fortnight – and shouted from the drawing room, 'Daniel, come quickly we're on the news!' It was the lunchtime local bulletin and in the space of only a couple of hours they had put a piece together about the murder. The reporter he had spent half the morning avoiding was reporting from outside the church (not shot, Daniel thought, from the best angle).

'A body was found last night in the parish church on the historic Champton estate, home of the de Floures family since the Norman Conquest.' The camera zoomed in on the lychgate, barred now by blue-and-white do-not-cross tape. 'It is believed the body was discovered by the rector, Canon Daniel Clement. It is thought to be a member of the de Floures family, although no one at Champton' – cut to a still of Champton House with Bernard and his then wife standing in front of it looking proprietorial – 'was available to make a statement. A police spokesman said an unexplained death was being investigated at an address in Champton and that the body of a male had been recovered…' There followed a shot of Daniel in the drive getting into the Land Rover. 'Canon Clement is the brother of the actor Theo Clement, who plays PC Heseltine in *Appletree End*.'

'Oh,' said Audrey, 'Theo will be pleased.'

Televisions all over Champton were flickering that afternoon, not only to see the house and the church and the rector, suddenly unfamiliar on the television screen, but also for the football: the League Cup final, Arsenal against Luton, a match expected not to overtax a spectator with the challenge of surprise.

Norman Staveley, with family origins in the hackney carriage trade, had been an Arsenal fan all his life, and after a rushed lunch of chops rather than a joint – for the solemn news of the discovery of Anthony's body and Dot's constant distractions on the telephone had disrupted the usual order – he pressed the button for ITV, and settled into his favourite chair, remote control, half of lager and an ashtray to his right. He nodded off during the pre-match chat, rice pudding from a tin as effective a soporific as a Mogadon, but with his semi-magical skill for waking up a minute before he had to, opened his eyes just before kick-off.

The teams were on the pitch, and he dozily looked out for potential danger in the Luton line-up, and for strength in the Gunners' – *O'Leary's still out, is Davis fit?* – while Dot talked in the background on the kitchen phone. 'I expect we'll have the police knocking on the door soon, the Porteouses have given a statement and the Achurches too, I think, so we must be next, only I hope it's not for a couple of hours because Norman's got the football on and God help them if they interrupt...' The whistle blew, and Norman came wide awake – hyper-awake, if you can be – after Arsenal missed a chance, then Luton, and then the wrong team scored ... 'Well, we didn't get back until after seven, I was doing the money with Margaret, and Norman did a sweep of the house to check no one was hiding under the beds or got lost in the attic. Alex – did you hear about Alex? Had a row with Anthony, in front of the visitors…' Norman lit a Benson and Hedges. Come on, Gunners, regroup! But they couldn't get through Luton's unexpectedly tight defence. 'Ooh yes, the Sharman sisters grumbling about the stairs and then disappearing before the clear-up. Mind you, the Stanilands didn't hang about either. And what about the Liversedges? Nathan's always creeping around, and I dare say the grandfather wouldn't think twice before cutting a throat…'

Norman got up and shut the door to the kitchen, just catching Dot's eye as it flickered towards him. It was half-time and he wanted the distraction of the football analysis rather than the murder gossip, which he could still hear leaking through the closed door. He needed to concentrate on the football, not on the events of last night, and the comings and goings, and whether he had been seen or not.

'Arsenal will be kicking themselves that they conceded that goal…' said someone on the telly, and it did not alleviate the intimation of defeat settling like low pressure over his afternoon.

13

The church was closed, and would be indefinitely, a crime scene inaccessible to the faithful. Theologically, it was a crime scene every Sunday, thought Daniel, with the body of Jesus broken and bloody on the altar, week in, week out; but theological matters had to give way to practical matters, for the faithful would have nothing for Holy Communion if Daniel could not find an altar. Bernard's offer of the house chapel at Champton was the solution to that problem. The house being old, its chapel was large, one of those structures at the centre of its nest of buildings built to accommodate the considerable retinue of clergy the de Floures family had employed over the years. At the end of the twelfth century it had been done up in the new Gothic style, with pointed arches and a handsome vault, but under its flags lay bones a century older. As the family grew grander and required memorials of greater splendour, the parish church was extended to accommodate their tombs; in the leaner eighteenth century an incumbent, full of post-Enlightenment zeal, had built another chapel for the house, really just another room on the first floor but Georgian and plain and lit with big sash windows by day and a sprouting chandelier by night. There another de Floures had gathered family and servants for morning prayers in one of the few flowerings of piety in their history. This had left the original chapel without much of a purpose and it was now, cold and austere, used occasionally for family christenings, for small marriages of the lesser or the shyer de Floures, for lyings-in-state of the greater, and for concerts which Anthony and Daniel had organised for the Champton Summer Arts Festival (and a production of *Murder in the Cathedral* so relentless Bernard had flatly refused to attend another).

It was not big enough for the unusually large congregation which turned up for that evening's Holy Communion – a congregation there for reasons both sacred and profane. Anthony's death, and the rumours of its violent manner, had shocked the parishioners of Champton, and the cannier among them, anticipating a crowd, turned up early to be sure of a seat. As Daniel prepared the altar, he saw the chapel was already full, parishioners pressing around the family pew at the front like standing commuters squeezed around the reserved seats on a busy train. The readings for the day, he was glad to see, threatened no jarring note, no grisly murder, or slayings with jawbones. Instead, Jesus, at his most obscure, tells the disciples, 'A little while and ye shall not see me; and again a little while and ye shall see me; because I go to the Father.' And the disciples have no clue. Uncertainty and cluelessness, the hallmarks of authentic Christian discipleship, thought Daniel, as he preached that evening about the necessity of learning to live with both mystery and promise. Mystery was easy, promise much harder. He said nothing about Anthony's death, nothing about how he came by it, but prayed for the repose of his soul in the proper place, for justice for those done wrong and for mercy for those who have done wrong – a little flutter as one or two shifted uncomfortably at the thought – and for the restoration of peace to the community. 'Amen,' the congregation replied.

He went to stand on the steps that led to the courtyard, but he was not first out, as usual, for during the last hymn – 'Faithful Vigil Ended', played by Jane Thwaite on the wheezing harmonium that served in the old chapel – the Sharman sisters and Mrs Shorely left for the kitchen. This evening there was no rush for the exit, no exchange of pleasantries. The whispery murmur from within grew louder and less sepulchral as speculation broke out, and half-heard phrases peaked above the undifferentiated din.

'… cut from ear to ear …'

'… Rector heard his dying words …'

'… hurrying along beside the brook …'

Honoria de Floures was first out. 'It's a scrum in there … oh, how we love a drama. Are you all right, darling Dan?'

'I'm OK. How about you? It's an awful thing.'

She shrugged. 'Awful. And I can't think why anyone would want to murder Anthony. He was so inoffensive. It *was* murder?'

'Everyone is saying so.'

Honoria gave him one of her 'don't be stupid' looks. 'Blue lights, lots of cops, do-not-cross tapes. Of course it was. Besides, Daddy said it was.'

Daniel said nothing.

'Oh come on, Dan, don't be obtuse. What I want to know is, was it opportunistic, or did someone have it in for him?'

Anthony might not have been universally loved, but could he have provoked feelings so intense that someone would want to kill him? Perhaps it was an opportunistic killing, someone in church, out of his mind, looking for a victim, any victim. It seemed unlikely; not because it was unthinkable – it had happened before, even in tranquil Champton, because human passions rise and clash anywhere, everywhere – but because of the death blow. Daniel had seen only one wound: surely an opportunistic killer would have struck more than once, and more wildly?

'Will you stay for a drink? In the library?'

'Will there be a crowd?'

'No, I think there's a glass of wine in the saloon for everyone. I suppose you'll have to go. But join us after that?'

Daniel nodded and Honoria left, just ahead of the phalanx of the faithful led by Bernard and Margaret Porteous. Bernard looked harassed, Mrs Porteous looked solemn, and Bernard rather skilfully steered her towards Daniel to make good his escape, if not for long. Bernard, for all his lack of graces, still held to the doctrine of *noblesse oblige* and for that reason the chapel and the saloon were open to the estate today. Another over-oaked Australian Chardonnay that he disliked had been made available from the cellar and the Sharman sisters would serve it unpaid in a spirit of Christian voluntarism which rather suited him.

'How awful, Daniel, to have to be interviewed by the police, and on today of all days.'

Daniel smiled wanly.

'And is there any suggestion as to who-m ...' (she had an annoying habit of turning whos into whoms) '... or why, or when?'

'I couldn't say, Margaret.'

'No, of course.'

She hurried off to the saloon to beat the queue for the wine and the nibbles, which turned out to be salted peanuts.

Later, in the library, it was champagne and dry roasted peanuts, which Honoria was nibbling on the wide fender in front of the fire. Behind her on the wall hung three small portraits of her ancestors, eighteenth-century beauties, white-fleshed and curvaceous, with the same coppery hair she had inherited. It glowed in the flickering light from the fire.

'Dan, join us! Champagne? I know it's not very funereal, but … life goes on,' she said, a little too brightly. 'And Anthony certainly wouldn't have minded.' She looked at Dan as she sipped, to see if he understood her. He did, but he was not going to be drawn.

'Oh Dan, you know he was a drinker? That was why he was here, poor thing. Daddy had him dried out, and then he came to stay and didn't go home afterwards. Now why do you think that might be?'

'I really don't know, Honoria.'

'*Really* don't know, or "Shut up, Honoria" don't know?'

'Can we talk about something else?'

Honoria had no intention of talking about anything else. 'What usually goes wrong with drunks, Dan? I've hung out in bars long enough to know. Debt, or gambling? Some secret life?'

'People drink for all sorts of reasons, I suppose,' he said, and immediately regretted being drawn after all.

Theo came towards them, put down an empty glass and picked up a full one without breaking stride, and sat on the sofa next to them.

'You didn't say much at the service.'

'I said the words I always say. From the prayer book. We don't improvise.'

'I know, I mean off script, something about what's happened. Anthony was murdered last night, after all.'

'We remembered him, we prayed for God to have mercy on him, and for justice. Don't you think that covers it?'

Honoria said, 'Do you think he was gay?'

The thought had occurred to Daniel. He remembered a moment once, talking to Anthony over a drink in his study after a parish church council meeting. The fire was glowing, the hour late and the whisky peaty; after some silence Anthony started to say something, but on the brink he hesitated and it went unsaid. At the time Daniel had thought that it might have been an inconvenient love that was troubling him (it so often was). If so, could he have had a secret life, and in that secret life could there be someone with a reason to kill him?

'I don't know. Do you think he would have told anyone about it?'

'Daddy? I don't think so. But then I can't imagine anyone telling Daddy they were gay. I would have thought him more likely to tell you.'

'No, not me.'

'Aren't you curious?'

'No.'

Theo said, 'Aren't you? Really?'

'I've learned not to be.'

Honoria nodded. 'Need to know basis?'

'Yes. If someone wants to tell me something, I am happy for them to do so. If not, I'm not running after them.'

Theo was puzzled by this. 'Even if what they wanted to tell you might be important? Something you could help them with?'

'I can only open the door, it has to be their decision to walk through it.'

'Sometimes you just know, though,' said Theo. 'A friend of mine was worried about her son – my godson actually, fey little chap, bullied at school – and she thought he might be gay. I said he's eight, he's not anything, but she asked me to have a godfatherly talk, you know. So I went down for the weekend and we were walking after lunch and, you know, to create a bond, I asked him what his interests were. "I *adore* Victorian neo-Gothic church architecture," he said. Gay as a goose, as it turned out. But I don't think Anthony was gay. I don't think he liked intimacy of any kind. Who would, after growing up like he did.'

'What do you know about Anthony growing up?' asked Honoria.

'We talked once or twice. Here once, and in London. Our paths crossed and we got pissed one night – very easy to do that – and he told me about it. It was quite heartbreaking.' His voice wavered for a second. 'I was glad when he hit the bottom, actually: he had to before he could sort himself out. I was glad Bernard took him in, although … well, what a sorry end. Is there anyone to carry on with his work?'

'His research? I don't know what exactly he was looking at. Maybe Daddy would know.'

Honoria beckoned to Bernard, who was making grudging small talk to a friend of Alex's who was up for the weekend and lacked the social sense to realise that an early departure is generally appreciated when a murder occurs at your host's. 'Daddy, need you over here!' she cried.

Bernard, glad to be rescued, came and lowered himself stoutly onto the sofa opposite.

'Daddy, what was Anthony *actually* doing here?'

'He was getting our papers in order – the archive.'

'Yes, but what did that involve?'

Bernard thought about it. 'I don't really know. I remember he said he was going through the house and estate account books from about a hundred years ago, although they go back five hundred years in some form or another. Anthony had the figures, rows and rows of them, kept meticulously by the comptroller – I think that's what we called him then.'

Daniel wondered how those bald figures might be interpreted to tell their tales. 'Do you know what areas he was looking at? He was a methodical person and I don't suppose he would have just picked up the first file that came to hand?'

'He said it all got a bit disrupted in the war. The last war, I mean. When the French went home, it was in a terrible state. Cost my papa a fortune to put it right. Yes, Anthony talked about that. Super-tax came along and wiped out a lot of the family wealth, and they never managed to put things back as they were. There are still rooms, whole wings, in fact, we've done nothing to since. There's an upper floor of bachelor bedrooms that went up in the reign of Queen Victoria for shooting parties and were used as the officers' quarters, which are just as they were when the French left. Except dustier. I dread to think what condition the roof's in.'

'It was a convalescent home, wasn't it?' said Theo. 'At least, that's what the French woman in the pub was saying yesterday…'

'It was – and they certainly made themselves at home, or tried to. They complained so much about the food that in the end they cooked for themselves. One had been a chef – Franck, lovely man – and he taught the kitchen girls how they liked things to be done. Except they kept arguing about it because some of the French were southerners and some were northerners and they liked different things. And there were some extraordinary characters here. I remember an artist – I think he had been quite famous before the war – they put him to work on camouflage, or making posters, or something. And there was a scientist, a chemist I think, who built a laboratory. We were warned never to go there, so we assumed he was making explosives or poison gas. You know de Gaulle visited?'

'I had heard that. Anthony showed me a photograph,' said Daniel. 'Do you remember it?'

'We weren't here. Anthony and I were both at school and in the holidays we went to Great Aunt Elizabeth in Argyll, or to Rudnam, our estate in Norfolk, although that became bit more difficult when they thought there might be an invasion.'

'So Anthony came too?'

'Yes, after his father died we took him in and... there was nowhere else for him to go. It must have been a strange experience for him. I wonder if that might have made him curious to find out more about it? And the papers were in a terrible mess because of all the disruption. I think people only want to preserve memory when they think there's a future in which they will have the leisure and inclination to look behind them. The war was very unsettling, especially after the fall of France, which felt very close here, when the French arrived.'

Honoria had an idea. 'Why don't we take a look at Anthony's study? Won't that tell us what he was working on?'

Bernard shook his head. 'The police took everything that was on his desk.'

Audrey appeared, buzzing from her circuit of the saloon, like a picky bee that had flitted from flower to flower, tantalising all with the promise of pollen, but settling on none. She had a remarkable lack of self-awareness, an almost complete lack of interest in the inner life, Daniel had often observed, and was blithely ignorant of the public mood a community adopts to mark the solemnity of events. There had been a death of one of their own – not only a death but a murder, and a murder on her own doorstep – and it had filled her with a brio that she made no effort to disguise. After the war her boredom with peacetime lifted only when she was finally appointed head of the local branch of the WVS, upgraded now to the Royal Women's Voluntary service, and in that role had to organise a response to a mock nuclear strike on Braunstonbury. Never had the vaporisation of a regional centre provided so much entertainment, and Audrey skipped from medical station to medical station with blankets, tea urns and biscuits, those invaluable defences against radioactive fallout.

'How *wonderful* to see the old chapel so full! How *wonderful* to see Champton really pulling together. Everyone's *so* devastated about Anthony's death. Everyone wants to know, darling, when there will be a statement.'

'I suppose the chief inspector will have something to say. Maybe tomorrow?'

'Didn't we meet the chief constable here once?' she said, looking at Bernard. 'Couldn't there be a hint, perhaps, a whisper, just to put people's minds at rest? And shouldn't we be vigilant, looking out for strangers or people acting suspiciously until they catch this chap?'

Bernard shrugged and made the half cough, half gargle noise he made when he was unsure what to say. 'Charlie isn't any likelier to know what's going on than you or me. Nobody tells him anything.'

Daniel recalled the bishop saying the same thing, that the higher you rise in an organisation, the further you are from what you need to know.

'But all in due course, all in due course,' said Bernard. 'And, naturally, we must be on the lookout...' And with that he wandered away.

They said their goodbyes and walked back home through the park. Audrey linked arms with her sons and Daniel noticed a slightly greater effort was necessary from him and Theo as they went along, the diminution of her energies in age requiring a little more of theirs. It was almost night and the path ahead of them became indistinct as the dark rolled in.

'Of *course* he's been in touch with the chief constable,' said Audrey. 'A murder? At the Champton estate? A member of the de Floures family? I wouldn't be surprised if the chief constable, high sheriff and lord lieutenant were all hiding behind the sofa.'

And then the flimsy dam behind which her sea of questions had been churning for hours, finally broke.

'Who killed him, Daniel? Why? Tell me *how*? And don't do your usual pained look, you know the one.'

Daniel knew when to mount a resistance to his mother and when to yield.

'Stabbed in the neck with a pair of secateurs. I suppose they came from the flower room.'

'The *flower room?*'

'I can't think where else they could have come from, unless the murderer had planned to do a little pruning after the killing. I'm sure I've seen Anne Dollinger using them.'

'Whatshername's sidekick? From the flower guild?' said Theo.

'Yes, her.'

'I can't see her murdering someone,' said Audrey, 'unless Stella Harper commanded her to.'

'The "how" is interesting, though. The flower guild had been in to water and tidy up for Sunday's visitors, but would they leave a pair of secateurs out for the murderer to find and … use? Or did he bring his own? Or she?'

'Do you think it could be a woman?' said Theo.

'How many men do you know who carry around secateurs?'

'Every gardener I know,' said Audrey. 'But I wouldn't want to try to cut someone's throat with them, even if I were a man.'

'It wasn't a cut, it was a blow. One blow I think, not a big wound, but it got the artery.'

'Doesn't that sound a bit surgical to you?' Theo said. 'One blow? And with secateurs? And they hit the artery?'

'I thought that too. I suppose in a rage you might lash out at someone and hit the right spot. But the blow came from behind.'

'How do you know?'

'He was praying. He was on his knees in a pew. The murderer must have come up behind him and struck.'

A common trope in Christian iconography, thought Daniel, a saint at prayer, composed as the knife falls, halfway to heaven before the blow; but Anthony was no saint, and if he had known his murderer was coming up behind him, he would surely have done something about it.

'Blood,' said Audrey, 'there would have been lots of blood. The spray.' Audrey had driven ambulances in the Blitz, seen enough of the messy frailty of the human animal in her twenties. 'A puncture wound like that would have caused the blood to jet out.'

'It did.'

'Two things, then. First, the murderer would most likely have been covered in blood. Second, it was someone who knew what he was doing. And *if* so, they might have known how to keep out of the way of the spray. Do you know, the more I think about this, the more I'm convinced it was a professional. So why would someone want to kill Anthony? What of his past? I know he had one, people talk about it in the village.'

'What do they say?'

'He was a drinker – you knew that? – his life had got sticky, which is why he came here. Perhaps it was drink? But perhaps he had made enemies. Gambling debts? Wouldn't Bernard have paid them?'

'I think he would, but he would need a very convincing sense of the urgency of repayment before he did.'

'It's something in his past. It must be.'

They came round a bend in the path and the rectory lay before them, the kitchen light left on to illuminate the way like a tabernacle lamp in a dark church.

Audrey made supper, Sunday-night soup and sarnie, as Sabbath tradition decreed. After dinner Theo, on his mother's instructions, went to the pub to see what people were saying; Daniel and Audrey watched a dull comedy on the television and not long after she had fallen asleep, Cosmo and Hilda looked to Daniel, with that dog-knowledge of the time, tails wagging in anticipation of prayer. The church was, for the moment, another's domain, and they whimpered as he made his way not for the back door but for his study. There he sat at his desk, which had been his father's and grandfather's before him. On its shiny surface were his pens, as neat as utensils at a tea ceremony: his propelling pencils, his pads, each in its place, ready for use. And let our ordered lives confess the beauty of thy peace, he thought as he opened his prayer book at the gold marker for Evensong, neither choral nor floral thanks to the murder, but said privately and late. Oh Lord, open our lips, he read silently, which seemed rather to go against the spirit of the invocation.

He had just got to the Nunc dimittis, the lovely canticle of Simeon, when there was a tap on the French windows. The curtains were not yet drawn and a figure was standing on the terrace beyond. It was Bob Achurch.

Daniel let him in.

'Are you all right, Bob?'

'Sorry it's so late, Rector, but I need to talk to you, I didn't want to disturb your mother.'

Tactful, thought Daniel, and invited him to sit down.

'The gossip is Mr Bowness was killed professionally. Now I don't expect you to say anything about that, but I did want to say something to you. I served in the Royal Marines in the war, I think you know, as a commando.'

'Yes, you told me.'

'I wondered if that makes me a suspect?'

'Why?'

'Because I know how to kill people, like Mr Bowness was killed.'

'You know how he was killed?'

'Throat cut. Everyone knows.'

'Have the police indicated that they suspect you?'

'The sergeant came and talked to me, and I told him about my military service and I told him where I was at the time of the murder, which was at home with Cynth. But no one else saw us. We didn't see nothing either. So am I a suspect?'

'Means and opportunity, perhaps, Bob, but what about motive?'

'None. Two out of three puts me ahead, though. But I'm not the only one.'

The only what?

'The only one who knows how to kill like that.'

'Didn't nearly everyone of your age serve in the war?'

'I mean kill like *that*. Expertly. I think you know what I mean.'

'I can't say anything about that, Bob.'

Bob nodded. 'I thought so. But I was thinking perhaps you could make a house call? Prick a conscience, if there's one to prick?'

'Did you mention any of this to the police?'

'I thought I would speak to you first, Rector.'

'That puts me in an awkward position, Bob.'

'But not as awkward as it would put me in.'

'I see. Leave it with me. Would you like a nightcap?'

'No thanks, Rector. Best get home. She's nervous left alone.'

'Of course.'

Daniel let him out and he walked away, without making a sound.

Daniel went back to his prayers. '… Give unto thy servants that peace which the world cannot give; that both our hearts may be set to obey thy commandments, and also that by thee we being defended from the fear of our enemies may pass our time in rest and quietness; through the merits of Jesus Christ our Saviour. Amen.'

14

In the morning Theo announced he was returning to London. He had a job, a voice-over, but he was also tiring of country life, as he always did after a day or two, and missing proper coffee from Bar Italia and snooker at the Groucho. 'But I'll need to see more of you at work, Dan. When would suit you?'

'I think it must wait.'

'Why?'

'There's been a murder, Theo.'

'Aware of that. I could help out.'

'I'm uncomfortable enough with your looking over my shoulder under normal circumstances, but these are not normal circumstances. People are anxious and upset and asking questions. We're in crisis, and I can't allow any spectators. Don't you see that?'

'I'm not a spectator, I'm already part of it. I've made a statement too, they might need me back.'

'You should come back when things have settled. I'm sorry, Theo, but I have to put the needs of the parish first.'

'Think it over?'

'I have. It will have to wait.'

'But I can't wait that long. I've got to prepare for my part.'

'Just watch old episodes of *All Gas and Gaiters* on video, it will tell you all you need to know.'

'That's not very helpful—'

Audrey interrupted him. 'Darling, would you drop me at the dress shop on your way? I want something cheerful and new for the spring. Something to banish the gloom, tra-la!'

Daniel did not find it so easy to dismiss thoughts of murder – they had kept him awake half the night – so after he waved off his mother and his sulking brother in the new Golf – 'go slowly past the post office, Theo, I want the ladies to see' – he took the dogs for a walk round the lake.

Daniel did his best thinking when going forwards under his own power. Once it had been through the medium of cycling – that's how he had come to grasp the elements of the hypostatic union sufficiently well to graduate with a first in theology. Now it was while walking the dogs. He often wondered how the way in which we do our thinking shapes what we think: Luther on the lavatory shouting '*Sola scriptura!*'; Thomas Aquinas rejecting his million-worded thought as chaff after a stroke; and now Daniel, his cycling days done, thinking over his pedestrian problems. And perhaps walking was a better way of confronting the issues of the day after all: it allowed him to notice details that would otherwise be lost to the wayside blur.

Cosmo and Hilda were meant to be on their leads, lambs still in the fields, but he picked his route carefully and as they approached the lake he let them off to explore the attractions of its bank. The lake was the work of two of the greatest landscape gardeners of England, Capability Brown – who moved mountains and divided the waters – and then Humphry Repton – who followed on a sales trip through the county, offering improvements to the improvements of his predecessor, which meant, in the case of the lake at Champton House, a strange little two-storeyed folly built on the bank furthest from the house, a cross between a thatched cottage and a ski chalet from which Daniel half expected Wham! to decant in Christmas jumpers every winter. It was actually a bath house, built around the stream that fed the lake, with a room designed for picturesque teas upstairs and a sort of grotto below, constructed around a pool into which the stream tinkled before making its way out. It was thought not only picturesque but healthful too, and in its day visitors were encouraged to lave themselves in the waters, until a neighbour caught something and died. A little landing stage connected the bath house to the lake and a rowing boat tethered to it by a painter was reflected exactly on the still surface with the folly behind. A perfect scene, thought Daniel, and wondered if he was at that moment being observed from the library half a mile away, a figure in the altered landscape, like the monks and hermits of the eighteenth century hired to add Romantic interest to the view (only in his case with two reddish-brown dachshunds circling his feet). And then he noticed something not behind him but in front, a figure, moving across the reflected ensemble.

Someone was in the bath house.

He looked up, but whoever had appeared in the window was no longer there. He wondered if it might have been Alex, who had at one time or another occupied or annexed every little building on the estate as a studio or for an installation (he had ruined the orangery the summer he discovered Yves Klein). Perhaps it was kids from the village, using it as a den to drink or to smoke or snog? Then he remembered the murder and his stomach tightened. He looked back and there again was a figure passing across the window, only this time it stopped, caught him looking and waved. Daniel waved back, tentatively, and deciding that a murderer in hiding was unlikely to offer a greeting, began to make his way round the lake to investigate.

Five minutes later he was walking through a clump of trees which gave on to the back of the bath house, hedged round by untidy laurels. He stopped to put the dogs on their leads and, as they walked out of the bushes into a tussocky clearing, the weathered back door of the bath house opened, and there was the waving figure again. The dogs began to bark, but it was only Ned Thwaite.

'Morning, Daniel!'

'Are you all right with the dogs, Ned?'

'Yes, go on, let them off.'

Daniel released Cosmo and Hilda and they ran to Ned, and as they leapt up at him for a moment his face betrayed less than full-hearted enthusiasm.

Daniel called them off, or rather, made some shushing noises to which they paid no attention, but something at the water's edge eventually became more interesting and they wandered away. Ned, a tireless walker, was dressed in hiking trousers and a functional sporty sort of jacket, with pouches and pockets for books and pads, and he was leaning on a stick cut from a bush, with a thumb rest where a branch would have forked. A camera (a Canon AE-1, Daniel noted) hung to one side and a small pair of binoculars to the other, which made him look for a moment like one of the heartier bishops of the Church of England on his way to Greenbelt.

'Lovely morning, Dan! Makes you glad to be alive!' Then he thought of Anthony. 'But not for some, eh? Poor Anthony. You know, it's partly thanks to him I discovered this place.'

'The bath house?'

'Yes. He showed me the Red Book, have you seen it?'

Daniel had not but remembered someone saying that they had in the archive the Red Book which Repton had made for Champton, in which he drew and described his plans for the improvements others would create after he had moved on. They were rather cherished by social historians and garden designers.

'It's from the 1790s. He built this for whichever de Floures it was back then. But it's an illusion, to be seen not lived in, although someone has.'

'Someone's been living here?'

'I'll show you.'

Ned opened the door wider and Daniel followed him in. It smelled of lake water and mud and damp, and he wondered if those rooms could really have ever cheered those summoned there for a picnic or a tea. The upper room was still handsome, its ceiling decorated with intricate plasterwork: some of it had fallen away, but still festoons of fruit and flowers hung dustily – except, on closer inspection, they turned out to be not fruit and flowers but seashells and seaweed. French windows gave onto a sort of veranda from where one could admire the view of the house, but they had not been used for years. Someone had made an effort to clean the glass, cracked, a pane missing. Perhaps it had been the same person who had lit a fire in the fireplace recently: an old kettle stood on a cast-iron trivet and there was a mug, too – one of the Champton estate ones, showing the house and crest, dating back to one of Bernard's short-lived efforts to make money from visitors.

'How recent is this do you think, Ned?'

'I don't know, but take a look at this.'

Ned, bustling with excitement, motioned for Dan to follow him out into the hall, where steps led down to the grotto. 'Careful, it's slippery…' Ned led the way, taking hold of the handrail. The dogs looked slightly comical as they followed, like Slinkies, round the corner into a gloomy space, open at one end. It reminded Daniel of a fairground attraction. It took a second to adjust to the darkness, but he saw he was in a sort of ornate cave. At the centre was a rectangular pool, fed by a little cataract which tumbled into it from the mouth of a stone fish. The pool emptied at the other end through a grille and into a brook which snaked into the lake beyond. If it had once been intended for therapeutic bathing, the smell of mud and slime would now deter even the most determined, although for the dogs it was a paradise of olfactory promise. Ned produced a torch. 'Look at this!' He turned, shining a light onto the wall behind them.

Daniel caught his breath in surprise. It was a mural, no longer fresh, darkened not only with age but with mould which gave it the shadowy, glowering look of one of Piranesi's etchings. The edges were indistinct, sketchy, as if seen through mist, but they were clearly figures in a landscape – a familiar landscape but in a nightmare version. It showed Champton –

the house half tumbled down, the park a cross between a cemetery and a battlefield. Swarming over it were figures, men and women, some in uniforms, some in what looked like streetwalker chic of 1940s Paris, but twisted and cartoonish, which made sense if it were painted during the war by a temporary resident, whose vision of the world was more Hieronymus Bosch than Delacroix.

The human figures might have looked cartoonish and grotesque, but, Daniel noticed, they were also carefully differentiated by their stance, or a facial detail, or their clothes. These were real people, he thought, like the gargoyles Canon Dolben had added to the restoration of the north side of St Mary's, still recognisable as caricatures of himself, the churchwardens and Bernard's father. Daniel looked more closely. The people on the wall seemed to be in conflict, growing more antagonistic, fighting desperately to the death as they moved towards the centre of the mural, where, like a Delacroix viewed from a distance, a tangled mound of bodies was topped by a golden cockerel crowing – the weather vane from his church. And there, right at the heart of it, two figures, a man and a woman: lovers surely, though neither lovely but mock-heroic, lifting up a cross of Lorraine. Above them the slogan IN HOC SIGNO VINCES was written on the reddening sky.

'The battle of the Milvian bridge,' said Daniel.

'What's that?'

'In the year 312, the Emperors Constantine and Maxentius met in battle at the Tiber. Constantine had a vision of a glowing cross and those words – *in this sign you shall conquer* – and so he had it painted on his soldiers' shields, and they vanquished Maxentius, so Constantine became sole emperor.

He gave Christianity imperial approval and the rest, as they say, is history.'

'But there's no bridge,' said Ned.

'No, it's just a reference. I wonder what it means?'

'The cross of Lorraine,' said Ned, 'that's the Free French, isn't it during the war?'

'Yes. It is not exactly propaganda.' Was it intended as a satire on war? A critique of religion and empire? Love among the ruins?

'I'm not surprised it was done down here. Not quite the message the officers would think suitable for the lads.'

'No, not really,' but then Daniel remembered more recent events. 'Ned, how long since the fire was used, do you think?'

'I don't know, can't be long, why?'

'The murder.'

Ned's excitement turned to surprise. 'Oh my God, I didn't think!'

'We must call the police straight away. Anything else you've found?'

'No. I don't think so. You think whoever killed Anthony might have been hiding here?'

'I don't know, but anything suspicious we must notify to the police.'

He called the dogs from their explorations in the tone he used when he meant it, and they came, their bellies wet, scampering up the steps after them.

'You stay here, Ned. Don't touch anything, don't let anyone in. I'll call the detective sergeant from the rectory.'

As it happened, DS Vanloo was in the village, taking statements, and came straight round to the rectory. The dogs ran at him barking, but he knelt to greet them and within seconds they were on their backs letting him rub their still damp tummies, which struck Daniel as slightly at an angle to the sombre purpose of the summons. They walked quickly back to the bath house, where Ned was waiting outside the back door, looking, Daniel thought, like Corporal Jones from *Dad's Army*.

'DS Vanloo, this is Mr Thwaite.'

'How do,' said Ned, sounding more Yorkshire than usual, which he did when he was nervous.

They showed him the fire and the mug, and Ned admitted he had picked it up and looked at it and maybe disturbed the dust and the damp in which a footprint may have been left.

DS Vanloo said, 'It's a shame you did that, sir. Always best not to disturb evidence.'

'I didn't think it was evidence,' said Ned, 'not of the murderer. I'm interested in the Free French who were here during the war and I thought it might be to do with that. The mural is fascinating. I wonder if anyone remembers it being done?'

The sergeant didn't seem to think of the mural as particularly fascinating: he just looked at it for a moment before calling for help on the radio. Once again a team arrived and produced blue-and-white tape to seal off the bath house, now a tiny but unignorable reminder of tragedy right in the middle of the artfully made landscape, to be seen from the windows of the library half a mile away across the park.

15

Alex de Floures was standing in the library window looking at the bath house across the lake, now, like the church, taped off. He stood, motionless, just looking, until the slap slap of Honoria's flatties approaching caused him to turn round.

'Hello,' he said, 'there's something happening at the bath house.'

Honoria stood beside him. Her breath made a little circle of fog on the pane of glass. 'What's going on?'

'Police tape. You can tell it from here. And I can see Daniel, or his dog collar ...'

'... and two little brown dots at his feet. Cosmo and Hilda. There's someone else.'

'I think it's Ned Thwaite.'

'The schoolmaster? What's he doing there?'

'He's interested in local history.' He grimaced.

'I wonder what they've found?'

'I don't know.'

Alex turned away, for the comfort of the fire and the sofa on which he had unfolded Repton's Red Book. It had been compiled in the 1790s and detailed the improvements to the improvements to the park at Champton, roughing up Capability Brown's tidy plan for the park thirty years earlier. Then he said, 'The mural!'

Honoria looked at him. 'It's nothing special, I grant you, but hardly a police matter.'

'That's why he was there, Ned Thwaite. He's interested in the Free French, for a project. He came to talk to Daddy about it.'

Honoria came and flopped down, symmetrically, on the sofa opposite. 'It must be something to do with the murder. Maybe the killer's been hiding out there?'

'Odd place to choose to hide, in one of Repton's most charming *cottages ornés* less than a mile from the scene of the crime.'

'You hide out there.'

'I haven't killed anyone, darling. Not *yet*. Anyway, someone else goes there.'

'Who else?'

'I don't know who, but someone does.'

'Kids from the village?'

'No, I don't think so. They don't leave a mess. Actually, they tidy it up, which is how you would know it wasn't one of us. I wonder if it was the murderer? The Tidy Murderer of Champton.'

'Do you remember when I took you there for the first time?'

Alex winced. 'I still have nightmares about it.'

Honoria laughed. 'Didn't I tell you it was a witch's house? And that the witch turned people into monsters and stuck them onto the wall?'

'Yes, you did. And one night you took me to see them and then ran away with the torch and left me screaming in the dark.'

'You actually wet yourself!'

Honoria's eye fell on the unfolded pages from the Red Book.

'So you've got it.'

Alex nodded.

'Anthony would have your guts for gaiters. He'd been looking for it since he arrived.'

'I know,' said Alex, 'but I've got plans too, and I didn't want *him* anywhere near them.'

She looked at him for a moment and then said, in a sing-song voice, 'My mother said – I never should – play with gypsies in the wood – if I did – she would say – naughty little girl to run away. Guess what?'

'What?'

'Hugh's coming home.'

Alex's face suddenly creased in a frown.

The Hon. Hugh de Floures, Alex's older brother and Bernard's heir, hated Champton so much he now lived in Canada, where he farmed vast and lonely wheat fields in a place as distant from his heritage as could be imagined. He had always hated being the son and heir, hated the house and its paintings and its furniture, hated Eton so much he had to be withdrawn and sent instead to a day school in the county. It was where the richer farmers sent their sons and he was happy there for the first time in his life: nobody cared that he could not tell the difference between the nominative or the accusative, or knew only the bare outline of English history, or anything about the economic importance of the coalfields of South Wales. Shy and awkward, he joined the Young Farmers' Club and discovered an aptitude for practical matters of baling and haymaking and driving tractors, and wearing waxed garments in pelting rain, and the brisk camaraderie of other young farmers. Not for him his father's and grandfather's old college at Oxford, but agricultural college; while there he had gone on an exchange trip to Canada and found under its big and indifferent skies a freedom he had never felt anywhere else. So of course he stayed. Bernard had wanted him to come home, for the day would come when he would inherit both title and estate and he needed to learn the rudiments of how to be a landowner and a peer, but Hugh hated the thought. 'If only you had been born a boy,' Bernard liked to say to Honoria, who would have been a much better choice, with her aptitude for business, her social confidence and glamour; but primogeniture permitted no prior candidate for Bernard's successor than his ill-suited son. Sometimes Honoria worried that Hugh might get trampled by horses, or fall under a combine harvester, or eaten by a bear, and it would be Alex upon whom the ermine would fall – and, even she, who loved both her brothers, could see how that might not work out well for the House of de Floures.

'What's Hugh coming home for? Surely not because of the murder?'

'I don't know,' said Honoria, but she could not think of anything more excruciating for Hugh: he disliked standing out as son and heir, but to be at the centre of a scandal too would be intolerable. 'He'll hate all this.'

16

It was not only Theo who departed for London, the press did too, once interest in the murder waned and other matters required their attention. After the shock of discovery, and the drama of the first days of the inquiry, Champton settled into a sort of limbo. Anthony's body, the property of the coroner while the police investigation continued, lay on a chilled shelf at the mortuary rather than in the enfolding earth of his ancestors, and the meticulous process of information gathering, supervised by DS Vanloo, ground slow and small.

Other excitements distracted Champtonians in the lull. Audrey was exercised for a while by the *Eurovision Song Contest*, a spectacle she rather enjoyed, its populist tropes more to her taste than the cup final of the week before. The British entry, 'Go', from the improbably named Scott Fitzgerald, had been her choice in the heats and was now strongly tipped to win. She and Daniel watched the contest live from Dublin, only to find the United Kingdom overtaken at the very last moment by Switzerland, with a song from a young woman called Céline Dion, whom Audrey described as looking like a Bulgarian air hostess who'd forgotten her skirt. Her win, by a couple of points in the last round, smacked of corruption, a suspicion reinforced when Audrey discovered she was not even Swiss but Canadian.

'Why not a tenor from Tasmania or a barbershop quartet from Quito?' she asked Daniel, and wrote a letter to the *Radio Times*, unpublished, to complain.

May began, Mary's Month, so named, Daniel thought, for the bursting forth of new life. 'If things grew at the same rate all year as they grow in May it would be a *jungle* out there,' his father invariably said when Daniel and Theo were boys, as the leaves unfurled, and the nettles grew, and the keck, as cow parsley was called in these parts, opened its cream parasols. Now he had started saying it too as if it were a phrase he had just thought of.

Change and routine: the school term continued, and every Thursday, at the end of the day, the bell went and from both ends of the school hall crocodiles of children, boys in blue sweaters, girls in blue-and-white check dresses, filed in and sat on the floor, cross-legged, in uneven lines. At the edges, teachers sat on grown-up-sized chairs, vigilant, looking with over-dramatised sternness at children who were talking or fidgeting. Mrs Buckhurst at the piano played the coming-in music, Schumann's 'Soldier's March', with all the repeats, and then some more repeats, until the little soldiers were all in place and Daniel was thinking again how quickly the charm of that piece could pall.

'Good morning, children,' he said.

'GOOD MOORNING FAATHER DAANIEL,' they replied in chorus with a rise and a crescendo on the MOOR.

It was a ritualised call-and-response, not unlike that in church every Sunday when he would say 'The Lord be with you' and the people would reply 'and with thy spirit' with the same inflection, although not so marked.

'Is it anyone's birthday today?'

Thirty hands shot up, fingers pointing to heaven.

'Has anyone *really* got a birthday today?'

Katrina Gauchet, head teacher, stood up and said, 'Where's Lily Weatherald?'

A gangly girl stood, looking shyly at the floor, wearing an over large badge which said 'birthday girl'.

'Father Daniel,' said Katrina, 'Lily is ten today.'

'Happy birthday, Lily. Would you like to come up and light the candle?'

There was a table dressed as a sort of temporary altar, on it a big Bible, one of the old ones from the clergy vestry, rarely opened, a brass cross, a frontal in the colour of the season (white for Eastertide) attached by Velcro to the front edge and a fat candle. To start assembly the candle needed to be lit, and so a box of Cooks' matches had been brought carefully by the assembly monitor from the school secretary and left on the table.

Lily blushed and picked her way through the lines of children to the front. Daniel handed her the box of matches and she struggled to take one out and then struggled to light it. The candle had not been trimmed and the wick was short, so it was fiddlier than he would have liked it to be.

'Happy birthday, Lily,' he said, and they all sang 'Happy Birthday', and then settled down, looking at him expectantly. Daniel had learned in his eight years at Champton to adapt to his congregation. In his last job, in London, he had a congregation of people like him and the stragglers of the English upper classes who had not yet given up on London (or given up the house in

Belgravia that was now worth more than the house in Sussex) and expected a certain kind of sermon delivered in a certain kind of way. He used to go into a preposterously grand prep school to give assemblies occasionally, but the golden-haired, peach-complexioned children there had a certain confidence. He had to take names for a school trip to Westminster Abbey once, the boys all Rupert and the girls all Caroline, until one little boy, when asked for his name, said 'Michael' and when Daniel asked for his surname, replied, 'I am Michael of Romania.'

In his first month at Champton, where school trips were few, the children less blessed than European royals in exile and assembly a weekly commitment, he had tried to introduce the children at school to the elements of Christian doctrine, but after the atonement and the Real Presence, Mrs Gauchet had tactfully suggested he try a different approach.

He tried several and found it more profitable to get the children to move around and make a noise, gratifying for them and for him, but annoying for the teachers who then had to subdue their boisterous classes as parents arrived to take them home. Mrs Gauchet therefore suggested he try to bring them down as well as up, so now assemblies finished with a song and a prayer. Today's theme was the Ascension – Jesus going up to heaven after the Resurrection, a promising theme with its potential for lift-off – and after he had got the children to jump up and down shouting, 'Grandmother, grandmother, JUMP out of bed!' (a game he had played with his mother when he was a little boy), he got them to sing a new worship song, 'Shine Jesus, Shine!' It was not to his taste, but was to theirs, and they sang it at the top of their high-pitched voices, something he would not have achieved had he stuck with his preferred choice of '*Viri Galilaei*'. He brought them down with a prayer, a prayer for anyone who was worried or upset, and the Lord's Prayer, which they said with a trustfulness that always moved him, and then AAMEEEEN!

Mrs Buckhurst played the going-out music, Mendelssohn's 'Song Without Words' in G minor (Daniel wondered if that was a judgement on what they had just sung), and they reformed into obedient crocodiles and departed whence they came. The hall was silent and empty, save Daniel and Mrs Gauchet, who helped him move the piano, abandoned by Mrs Buckhurst, who had a bad back.

'Are the children all right? What have you said to them about the murder?' asked Daniel.

'Some are upset, some don't really understand what's happened. We've never had one before. We try to say reassuring things, but it's affecting teachers more. And parents.'

'What's the mood at the school gates?'

'Is it safe for the children? There's a murderer on the loose. Gossip. Who could it be? We give reassurance, but what do I know?'

'And in the staff room?'

'The same. We had a staff meeting yesterday. I think it will be better when we know what actually happened and why. Didn't you discover the body?'

'Yes.'

'What's it like to discover a body?'

Daniel could not immediately think of an answer.

'Sorry, Dan.'

'I try not to dwell on that too much. Business as usual, don't you think?'

'Yes. What about the police? Any ideas?'

'They're not saying much, apart from asking questions. I suppose they have to put together a picture of who was where and when.'

'Someone said the bath house was taped off.'

'Yes. Maybe they found something there?'

'I haven't been there for years, I thought it was closed up. You know about the painting there?'

'Yes, I've seen it. I didn't think anyone else had. How do you know about it?'

'Because of Hervé.' Hervé, Katrina's husband, fathered by one of the Free French, mother unknown, taken in and brought up in the village. 'He has always known about it. He thinks it has something to do with his father.'

'His father?'

'There's a story that his father was an artist of some kind, sent here to recover from injuries, but he died. That's where the name Hervé came from. He's named after a man he never knew.'

'Oh yes, I think I'd heard that.'

'His mother's a mystery, though.'

'I think I knew that too.'

'Probably a local girl he banged up. Hervé never knew her either; he was fostered.'

The fortunes of war, thought Daniel: it blew people in and out, and when they settled they were someone different, somewhere different. 'Does he want to find out who they are?'

He remembered a former parishioner who had been adopted as a baby and only found out when he was in his twenties. He had tracked down his birth family and knocked unannounced on a front door in a town he didn't know. It was answered by a man who looked just like him; they had stared at each other, saying nothing, and after a few seconds the man had gently closed the door.

'Sometimes. We're doing a special commemoration next year for the fiftieth anniversary of the war. We're going to take the whole school back in time, dress up, eat Woolton Pie and powdered egg, if we can find any, and get some of the older people in the village to come and talk about what it was like. I asked Hervé if he fancied doing something about the Free French and now he's obsessed with it. He's been talking to Ned Thwaite. He's the expert round here. He's been knocking on the doors of the older people who used to work on the estate and in the house, and taping them on his tape recorder.'

Anthony had once shown Daniel a photograph of de Gaulle's visit to Champton in 1943. There sat the tall general, looking aloof in his kepi, surrounded by officers and men from the Free French Army on the steps of Champton House. There was something almost jarring about it, seeing Frenchmen plastered across the English baroque. Was one of them Hervé's father?

'You know the photograph of de Gaulle when he visited?' Daniel said. 'Can't be the only one. But I've never seen any others. Perhaps you could try the French Embassy?'

'When I have a minute, I will. Do *you* have a minute? I'd like to show you something,' said Mrs Gauchet.

They went upstairs to her office, where a rolled-up scroll of canvas had been laid on the table.

'We found this.'

She unrolled it. Beneath a painted crest – showing the Union Jack and the French tricolour combined, with the cross of Lorraine and a V for Victory – was a text, which Daniel half recognised with a mixture of familiarity and dismay.

Arise ye children of the Fatherland,
The day of victr'y is nigh;
The bloodstained flags of the tyrant
Are flutti'ring, raised on high.
Do you hear them in the vale?
Do you hear them on the hill?
Come to slaughter friends and neighbours,
Come to butcher and to kill,
Come to butcher and to kill?
To arms, against the foe
To battle we shall go!
March on, march on,
Foemen be gone!
To battle we shall go!

'That's quite a change of mood from "Shine Jesus, Shine",' said Daniel.

'Do you recognise it?'

'I think it's the *"Marseillaise"*. I had no idea it was so gory.'

'In the war the children used to sing it every morning after the national anthem out of respect for the Free French. There were French children here, too.'

'I didn't know that.'

'Yes, some of the civilian staff up at the hall had children, so they came to school. Champton was surprisingly cosmopolitan in the 1940s.'

17

Audrey was taking her time in Stella's: High Class Ladies' Fashion, not least because Anne Dollinger was on the till and she was easier to intimidate than Stella, her more equal adversary. It was not a big shop, but there was new stock in, looking towards summer, and Audrey wanted to give everything the most thorough consideration, and had Anne going to and fro between the back of the shop and the racks, while she amused herself by putting things back in the wrong places, if putting them back at all. Soon Anne was laden with a bale of dresses that Audrey wanted to try, so she hung them, as best she could, in a changing room. Audrey closed the door behind her, open at top and bottom and sat down on the little bench to get her breath back and ease off her too-tight shoes.

As she sat, thinking whether she should go for two mid-priced Country Casuals frocks or one splendid Tricoville, she heard the ding of the door opening and Stella speaking in her shop voice – a strangled Joan Fontaine which Audrey liked, very subtly, but noticeably, to mimic.

The shop voice was for the benefit of a customer.

'Anne, would you be a dear and pop to the post office with that parcel for Gillian Thwaite? It's addressed but you'll need to pay for the stamps, I'll reimburse you. I just need to sort out Mrs Lee…'

'Yes. Do you want me to get a slice of cake, and …'

But Stella was already fully occupied with Mrs Lee. She was the wife of a travelling family's patriarch, now settled on a site on the other side of town and, thanks to Mr Lee's enterprise, dreamed dreams of a glamour Mrs Lee's mother would not have dared to dream. She was one of Stella's best customers and although Stella was sometimes unkind about her behind her back – 'she makes Nellie Boswell look like Grace of Monaco' – to her face she was as accommodating as Norman Hartnell to the queen.

'To business, Mrs Lee: what arrangement would you like to make?'

Audrey would normally, in these circumstances, cough politely to make others aware they were not alone, but not, of course, for Stella: every potential advantage needed to be pursued.

'I've a grand in cash in my bag to clear my account.'

'I can't possibly, Mrs Lee, I would barely break even.'

'Twelve hundred? Call it quits?'

There was a pause.

'Quits,' said Stella, and if they did not actually spit on their palms and shake, the deal was done, and the door dinged as Mrs Lee departed, twelve hundred quid lighter. Only then did Audrey emerge from the dressing room, the Tricoville draped over her handbag arm.

'Audrey!'

'Stella!'

'I didn't know you were here.'

'Trying this on,' said Audrey. 'I'll take it.'

'*Excellent* choice,' said Stella. 'How would you like to pay?'

'Perhaps I should ask for your cash terms?' trilled Audrey.

Stella, unusually, had no comeback.

'I think I'll use my flexible friend. Credit card, Stella, not you.'

Stella went to find the card machine and proceeded to fill in the slip rather unsteadily.

Audrey said, 'Oh, don't worry, Stella, did you think I would report you to the VAT man?'

'I can assure you, Audrey, that my accounts are in order,' said Stella, using her shop voice, which did nothing for the credibility of her assertion.

'I would expect nothing less. And I wouldn't dream of calling your probity into question. Not even a typhoon of gossip could dent that.'

Stella took the impression of Audrey's Access card with the sound of a distant guillotine.

'Is there anything else?'

'No, dear, thank you.'

Stella handed her the dress in a smart bag.

'"High Class Ladies Fashion",' read Audrey. 'Oh, there is one thing.'

'What?'

'Could I possibly use your loo?'

And Stella understood.

18

Daniel called in at The Flowers, reopened for the season, and saw that Dot Staveley had walnut cake, his favourite; it looked like one of Kath Sharman's, by far the best baker in the whole village. It was set out on a fussy counter, all doilies and cake stands. His mother had once described what Dot called the 'design concept' as the spoilt child of Laura Ashley and Billy Bunter.

'Hello, Daniel,' said Dot, 'we had your famous brother in this morning.'

'He said he was going to call in. He wilts without his espressos.'

'Caused great excitement,' she nodded at the corner table where Dora Sharman was sitting, in her coat and hat, back to the wall, handbag on the opposite seat, looking at him in her characteristic pose, which always reminded him of an attentive pigeon.

He waved. She waved back, so he took over his cake and his tea.

'Hello. This is one of Kath's, I think, Dora?'

'Yes. Why wouldn't it be?'

'Oh, no reason at all.'

'We may not like her, stuck-up Dot Staveley,' said Dora, 'but the customers like the cakes and we like the money.'

'They are wonderful,' said Daniel, hoping this would not be taken amiss, but you never knew with the Sharmans. 'And your apple tart is the best I've ever had, Dora. Cordon-bleu standard.'

'Did you think it would be all spotted dick and custard round here?'

Daniel opened his mouth to say no but realised he had, so he said, 'Yes, I think I did.'

'It was the French. There was a chef at the big house, he taught me the apple tart. And lots of things. And the Eyeties. Thanks to them we can get a decent cup of coffee.'

'Italian Prisoners of War?' asked Daniel, mildly.

'Of course,' said Dora, 'they were marched through town on their way to the camp at Little Frimmington. Handsome they were, and jolly. You wouldn't think they'd been in a war. All us girls came to wave.'

Daniel recalled talking to an American air force padre who had been on the base from where Flying Fortresses flew out from the flatlands of Northamptonshire to bomb the towns and cities of northern Germany. Thousands of Americans had been based there, and came into Braunstonbury for the pubs and the pictures – and Braunstonbury came out to them too, its women enchanted by their accents and their generosity and their predicament. In the harsh and loveless world of warfare, such comforts and pleasures they were capable of exchanging were exchanged. He had often wondered what would have been worse for those Italian boys and men, the horrors of war and surrender and capture, or being stuck in wooden huts in the English Midlands on a wet, dark afternoon with nothing to drink but stewed tea. And then he wondered if Kath and Dora Sharman, girls themselves back then, had fraternised with the Americans and for their trouble been rewarded in nylons and chewing gum and coffee?

'Bad business, Rector, with Mr Bowness.'

'It is indeed, Dora.' They sat in silence. 'Did you know him? From before, I mean.'

'I can't say I knew him. I remember him, when he was a boy. He spent all his holidays here before the war. Him and his lordship were cousins, you know about that, and they were close after his father died. We used to see them at Champton until the French came. Then the family were mostly in Norfolk.'

'What about you?'

'What about me?'

'Weren't you in service in the house?'

'Yes, we were, but everything changed with the war.'

'Weren't you lady's maid to Lord de Floures' mother?'

'I was. Kath was parlours. Uniform in those days, cap and a pinny. We used to have to bob to his lordship and her ladyship.'

'What happened during the war?'

'We were split up. I went to Rudnam with the family to the house there to take care of her ladyship, and Kath stayed here to help out in the kitchens. And then Kath went to Rudnam and I came back here. They moved us around.'

'Did you mind being split up?'

Kath shrugged. 'Wasn't ours to mind. They needed people here to keep an eye on the French, you see, and to show them how to run the house. A few stayed. After the war everything was different. Most of the staff didn't come back. No footmen, no under butler. No lady's maid after her ladyship died. Never thought it would all go so quickly, but it did. It just didn't seem right any more.'

'What do you mean?'

'The bobbing and the yes m'lady, no m'lady. The old order passeth. And I enjoyed it when the French were here. I didn't want to go back to how we were.'

By the time Daniel arrived at Champton there was a cook, a housekeeper and a butler at the big house, all of them long gone. Now Mrs Shorely and dailies and the Sharman sisters and whoever could be mustered kept the great house going, though the loss of hands to lay fires, and air rooms, and change bedlinen, and polish silver, changed the lives of everyone connected with it. It felt like a clock slowing down.

'I would have loved to have seen it in all its splendour,' said Daniel.

'It was one of the finest houses in all of England,' said Dora, sitting up a little. 'When I was a little girl we had the coming-of-age ball for his lordship's father. There were flares lit all the way from the gates to the house. Car after car arrived, all the best people. Prince of Wales came. White tie, tiaras, the house all lit up like an ocean liner. An orchestra played till midnight and the party went on till dawn. It was written about in all the papers.'

Daniel had seen the newspaper cuttings in the archive, and photographs mounted on a thick board, showing the great and the famous dressed in feathers and tails and a look of innocence, like a Romanov ball in 1913.

'Anyway, must be going,' said Dora suddenly, and before he knew it she was up and at the till, fetching her purse from her handbag.

19

Daniel called in at the post office before going home; 'Post Office and General Store', it said, in Champton beige, although the 'general' was misleading for there were barely three shelves of goods on sale: some bags of sugar, teabags, Players No 6., biscuits from the cash and carry, tins of terrible meat, and a chest freezer with choc ices, Orange Maids and fish fingers. Half the counter was plain, the other was for post-office business, and Mrs Braines had to shift between the two, legally constrained from selling stamps and dog licences alongside Silver Spoon and Garibaldis.

The chimes over the door rattled as Daniel pushed it open, but Mrs Braines was already behind the counter and the tiny shop full, thanks to the presence of Dot Staveley, Stella Harper, Kath Sharman and Jane Thwaite. The chatter he could hear from the street ceased the moment he walked in, but the Sharmans' Jack Russell jumped up and barked at him.

'Scamper, hush!' snapped Kath, and the little dog gave a tiny growl and sat down. 'It's your two she's smelling, Rector; you know what little dogs are like with each other.'

Daniel felt an impulse to defend Cosmo and Hilda, but he knew Kath was right. They hated Scamper and Scamper hated them.

'Good morning, Rector,' said Mrs Braines. Why the formality, he wondered. Was it to dispel the wild energies of gossip?

'Good morning, ladies,' said Daniel, formal himself, and moved to stand behind Jane Thwaite in such a way as to suggest he was forming a queue.

'Go ahead, Daniel,' said Jane. 'We've been served.'

Mrs Braines gave her a glance of reproach. 'We were just chopsing, Rector,' the colloquialism at odds with the formality of the address.

'Stamps, please, Mrs Braines,' said Daniel, and she moved, formal again, from behind the plain counter to the post-office counter, with a pane of glass separating her from him like the grille of a confessional.

'Fifty first and fifty second, please.'

She opened the fat books of stamps. 'Do you want plain or fancy? Only the fancy are about the Welsh Bible, and you might like that.'

Daniel, particular about stationery, had a preference for uniformity where correspondence was concerned. 'Plain, I think.'

As she detached the strips of dark blue and bright red from the pages, Dot Staveley said, 'Parish in good heart, Rector?'

'I think so … under the circumstances.'

Jane Thwaite said, 'Ned is still very shaken, Daniel. To think the murderer had been camping out in the bath house and none of us knew!'

'Oh, that would be jumping to conclusions. We don't know who's been there – we don't really know much at all. It could be nothing.'

'Nothing?' said Stella. 'A man's been murdered! A smoking gun in our midst!' Daniel thought for a moment of steam rising from the abandoned mug in the bath house.

'That's not quite what's happened. And isn't it better not to speculate too much until we have a clearer picture?'

'I suppose …' said Stella, 'but the fact remains there's a murderer on the loose.'

Dorothy butted in. 'Norman's at County Hall today and he's going to call on the chief constable to find out if anything's actually being done.'

'Yes,' said Stella. 'We want some *action*.'

Mrs Braines and Mrs Thwaite nodded.

'Easy to call for someone to do something – but what?' said Daniel.

'Catch him,' said Stella. 'Until he's caught I don't see how we can even begin to get back to normal. And that's what we want, isn't it, for things to be *normal*.'

'Everything's suspended,' said Jane. 'What about Whit? The flower festival? The new buttery… Oh.' She checked herself.

A faux pas, a short silence and then Stella spoke. 'Our plans seem so very insignificant in light of what's happened. Perhaps we'll look at them when this is over and think again?'

Daniel said, 'Really? You seemed very certain about them, the last time we talked. Have you changed your mind?'

'No, Daniel, I've not changed my mind. But, on reflection, I can see merit in considering different views.'

Silence again. Daniel broke it. 'How much do I owe you for the stamps, Mrs Braines?'

'Sixteen pounds fifty.'

Daniel paid with the twenty he had put into his wallet that morning for precisely this transaction.

'Good morning, ladies. I hope it won't be long before the most we have to worry about is pews and loos.' They squeezed together to let him pass, and Scamper growled, as if to remind him that in spite of this unexpected concession he was still very much *persona non grata*.

When he got back to the rectory, DS Vanloo was in the kitchen with his mother.

'Darling,' said Audrey, 'Detective Sergeant Vanloo called to see you and I asked him to wait.'

Daniel scanned the detective's face for signs of suffering endured, but he was, as usual, impassive. 'If we could speak somewhere privately, sir?'

They sat in Daniel's study and waited briefly for the indignant scratching of the dogs, temporarily barred by the closed door, to die down.

'Just a couple of questions, sir. About timing. We know you discovered the body a little after nine. We know that Mr Bowness was last seen in the Royal Oak about seven. So death occurred between those two times. Where were you, exactly, at seven?'

'I was home by then. I was having supper with my mother. I think I told you this already.'

'When did you last see Mr Bowness?'

'I saw him at Champton House. It was Open Day, which Anthony would have done his best to avoid. We all met in the morning, about nine, before people started arriving, I remember seeing him then. And I saw him leave, must have been at lunchtime. I think he had a confrontation with Alex de Floures in his office, near the old kitchen. Early afternoon.'

'A confrontation?'

'Nothing of note. Alex was just being annoying. I don't think there was anything more to it than that.'

'Any idea where he was going?'

'The pub, I assumed.'

'Yes. He was there all afternoon. We spoke to Mr Thwaite, who had been on duty in church until the end of the day. He left at about five thirty. Mr Bowness was due to come and lock up. But we know he was in the pub until after seven – so the church would have been open and accessible to anyone?'

'Yes, it would. I wonder why Ned didn't call round and ask me to lock up?'

'He did, but you weren't yet back from the house. Your mother told him she'd pass on the message when you did get back.'

'But she didn't.'

'Any reason why?'

'She would have forgotten. But you should ask her.'

'I did. She did forget. Is the church normally locked?'

'It is at night. One of us locks up, me or Anthony.'

'Do you remember seeing anyone after you left the house to go home?'

'No, I don't think so. I said goodbye to Margaret Porteous and one or two others – people were coming and going – and I walked home through the park. We must have left about the same time, but they all live at the other end of the village and would have gone a different way. Margaret Porteous would know.'

'When you discovered the body, you're sure the blood was still wet?'

'Quite sure. I distinctly remember the dogs leaving a trail with their paws, and you are aware, I presume, of the state of my clothes?'

'What would you surmise about the blood being wet?'

Daniel thought about this.

'It must have been quite recently shed. I had not really thought about it.'

DS Vanloo made a note, then continued. 'One more thing. It sounds ridiculous, but is there anyone you can think of in the village who would be an expert in hand-to-hand combat?'

'Yes. Bob Achurch, former commando. But he's not the murderer.'

'How do you know.'

'I'll eat my hat if he is. Combat in Champton tends to be more genteel.'

'How do you mean?'

'I mean nothing, except that this is not a violent place. But some might say parish politics are a continuation of war by other means.'

'Was Mr Bowness involved in parish politics?'

'Yes, we all are, but I can't imagine anyone doing violence to another over ... The last argument we had was over installing a lavatory in church. It's hardly the assassination of the Archduke Franz Ferdinand.'

'Was Mr Bowness involved in that argument?'

'Yes, in so far as he is a member of the parish church council.'

'We will need to talk to the other members, if you could let me have a list?'

'Of course.'

DS Vanloo made another note, then looked up at Daniel. 'How are you, by the way?'

'Me? Oh, I'm all right, I think. It's still very raw. You know how a violent death affects communities. It brings to the surface all sorts of things.'

'What are you seeing?'

'Nothing that defined just yet. But there's a rise in tension. The parish pump is … cranky.'

'Anyone in particular?'

'Too early to say. Do you really think the murderer may be one of us?'

'I don't know. But…' Daniel noted a change of tone in the policeman's voice '… the murder looks professional. One stab wound, hit the mark exactly, cut the carotid artery. And a stab wound made with secateurs, not that sharp. So the murderer knew not only where to strike but how to strike. He must have bent the head back to stretch the neck and bring the carotid nearer to the surface. Imagine that, creeping up behind someone on his knees, with stealth, yanking his head back, stabbing him in the neck with enough force to puncture the carotid with a blunt blade, and then holding on to him in his death throes and directing the spray of blood so they didn't get covered in it. Does that sound like an opportunistic killing to you?'

'It does not. But secateurs… If you set out to murder someone, presumably you would go equipped for the task.

Isn't it leaving it to chance to improvise a weapon at the crime scene? It doesn't fit.'

'Things don't always fit, sir. It's not like the novels.'

'What did you find at the bath house?'

'Just what you saw. Someone has been there, probably more than once. They seem to have made themselves at home. Left no evidence, no prints, no forensics. There's no reason to connect that with the murder, nor to rule it out. Can you think of anyone who might go there?'

'Yes, Alex de Floures. The second son. He's an artist, lives in London, but when he's here he lives in the lodge house and uses sites all over the estate for his... I think he calls them installations. They're quite the spectacle. He's used the orangery and the old stables, so I wouldn't be surprised if he's been using the bath house.'

'What about Ned Thwaite?'

'Local historian. He's been doing some research on the house during the last war when the French were here, when the mural was painted. But it was a recent discovery. The bath house hasn't been used for years. It's been visible, but inaccessible, really, since the war, one of those things the estate let slip.'

'I don't think it's of any more use to us, so consider it no longer out of bounds.'

'What about my church, Detective Sergeant?'

'I'm afraid we're going to need to hang on to it for a bit longer.'

'Any idea when we can get it back?'

'No. And when we do there will be quite a bit of clearing up to do. There are specialists who deal with this sort of thing, we can give you their contact details.' He finished his tea. 'Not something you expect to come across in a church.'

'It's not the first murder here,' said Daniel. 'We killed a Quaker who came through in the seventeenth century. Called down one of my predecessors from the pulpit and accused him of heresy. Some of the parishioners took him outside and beat him to death. And in the Civil War some Royalists came through Champton after Naseby and were caught and massacred.'

'And I thought it was all flower arranging and Evensong.'

'Man's inhumanity to man, Sergeant, in evidence everywhere, anywhere. And the Civil War wasn't really that long ago.'

'What would you have been, sir?'

'What do you mean?'

'Roundhead or Cavalier?'

'I would have been for the Crown, Sergeant, I suppose. My predecessor at that time was and so were the de Floures, or most of them.'

'I would probably have been a Roundhead,' said the detective sergeant. 'We're nonconformist, my people, Moravian Brethren from Manchester.'

'Still in the church?'

'Not me, no. Though it left its mark.'

'Long way from Moravia to Manchester.'

'I'll tell you about it some day. Thanks for the tea, sir.'

'It's Daniel. And you are …?'

'Neil.'

Daniel saw him to the door. 'I'm glad we've had a chance to talk. If I can help at all, just ask.'

'Where can I find Mr Achurch?'

'Sexton's Cottage, just past the lychgate.'

20

The Old Vicarage at Pitcote closed its lovely doors on its last vicar in the 1960s. It was sold to raise cash by the diocese during one of its frequent periods of financial crisis and was eventually converted into an old people's home. It opened its lovely doors to admit a clergyman again in the 1980s, when Canon Dolben – Daniel's predecessor but one as rector of Champton St Mary – finally retired in his nineties.

Daniel went to see him once a month, on the first Saturday usually, to give him Holy Communion and talk about the cricket when the cricket was on, and it most certainly was on, for the day before Hick had scored 405 not out for Worcestershire against Somerset, and the old canon was as lively with excitement as Daniel could remember. More excitement was to come when Daniel took him for a spin in the Land Rover, an entertainment his mother thought reckless for a man of that age and frailty, but the old canon was practically blind and enjoyed the creaking and braking and surging of Daniel's terrible driving. 'It's the only physical thrill I get now!' He liked most to be taken back to Champton and to sit in Daniel's study, which had been for so long his own talking shop.

Canon Dolben had been rector for thirty years – from the Battle of Britain to the Three-Day Week, as he put it – and in age showed no mental fatigue or lapses of clarity. He also had a feel for the parish which extended beyond his years of incumbency. Once, he mentioned another incumbent, Geoffrey something, whom Daniel could not place. 'When was he here, Father?' he asked. 'Installed in 1217,' he said, as if it were in living memory.

Audrey brought them tea and chocolate-chip cookies from the post office, which the Canon adored, and hovered too long in the doorway discussing the death, recently announced, of the former Archbishop of Canterbury, Michael Ramsey, who had been Canon Dolben's neighbour in Lincoln diocese in the thirties, and whom Daniel had known as a venerable and unworldly resident of his old theological college in the seventies.

When she had retreated, he asked Daniel to tell him everything that had happened.

They sat in silence for a while and then Canon Dolben said, 'A parish can suffer a trauma, like an individual. It happened during the war. The wars, both wars, had an incalculable effect. I am of that generation of young men – teenagers, really – who witnessed the wholesale slaughter of their peers. Shells, interlocking machine-gun fire, gas. And then we all came home. And then it happened again, only the second time I was at Champton. A long way from the cannon and the bombers, but of course it arrived in the form of those people who came back. And those who didn't. And even worse than that.'

'What could be worse than that?'

'A Frenchman, I don't remember his name, an officer who was up at the house. He was a painter, I think quite a famous

one, before the war, a surrealist, if they had them then? He was
exactly what one expected a French painter to be like: he wore
a sort of cravat and peculiar trousers, smoked constantly and
walked with a very pronounced limp from his wounds. I think
he had something to do with camouflage, but he loved to put
on shows and paint sets and design the costumes. He did a
wonderful *As You Like It* in the bath house and in the woods,
we all had to move around, French and locals in the cast.
He played Jacques, and there was a terrible argument when
we said it was pronounced Jay-queeze rather than the French
way, but in the end we gave in, for he was so insistent. He had
that sort of personality, explosive, charming, divisive. And
he had an extraordinary appetite for other people, utterly
indiscriminate. He wasn't bothered by people's class, he was
just the same with the village folk as he was with the gentry.
You can imagine the effect he had on Champton. Bernard
would remember him. He and Anthony idolised him, when
they were up.'

The old priest tailed off.

'What happened to him?'

'Killed. Killed here. It must have been more than camouflage
because he was in the plane that crashed in the park and
everyone was killed. I can still remember the sound and the
impact. It blew out half the windows at the house.'

'Oh yes, Alex told me about it.'

'Well, I suppose he would know that story. What's he up to?'

'He's still trying to be an artist, although not really painting
now. He's a sort of impresario, rather like the French chap.
He puts on events, shows, and invites people to come and
see them.'

'Like a barn dance?'

'Not like a barn dance, no.'

Daniel sipped his tea. It came in a mug that bore the legend Britain's Best Mum.

Canon Dolben nibbled his cookie. 'These are really very good. So the war blew in and blew out all sorts of characters, and, it being war, there were dalliances that seemed to come out of nowhere. The Free French, a pool of men, damaged, glamorous, different from us. And there was plenty of attention from the ladies of Braunstonbury, who came up on a Saturday night for dances. And plenty of broken hearts and sometimes babies that had to be discreetly dealt with – Bernard's father was most understanding – and sometimes girls from the village were whisked away, to work on another de Floures estate, and' – he gave a gesture which looked like Mary of Teck waving – 'arrangements were made for the children to be adopted. It was not unusual. Actually, it has never been unusual.'

Daniel thought of the baby bones that turned up sometimes when the churchyard earth was turned to bury ashes, unbaptised children who were not allowed burial. Whether his predecessors had turned a blind eye, or actively encouraged the mothers to bring their children to be buried, he did not know, but they went in alongside their ancestors without much ceremony or even a marker, often against the unvisited north wall of the church. 'The wall of tears,' Bob Achurch called it, the memory of those unofficial disposals still carried by the community.

'Young Canon Segrave, I remember him saying that in his father's day the clerk used to enter "Born into Bastardy" in the baptism register for children whose parents had not married.'

'Now baptisms precede marriages,' said Daniel.

'Does it bother you?'

'No, I'm just pleased to see people. And so much of what we do, as parish priests, is off the books, if I can put it that way.'

'It is indeed.'

They sat, in silent solidarity, thinking of things they could not say, not even to each other.

When Daniel got back from Pitcote, having delivered Canon Dolben into its care like a piece of delicate furniture, instead of going to the rectory he went to church, restored by the police to his custodianship. In the vestry he opened the safe and took from it one of the bunches of keys that hung on hooks glued to the inside of the door.

There were far more keys than locks for them to turn – ancient keys made of iron hundreds of years old for the exterior doors, tiny little keys to open alms boxes and aumbries and the old Bechstein piano that once belonged to Canon Segrave and on which the Misses Segrave played Clementi sonatas and Czerny exercises as young ladies of accomplishment. There were modern keys too, deadlocks and snib locks, and he took a ring with one of both, and made his way to the south porch, where he opened a little door at the bottom of a turret stair that led to the parvise, the room over the porch. It had once been a schoolroom, although the master could not have fitted in more than half a dozen of even the scrawniest children; in the eighteenth century it had been made into a parish library with a donation of books from the then Lord de Floures, and the shelves were stuffed with volumes, bound in dark leather, most of the spines now unreadable. When opened, they released a mouldy odour, and the generous donation seemed suddenly less so, for they were mostly of Puritan sermons, austere and forbidding, at odds with the exuberant *Ex Libris* pasted on the inside covers. Daniel had often wondered how they came to be at Champton, the least Puritan of parishes; even the doughtiest would have struggled to finish the 112 lectures in Caryl's *Exposition on the Book of Job*. But there were unexpected delights: once he had found a few leaves of paper stuck in an unpromising volume with handwritten remedies for various complaints, including brimstone and butter for purpled-face.

Another key on the ring opened the metal doors of the fire-proof safe where the parish records, going back to the sixteenth century, were kept and through which he would occasionally browse, noting a predecessor's minute hand, in ink faded to brown, recording every farthing paid and owed by parishioners with the same surnames as Daniel's parishioners today.

But he was not here for the remedy of soul or body, but to satisfy curiosity. He found the baptism books for the 1940s, laid them on the table, switched on the lamp and began to read.

And then he heard the door at the foot of the turret creak open, and his mother's voice floated up.

'Daniel? Are you up there?'

'Yes.'

'You must come AT ONCE!'

21

Daniel rang the bell, and wondered if Jane Thwaite would see, through the frosted glass of her front door, the dread shape of a policeman and a parson on the threshold.

The door opened. She was wearing an apron, dusty with flour, and looked confused. 'Hello, Daniel?' She wiped her hands on the apron, then looked at PC Scott. 'Constable?' she said, and wiped some more, unnecessarily.

'Jane,' said Daniel, 'something awful has happened. May we come in?'

At midnight her daughter Angela – who had driven up from London after Daniel had retrieved her card from his pocketbook and called her with the terrible news – found pudding batter resting in a jug in the fridge but could not imagine it being used now. She poured it away into the sink, where it pooled oozily over the drain before trickling away.

22

Nathan Liversedge, even more nervous than usual at the thought of being interviewed by the police, had checked and double checked his flies before Daniel and DS Neil Vanloo caught up with him in the old potting shed Nathan used for his various and mysterious purposes.

'In your own words, sir, tell me what happened?'

'I already told the other one last night.'

'Same again, please, sir?'

Nathan looked at Daniel, who nodded reassuringly back.

'I was out with the gun teatime to look for mink and otter because they kill the ducks and eat the eggs.'

And maybe hunt the odd rabbit or pigeon or deer, thought Daniel.

'I went up to the lake and I saw summat floating in the reedbed near the bath house. I though it were a fertiliser bag or summat, but it weren't, it were Mr Thwaite.'

'How did you know it was Mr Thwaite?'

'I didn't at first, I saw it were a body, so I went round to the bath house and got a boathook and pulled it in and it were Mr Thwaite.'

'What did you notice about him?'

'He were dead. Drowned, I thought, but then I saw he had tekken a knock on the back of the head, beaten in, like. So I left him up on the bank and ran home and told Bap and he told me to fetch the rector.'

'And I telephoned you.'

'What did you do?'

'We came straight away to the bath house. I saw Ned's body, I said a prayer. And then we kept away until you got here.'

'What did you notice?'

'There were footprints in the mud on the bank, I couldn't say whose they were, probably ours. Ned's jumper had been yanked out of shape, but I think that would have been from the boathook when Nathan pulled him in.'

Nathan nodded.

'What about injuries?'

'I couldn't see any. Ned was lying on his back.'

'It were disrespectful to leave him just like I'd pulled him out of the water, so I put him on his back and folded his arms on his chest, like, and went to fetch help.'

'You'd seen he had injuries to the back of his head?'

'Yes. He'd been hit. The blood had been washed away like, but it were a big knock.'

'Any ideas what could have caused it? The boathook?'

Nathan thought for a moment. 'Doubt it. It must have been summat bigger, heavier, than a boathook.'

'Did you see anything that could have caused the injury?'

He thought some more. Then he said, 'The grapnel. It's like a small anchor they use on tenders, it folds up. It were kept in the bath house, near where the boats tie up ... I don't think it were there.'

'Why did you not say this before?'

'I only just thought on it.'

'What does it look like?'

'It's about so long' – he indicated two feet or so – 'and it has these prongs, but they fold up, like, and you can lock them in place, so it's like a weapon, a sort of club. If you hit someone with that, they'd know about it.'

'How did you know about it?'

'Me?'

'How did you know about the anchor?'

'I know about lots of things, I work all over the estate, I have to fix things. I know where tools are.'

'Did you often go to the bath house?'

Nathan looked uncomfortable. 'Not often. I know about it. When I come to shoot mink, I sometimes sit up in there, have a brew. I notice things.'

'Why are you saying this now? You know we've been making enquiries about the bath house?'

Nathan looked more uncomfortable. 'I don't know that I should be there. I sometimes take duck. To sell, like. I don't want Mr Meldrum to know.'

'Mr Meldrum?'

Daniel cut in. 'Estate manager. But Nathan, this is more important than a few ducks. No one will punish you for it. Tell the detective sergeant everything you know.'

'That's all I know. I ent never seen no one else up there, apart from Alex. He got me to show him the bath house when he got interested.'

'This is Mr de Floures?'

'He's his lordship's son. I have to do as he says.'

'What do you mean "he got interested"?'

Nathan paused and thought. 'He takes an interest in the old places: the lodge, the folly, the bath house. He likes to use them for his art shows. He likes me to show him round.'

Daniel saw that Nathan had slightly braced himself when he said this, as if he was squaring his shoulders for a fight. And then he understood something he had not understood before: Alex's interest in Nathan was not only for his knowledge of the estate.

DS Vanloo wrote a few lines and then closed his notebook. 'That will be all for now, sir. We will need to speak to you again. Do you have any plans to leave Champton in the near future?'

'No. I don't go anywhere.'

Daniel saw him to the door.

'Something he's not saying, Dan?'

'I suppose so. Isn't there always?'

'Let me know if anything comes up.'

Daniel watched DS Vanloo set out to walk back across the park to the bath house, once again taped off, only now with a bigger team coming and going in their boiler suits, walking in and out of one of those little white tents that go up like a folding mausoleum when a body is discovered.

Another murder. Harder, somehow, to deal with the second time round – because it was the second time and the routine around it had already become tragically familiar, and that obscured the horror of Ned's death. Daniel didn't want the horror of Ned's death to be diminished at all.

Nathan was rolling a cigarette. His hands were shaking and the smoothness with which he usually rolled the stringy tobacco into a neat paper-covered cylinder failed him. He started again.

'Are you all right, Nathan?'

'No. I've never seen a dead 'un before.'

He lit his cigarette and took a drag of its sour smoke.

'Will I be in trouble with Mr Meldrum?' he asked.

'I don't think so.' Highly unlikely, thought Daniel, when you consider how much more the estate needed Nathan than Nathan the estate.

'What will the coppers want to know?'

'What you saw, what happened. It is really important that you tell them everything. It might be something that means nothing to you but could mean a lot to them.'

'I didn't see no one there. I wasn't with Alex, like, if that's what you're thinking.'

'You've been up there with Alex?'

'A few times.' It came as 'foo toimes'. 'He wanted me to show him how to get in there, but people have always been getting in there, from the village. I never saw no one else, but you could tell they'd been. Cans, fag ends ...'

'But you went there more than once with Alex?'

'Once or twice.' Nathan again looked like he was bracing himself.

'Why?'

'He ... liked the company.'

I bet he did, thought Daniel, the company of Nathan, so handsome, so unknowing, so curiously open, like his wayward flies.

~

Another Sunday and another scandal. St Mary's, open again for business now the police had concluded theirs, was unusually busy, not only with parishioners seeking solace in a terrible time, but with journalists who had returned in force to Champton, scene now of a double murder and redoubled interest. They had set up camp in the village, staking out the gates to the house, taking pictures with long lenses over the walls and through the trees, occupying every room at the Royal Oak. And this morning here they were, in a mood of unusual piety, annoying the regulars by sitting in their places at the back.

Bernard was furious when he arrived and wanted them chucked out, but Daniel said he could not do that, which made Bernard even more furious, and he had stomped off, causing an exodus of as yet unshriven journalists and photographers. Audrey had seen this coming and scooted out to rescue him, diverting him to the rectory and closing the gate on the fourth estate with a look of stony reproach. She put him in Daniel's study, from where he called the house and had Mrs Shorely send Honoria to fetch him in her car.

As he telephoned, Audrey went to make coffee and to fill a plate with biscuits, but the tin, alas, was furnished only with the dreary sort, taken as an economy from the supply ordered for church from the cash and carry at Braunstonbury, and not of noble standard. She had no choice but to take the Victoria sponge made for the Thwaites' funeral visit later that afternoon, put it on a stand, and offer it to the de Floures instead, on the grounds that it was better to be too magnificent than too mean. Hilda and Cosmo, confined to their basket by the Aga, whined as she shut the kitchen door on them.

'Wonderful cake, dear lady,' said Bernard, for he had forgotten her name, as blobs of cream and a shower of icing tumbled down his tie like a tiny avalanche.

Honoria put her cup down on the saucer. 'We are going to have to give the journos *something*.'

'Why give them anything? Can't they mind their own fu— … blasted business?'

'It *is* their business, Daddy, and they won't go away until they've got what they want. Perhaps I should talk to them? See if we can work something out?'

'Just make them go away.'

The cost of being left alone was a press conference, which Honoria arranged to take place at the gates to the house at half past twelve, so that Bernard would have the incentive of lunch to get him through it, and the representatives of the press the incentive of a pub open for their refreshment to speed matters along. Bernard had insisted Daniel accompany him and they walked together down the long drive towards them, photographers and cameramen and reporters. 'The barbarians at the gates,' muttered Bernard, 'and Alex in the lodges. That doesn't bode well.'

Bernard in his country tweeds and Daniel in his clericals looked like representatives too, of the *ancien régime*. Mindful of his standing, Bernard had tried to appear dignified and reticent. But not for long; under the barrage of questions, he soon blustered and chose an easy escape. 'I think, ladies and gentlemen, you may better direct your questions to the rector, Canon Clement.' The cameras had turned to Daniel and the questioners too.

'Do you think evil has come to Champton?'

'What's it like to have a killer in your midst?'

'Do you wonder who's next?'

As soon as he could, Bernard thanked them all for coming, in a rather *noblesse oblige* sort of way, and he and Daniel went back through the closing gates to walk up the drive towards the house. They did not speak; Bernard did not want to, and Daniel knew when to remain silent. Instead he watched the ewes and the lambs dotted along the drive, half on half off the asphalt, oblivious to the world and its dangers until they were nearly upon them, when they would start and get up, the lambs wobbling upright, the ewes creaky, and amble stiffly away until they had passed and then settle again behind them.

Alex and Honoria had been watching the interview take place from the north lodge.

Alex said, 'Is that why you're here? To discourage *me* from talking to the press?'

'As if I could,' she said. 'But you mustn't, darling. They wouldn't be kind to you. And it would upset Daddy.'

'I'm not a complete idiot.'

'I know you're not. But what are these morbid drawings?'

At her feet lay small piles of A2 sheets of paper covered with what looked like tombstones and funeral wreaths and solitary ravens drawn messily in charcoal.

'Ideas for my new piece.'

'I'm not sure it's in the best possible taste, given our circumstances. But then good taste is not really your thing.'

'It's not meant to be about present circumstances ... Actually, maybe now it is a bit. Do you recognise them?'

Honoria squatted to look. 'I don't think so. Are they from the churchyard?'

'No. But I may want to do the performance there and I may need you to use your charms on the rector.'

'Oh, I see what they are. Don't die of ignorance?'

There had been a government information film on television warning of the dangers of AIDS – unnuanced but powerful – after the Department of Health realised the potential of the virus to infect and kill anyone. DON'T DIE OF IGNORANCE, the slogan solemnly advised, chiselled into what looked like a tombstone, which thudded to the ground in slow motion. As a cloud of dust rose in the air, to crashing synthesiser chords, a bouquet of lilies dropped onto it. 'Don't die of ignorance,' intoned John Hurt in voice-over.

'People are more likely to die of cholera than AIDS in Champton, darling,' said Honoria.

'That may be precisely the kind of ignorance from which you may die.'

'Hardly me, Alex.'

'Why not you? You only have to sleep with someone who slept with someone who slept with someone.'

'You make it sound like pass the parcel.'

'It *is* exactly like pass the parcel.'

Honoria stood and went to the window, in need of a little air and light. 'I just don't think it's me who has to worry about catching AIDS.'

'Do you remember when the first cases started to appear in London and I came up and you thought I had been infected because my cuticles had turned blue, but really it was because I had just dyed my hair?'

'Oh yes. We were all a bit worried about you. Well, I was.'

'I don't suppose Daddy noticed.'

'Hard to know what Daddy thinks, behind the bluster and the show.'

At teatime the Thwaites came to call. Jane sat on the Sofa of Tears, flanked by her daughters. There were tears, so they dabbed at their eyes with the grief-absorbent tissues Daniel had left on the otherwise empty coffee table.

'I don't know what we came here for,' said Angela, the elder daughter, 'it's not as if there is anything you can do.'

People like to have something to do, thought Daniel, when their lives are suddenly wrecked. The boring and arduous admin of death was actually quite helpful to those in the first shock of loss – cancelling driving licences and bank accounts so much easier to deal with than a life cancelled inconceivably.

Jane winced. Daniel said simply, 'No, there's nothing I can do.'

A knock at the door, and Audrey came in pushing a tea trolley.

'I suppose there's always tea,' muttered Angela.

A cup of tea, Daniel had offered, but Audrey had interpreted that liberally and the trolley was laden not only with a teapot, four cups, a milk jug and a sugar bowl (best china), but with an array of silver cutlery and side plates. A date-and-walnut cake stood on a pedestal, a rectangle on a circle; it looked somewhat wrong, but the specially made Victoria sandwich had been sacrificed to the aristocracy that morning, and besides, Audrey thought, it might look a little *en fête*, and no one would think her date and walnut was that.

Funeral meats, thought Daniel, and said, 'Thanks, Mum.'

'I won't stay,' she said, 'but I just wanted to say how sorry I am at the news. We adored Ned, and I can't imagine Champton without him. And the manner of it. So awful.'

As Audrey turned to leave, Jane began to weep again and Daniel thought, not for the first time, how well-chosen were his mother's words. Some people are good in a crisis.

'The manner of his death,' said Gillian, the younger daughter. 'Beaten unconscious and drowned in a lake. That's not what's meant to happen in places like Champton.'

'I'm afraid evil can flare up anywhere,' said Daniel. 'Jane, I want you to know, I want all of you to know, that you are in our prayers, and th—'

'Very well meant, Rector,' said Angela, 'and we're grateful of course,' though she sounded anything but. 'However, right now all I want is whoever murdered my father, and I suppose murdered the archivist chap as well, to be caught.'

'But who would want to murder, Ned?' wailed Jane.

'I don't know,' said Daniel. 'I cannot think of anything in his life that would have made anyone want to hurt him at all.'

'He was a good and kind and gentle man, he would not have hurt anyone,' said Gillian.

'The nearest he ever got to violence was on the rugby pitch.'

There was a pause. Then Jane said, 'He had not been quite his usual self lately. Had you noticed he was getting forgetful?'

Gillian and Angela looked at each other. Angela said, 'We had. Forgetful, struggling for words sometimes. But there was nothing in his behaviour that felt off. Had you noticed anything at all, Mum?'

'He knew his mind was not what it was. We joked about it. At first. But his grandmother lost her wits – Alzheimer's or something – and he dreaded the thought of losing his. His wits were what he was all about, you see. That's what he thought. But apart from that he was still the same. No outbursts of anger like you see sometimes, nothing like that. I suppose there is no need to worry about that now.' She began to cry again. 'The thought of him being hit over the head!'

Her daughters drew closer and tried their best to comfort her, but there was very little comfort for the Thwaites to be had in that moment.

After a while, Angela said, 'What have the police said?'

'Nothing more than we know already,' said Daniel, which was not strictly true. He and Neil Vanloo had started to work together, not formally and without official sanction, of course, but sharing thoughts and sharing information which, strictly speaking, neither of them had any right to share. But they were growing to trust each other, and trust normally withered quickly in the anxiety and suspicion generated by two murders, probably committed by the same hand. Both attacks had the mark of a professional – the expert stab wound, the opportunistic use of the grapnel anchor. Neither had been done in a frenzy: in both cases one blow, carefully aimed. Someone who knew what they were doing was picking off people in Champton, but if there were a connection – and how could there not be? – it led to no one person in particular. It was likely, Daniel and Neil agreed on this, that the murders were linked and had something to do with Champton's history: an archivist and a local historian, turning over the past, perhaps turning up things long buried but still potent.

'Had Ned said anything to you about what he was researching?'

'The war,' said Jane. 'He was fascinated by the war in Champton, the men who went out to Dunkirk. And Burma – we have a Chindit, he said – and the men who came here, the Free French at the hall. He wanted to talk about the impact they made on the locals, these Frenchmen. He said he'd found a newspaper report in the *Braunstonbury Evening Telegraph*, about a sentry at the crossroads one dark night challenging a stranger who came out of nowhere. The stranger didn't acknowledge him, didn't reply, so he shouted at him again – still no reply, so he took aim and was about to shoot when he saw it was General de Gaulle. Sounds too good to be true?'

'Anthony told me about it, actually.'

'Yes, he did, and there were photographs. Anthony found them in the archive and the *Telegraph* had some too. De Gaulle, in his ... what do they call their army hats?'

'Kepi?'

'A kepi, that's right, surrounded by these wounded men and some of the locals who looked after them, or looked after the house.'

'I've seen it. Anyone he recognised?'

'Yes, Gilbert Drage, who was the estate carpenter then. He'd helped convert the house for when the French came, but he's very old now and his mind's gone, and when Ned asked him about it, he just ranted. Didn't make any sense. I think Ned found that a bit difficult to deal with.'

'Why?'

'He didn't like it when people were – would you call it racialist if it's against the French? And people who've lost their marbles were difficult too, because he feared he was losing his.' Jane began to cry again. 'He was frightened that he would end his days in a chair looking at the wall not knowing who I was.'

No one spoke, and what would have been silence was broken only by her stifled sobs, until Angela said, 'This cake's a bit dense.' She finger-wrestled the slice on her plate. 'Is it date?'

'Among other things,' said Daniel.

Silence again, broken this time by the distant sound of dogs growing less distant, and then a barking at the door on the other side of the hall and furious scratching.

'Oh, do let them in, Daniel,' said Jane.

'I'm not sure that would be wise. They're not very well behaved.'

'Aren't they sausage dogs? We had a sausage dog. Caspar, do you remember him, Mum?' said Gillian.

'Yes, a miniature smooth-haired red. Same as yours, Daniel. I'd love to see them.'

'Well, if you're sure.' Daniel let them in and they exploded into the room. Hilda threw herself onto Jane's lap with such force she spilled her tea; but before she could do anything about it, Hilda rolled over onto her back in a passion of self-indulgence and waited, her nipples like rows of buttons, to be rubbed. Cosmo sat himself in front of Gillian and barked, not especially aggressively, but insistently. Dogs, ignorant of human weal and woe, did what dogs do, demanded what dogs demand, and – ignorant of the terrible loss of Ned – broke the spell of the moment.

Daniel loved the indelicacy of dogs, the enthusiasm with which Cosmo would try to shag the bishop's leg, or Hilda lick the unlovable face of Stella Harper.

'Who's a good girl?' asked Jane, rubbing Hilda's belly. 'Who's a *good* girl?'

Gillian nervously patted Cosmo's head, who responded by licking her hand.

While her mother and sister were preoccupied with the dogs, Angela spoke. 'Funeral arrangements. What happens now, Daniel?'

'Nothing, I'm afraid, until the coroner's business is done. There will have to be a post-mortem and an investigation. There's no way of knowing how long it will be before we're able to have a funeral.'

'And meanwhile?'

'Meanwhile you get through each day one at a time, however you can. Try to be kind to each other. Emotion is high and behaviour erratic.'

'You're becoming quite the expert in this, aren't you? Pastoral care of the criminally bereaved.'

There was something astringent, corrosive even, about Angela's directness; she displayed it like an accomplishment, but those around her did not enjoy it as she did.

'We deal with what arises.'

'But two murders, Daniel, in as many weeks. That must surely be way above the odds for an English country village, even St Mary Mead. What on earth is going on?'

'Humanity. Or inhumanity, rather. It happens everywhere.'

'*This* inhumanity has happened *here* and it has killed *my* father and I really want to know who did it and I want them to be punished for it. I want them to suffer for it. I'm sorry, but I do. I have never believed in the death penalty until this afternoon. Do you know what that feels like?'

'When I was a student, I was sent on a placement at Winchester Gaol. I was barely twenty years old. One of the prisoners had been convicted of murder. He'd killed a farmer in a robbery – I think he got away with five pounds – and for that he was condemned to death. I remember I played draughts with him the day before he was hanged and he made a joke about a rematch. I did not attend the execution – the chaplain wouldn't have allowed it even if it had been permitted, which it wasn't. He told me about it, though. The awful drab of the condemned cell, the solicitousness of the executioner, the white hood, the lever, like the ones that work the points on the railway. Eight o'clock struck and the trap opened and a thud that he could feel through the floor as the rope took the weight. I've never forgotten it.'

'That's exactly what I want for the person who killed my father.'

It was still bright when Daniel returned to church. The choir had not yet arrived for their pre-Evensong practice, and he wanted to be there before them, to see what it felt like, to see that the shadows and echoes of the terrible murder that had occurred there were now dispelled. He remembered a Romanian visiting his church in London who was horrified to find Cosmo and Hilda running around, for in his country dogs in church were considered a profanation requiring the remedy of prayer. Perhaps the same impulse had brought him to church too, to correct and cleanse and rehallow? He sat once again in his stall, prayed and then sat back to watch the effect of the sun shining through the stained glass in the north windows of the chancel. One window was exceptionally gaudy, typical of its period and maker; Daniel often thought it looked rather like Tom and Jerry, not that the artist could have foreseen that. Its colours were intense and even, the glass without the imperfections that gave glitter and grain to its neighbours. It threw a vividly coloured smudge on the opposite wall which crept across the whitewash as slow as the dawn – too slow to see moving, but look away and then look back, and it *had* moved, like a game of grandmother's footsteps.

The past weeks had been extraordinarily turbulent. Daniel had felt that turbulence turn not only in the parish but within himself, disturbing the balance which he normally sustained through the discipline of prayer. Part of that discipline was its regularity, and being displaced from church had isolated him from the ordering pulse that otherwise prevailed. And the unsteadiness within had met the unsteadiness spreading through Champton, as the village reeled from the two violent deaths visited upon it. It was not simply the shock of loss and horror at its cause, but the interruption they caused to the community's own steady heartbeat, now fluttery and uneven. Arguments about lavatories, the flower rota, car parking, had suddenly become unmanageably intense as the sense of threat had grown more severe. It affected people in different ways, too. The Sharman sisters had become quiet and withdrawn; Bernard had grown morose; Alex – on the other hand – had been lively, sucking up disquiet like a growing crop the rain.

But it was the unanswered questions hanging over the community that had come to Daniel again and again as he said his prayers and then waited in silence for the unexpected returns of that enterprise. Neil was piecing together the movements of everyone in Champton, and anomalies were beginning to appear, perhaps because people forgot where they were, perhaps because, like Nathan, they had reason for people not to know their business. Somewhere in those accounts an anomaly would point to the murderer, thought Daniel. Two victims with a common interest and purpose, both looking into the past: the motive for whoever did it lay, he felt sure, in that common purpose. He was all but convinced that Anthony and Ned had been killed because they had trespassed on the past and discovered something buried there that needed to remain a secret at all costs.

What was certain was that Anthony had been killed by a single blow to the neck with a pair of secateurs that had severed his carotid artery; he had bled to death in seconds. Time of death was sometime between seven and nine; Neil Vanloo had said there was a question over the exact time because his blood had been thinned by alcohol, widening the window provided by the forensic pathologist. They knew that at around five or six o'clock in the evening Ned had been stunned by a single blow to the back of his head from a grapnel anchor (it had eventually been found by a diver), then had fallen, or been pushed, into the lake and had drowned. One question that needed answering: Ned usually carried a notebook, a camera and a dictaphone on his historical expeditions, and none of those items had been found, either on him, or near him, or at home. Had the murderer taken them? Why?

The times of death, if accurate, did not help much. Anthony
had died while most of the locals were at home, settled for the
evening. Ned had been killed when most people would have
been on their way home from work (and those who weren't
could very easily have been walking unobserved up by the lake
and bath house). If it were someone outside the community
who was responsible for their deaths, then they had come and
gone and left no trace.

Eventually Daniel rose from his stall, the dogs uncurling
from his feet, and walked with them down the aisle to where
he had discovered Anthony's body. The crime scene had been
cleaned by the specialist team; they had done such an excellent
job that any ghouls in search of bloodstains would have to use
their imagination. They would, of course, and the murders
would enter local folklore, generate tales of dogs refusing to go
into church, or birds no longer singing in the trees around the
bath house. He and Neil would have to save the duller facts of
the matter from the brew of conjecture and myth into which
the murders were already disappearing.

23

Monday was meant to be Daniel's day off, but he rarely took it because he did not think of his employment as a job, or not quite. He did what needed to be done when it needed to be done, when and where possible; and if there were nothing that needed to be done, then he would do nothing, for he thought inactivity as important as activity, perhaps more important if Mary and Martha of Bethany in the Fourth Gospel were offered as an example to follow. But it was harder to justify doing nothing in a world which measured achievement more and more narrowly, and there was no credit granted to those who looked like they were idling. On the contrary, they were looked down on, or with suspicion in a brave new world of balance sheets and productivity. Our measurements will only be as sound as the measures we use to establish them, he once said to a keen rural dean who wanted to apply the methods of business to the calculation of souls saved. He gave Daniel rather a sour look, and ever since Daniel had found himself more and more tempted to the sin of dissembling a busyness he did not actually believe in. He was not the only one. He remembered once in London having nothing in his engagement book, going to the pictures in Leicester Square, to a lunchtime screening of *The Eagle Has Landed*. He thought he was the only person there until the lights came up and he saw there was another: the Secretary of State for Energy, Mr Benn, who looked sheepishly at him and he sheepishly back, shrugging in the manner of a guilty man offering no defence.

This Monday morning, however, was not for leisure. Daniel was walking through the woods at the edge of the estate – not with the dogs this time, for once when he had visited this parishioner he had found him boiling the severed head of a Rottweiler in a pot on the stove (he had shot the dog 'for worrying sheep' and taken it home 'to see what the skull looked like').

The Liversedges' cottage stood in a clearing that was gradually becoming less clear, partly from encroaching nature, partly from the detritus that Edgy had collected over the years – broken-down machines awaiting repair, oil cans, tractor tyres. Smoke rose from the chimney and Daniel knew Edgy was in because his boots were at the front door. He knocked. 'Mr Liversedge? It's the rector here.'

He heard slow movements from inside, a creaking and a rustling, and then the door opened. Edgy looked at him from under the rim of his smoke-darkened cap. 'You'd best come in, Father. I wondered if you'd call. Kettle's boiled.'

A black kettle stood on a rack over the fire in the kitchen range and the old man laboriously made a pot of tea. The mug, when it came, was another of Bernard's unsold souvenirs, although not in a condition likely to provoke fond memories, for the brew it contained was as dark as teak, smelt like creosote and left a stain beyond the power of any detergent to shift. It would take an effort to drink it, but drink it he must, for there were formalities to be observed here as rigid as any Japanese tea ceremony. Edgy, in person, was always Mr Liversedge, and any offer of hospitality, from either party, must be accepted. Face was important: Daniel observed *toujours la politesse* in his dealings with gypsies and travellers.

'Has Nathan talked to you at all, Mr Liversedge, about the murder?'

'He was quite shook up. He liked the old schoolmaster. He took some trouble with him, now and again, learned him up about the house and the family.'

'He was worried, I think, that he might be in trouble if people found out – Mr Meldrum, I'm thinking of – that he had been… um… going beyond the formal terms of his employment. He need not worry about that.'

Edgy nodded again, but his instinct, and the judgement of experience, was to steer clear of the law altogether. He had been steering clear of it all his life, a necessary tactic for a travelling man, disconnected from the structures that settled people knew. He had learned a different code, more exacting than that of the mainstream, for it was founded on plain principles of survival in a hostile world. Nathan, who had grown up differently, was neither fish nor fowl, and his life was defined by uncertainty, uncertainty about who he was, and where he fitted. His outlook lacked the clarity of his grandfather's and one of the effects of this was his willingness to please. Too willing sometimes, especially with someone looking for an advantage, and in Alex de Floures Nathan had met someone who was always ready to exploit such weakness.

As a child, Alex had been fascinated by Edgy: he used to come and sit with him outside when he chopped wood and when the split log separated and the splinters flew, he would cry with delight. When he was a bit older, Edgy would let him watch him wart-charming, rubbing the disfiguring eruptions with a split pea pod and then saying a prayer, or a spell, and burying the pods in earth. Then Nathan arrived, from down south, a 'troubled teen' as he had heard it called, in circumstances which had obliged a quick and discreet removal to his grandfather's. Alex, home for the holidays, came to see Edgy one day and found there a boy nearer his own age, but with his grandfather's mystery and glamour and allure.

Daniel took a sip of his tea. 'I was wondering, Mr Liversedge, when the police came to speak to you, if you had said much about Nathan and his past?'

'I answered the questions, Father, about where I was, and about where he was. That was an end to it. Someone else been talking?'

'Not to my knowledge.'

'Good. Would you light me up one of these?'

Edgy nodded at a tin half full of roll-ups. Daniel took one and a spill from beside the fire; he lit the roll-up with it and passed it to Edgy, who grunted his appreciation as Daniel pinched away a straggling thread of tobacco frond from his bottom lip.

'I don't want Nathan to come to any more trouble than he's already come to.'

'Of course not, but if he were to know anything that might help find the murderer, then all other considerations, I'm sure, would be put to one side.'

'What about my other considerations, Father?'

'I don't think they come into it, Mr Liversedge.'

'The coppers might think differently.'

What the coppers did not know – what neither Nathan, nor Alex, nor anyone else in Champton but Daniel knew – was that Edgy once had another employment. As a young man he had been a prize fighter, but when he grew too old for the ring, he developed a sideline in debt collection. When other means failed, Edgy would be sent for to persuade a slow payer to speed up. That eventually led to a more specialised service, exclusively for overseas clients, an extreme solution when a failure to pay, or some other lapse, became unforgivable.

Edgy's choice of tool for this work was the cut-throat razor – hence his nickname – and he would arrive at his destination, discharge his duty, collect the cash and be back home before anyone noticed. Edgy considered it a professional service for professional clients only: he gave no hint of menace and sought no notoriety for it. He had retired long ago and had made himself useful at Champton, as his father and grandfather had done; in age he had not exactly mellowed, but he did not seek trouble and wanted for his grandson an easier life than he had known. His failings as a father were a cause of trouble to him and, while he could do nothing about that, he could do his best for Nathan, who needed looking after and putting right and – above all – keeping safe.

'One of the lessons of life, Mr Liversedge, is that we cannot hide forever from the consequences of our actions, wouldn't you say?'

'You would say that, Father. It's your job. Mine's the opposite.'

'Isn't it your job to take care of Nathan?'

'It is, and I do.'

'Well. Thank you for the tea, Mr Liversedge. You'll let me know if I can do anything for you, won't you? And if you should hear of anything that might cause concern ...?'

'My regards to your mother. I'll have the boy paint your fence as soon as the weather settles.'

Edgy saw him to the door and closed it firmly behind him. As Daniel left, he noticed a warm draught, as if someone had opened an oven door, and the faint smell of burning tyres with it, a scent that often hung over Edgy's cottage like the smell of bread over a bakehouse. He saw that something had been burning in one of the old oil drums that Edgy and Nathan used to get rid of pieces of old wood, or rat carcasses, or the combustible relics of tractors, or all the other unusable or unmentionable things their daily work unearthed. The smell reminded him of the crematorium at his first parish, when it had started doing Hindu funerals after the first generation of Indian immigrants had begun to die. It is the custom in that religion to watch the cremation – all those pyres burning beside the Ganges – but the law did not allow such a spectacle in England, so the family would gather outside, looking expectantly at the chimney to see the soul of the departed ascend to mukti, only to be disappointed, for cremators burn without producing smoke. After discussion with the funeral directors, the lads decided to throw in an old tyre with the coffin to produce a satisfactory plume. *Non habemus Papam*, thought Daniel every time he saw black smoke rising from the chimney and smelt the terrible smell.

On the way home he called in at the post office. Writing marginal notes in *After Virtue*, which almost a decade after publication had finally come to the attention of his Theological

Club, he had noticed his pencil eraser had lost definition (so had the thought of Professor Macintyre on embodiment, he maintained); pencil erasers – his favourite kind, Faber-Castell, latex-free so they did not smear – were one of those items that Mrs Braines kept in a drawer, along with playing cards and birthday-cake candles, to meet slow but steady demand.

A small village parliament was at the counter: Margaret Porteous, Anne Dollinger and, towering over them, Bob Achurch. Silence fell when he came in.

'Good morning, ladies. Bob,' he said.

'Shop or post office?' asked Mrs Braines.

'I don't want to push in...'

'You're not. We were just chopsin'.' Margaret winced at the colloquialism.

'Shop, please, Mrs Braines: one of your pencil erasers.'

He never asked for a rubber in a shop lest it cause sniggering. Unlikely in this company, but it was a habit all clergymen acquire quickly: not to provide an open goal for humorists.

Mrs Braines went out to the back and Margaret said, 'You just missed your brother, Rector.'

'My brother?'

'Yes, he popped in for cigarettes. He was telling us he's playing a parson in a new programme on the television, and you're helping him.' Daniel frowned. 'He picks his moments, doesn't he?'

'He does.'

'Didn't you know he was back again?'

Daniel wondered for a moment if he had been told and forgotten, but he would never have agreed to Theo coming back at a time like this. 'No,' he said. 'I didn't know.'

Anne Dollinger said, 'Your mother knew. She mentioned it the other day, in here.'

Mrs Braines was back with the pencil eraser. 'Yes, she was in yesterday, buying his favourites.'

'His favourites?'

'Uniteds.' She put the eraser into a little paper bag. 'That's 75p. Anything else?'

'No thank you, Mrs Braines.' Uniteds were not Theo's favourite biscuit bars – Club Fruit were – but Mrs Braines only had Kit-Kats and Penguins and Uniteds. Audrey would have said Uniteds were Theo's favourites as a pretext for announcing his visit.

'Very thorough, your brother, Rector,' said Bob. 'Don't they call it method acting? Getting under the skin of the character. It must be like living different lives.'

'We all do that,' said Margaret. 'A man in his time plays many parts, isn't that so, Rector?'

'Shakespeare says so. And entrances and exits – and I must be going.'

'Rector,' said Anne Dollinger, 'will we see you tonight?'

'Tonight?'

'Yes, flower-festival meeting at seven. Had you forgotten?'

'I had. But can it go ahead?'

'Why should it not?'

'As I recall, the purpose of the meeting was to consider Anthony's report on the pews. And… well, there is no report.'

'No report because there's nothing to report,' said Anne.

'Perhaps it would be best to postpone any further discussion about pews until we know exactly what we're dealing with?

And don't you think it can wait until after Anthony's funeral, which is, if I may remind you, tomorrow?'

Anne shrugged, 'I don't see why—'

'Don't you think it would be a little peculiar to have that discussion literally over Anthony's dead body, which will be lying in its coffin in the chancel from six?'

There was a silence, interrupted by Bob Achurch, who said, 'That's right, Mrs Dollinger, body comes into church teatime.'

There was another silence.

'Well,' said Anne Dollinger, 'I do think someone might have said. Stella's done an agenda. I had to have it photocopied at Coleman's.'

'Murders are very inconvenient things, Anne. Perhaps you would be so kind as to let Stella know? And I'm sure – between you – you can stand everyone down?'

'It's very last minute!'

'Thank you. See you all tomorrow at the funeral. Bob, I shall see you later.'

'You will.'

Daniel left them to it. He had indeed forgotten the flower-festival meeting, not because it had slipped his mind, rather it had been displaced by an immeasurably more important matter. No one can seriously have thought it suitable to hold such a meeting on the eve of Anthony's funeral? Stella, he reflected, would not lightly let an opportunity pass to play her hand, but not even she would try to trump Anthony's obsequies with flower-festival business.

He offered a silent prayer of thanksgiving to Almighty God, but as he turned into the rectory drive, gratitude turned to apprehension when he saw his brother's Golf.

Theo was with his mother in the kitchen.

'Dearest brother of mine,' said Theo extravagantly, getting up from the table and advancing, his head to one side, arms open, threatening an embrace.

'Theo,' said Daniel, dodging the embrace by dropping to his knees to rub the dogs' ears, leaving his brother standing like an outflanked back, 'what a surprise.'

'Mum's idea,' he said, his arms dropping to his side. 'I thought she'd told you.' Daniel knew that was a lie. 'You don't mind?'

'Some notice would have been helpful. And your timing is ... extraordinary.'

'Oh, come on, Dan ...'

Audrey came to Theo's rescue. 'There's never a good time, is there, not for you. But what about the rest of us?'

'I would have thought this might not be an obvious time to pay an unexpected call, with a double murder inquiry still ongoing, the community in shock, two dead parishioners to bury and their grieving families to console.'

'It's *perfect*,' said Audrey. 'I can't think of better circumstances for Theo to get a feel of what you do! And he is going to solve crimes too, so he can ask that nice detective questions.'

'I've done it before, Dan, when I was preparing for PC Plummy Plod. I spent a week at the nick. They rather liked having me there.'

'And Bernard said it was fine. Honoria asked him,' added Audrey.

Daniel stood still, only blinking as he did when he was

trying to master a surge of anger: they came infrequently, but one had come now. He wanted space to think.

'I'm going to let the dogs out.'

Cosmo and Hilda bolted through the back door, their uninhibited progress transporting Daniel's unexpressed anger away from his mother and brother to the soothing tranquillity of the garden. He closed the door behind him with a sort of mild slam, a firmness that betrayed his temper, and went to stand where there was still sunlight as the lengthening shadows encroached.

Watching the dogs scampering in and out of the shadow, his anger began to disperse. He thought about his mother. How often had he come home, the cares of the parish on his shoulders, only to find someone for whom those cares meant nothing. Sometimes that was a relief, because he did need a rest from his worries, and his mother's delight at Stella Harper messing up her Gansey because she couldn't manage the long double-pointed needles – 'la tricoteuse interrompue!' Audrey had triumphantly exclaimed in a paraphrase of Debussy – was an antidote to the woes of others. But more often, when tragedy befell and the jungle drums beat wildly, his mother's shallowness of empathy disturbed him. He was never sure if it was because she genuinely felt nothing – lacked the emotional apparatus – or if she was just fully absorbed with her own causes.

Theo appeared, boyishly awkward, beside him. 'Are you OK?' he said. Then he squatted and for a moment Daniel thought he was exacting a peculiar revenge for the dodged hug, but he picked up a length of yellow rope with a rubber ball at one end, frayed and chewed. It was the Yellow Thing, the dogs' favourite toy, and as soon as they saw it they ran towards him, only to execute handbrake turns when Theo threw it with an athleticism his brother did not possess. It flew further down the garden than the dogs were used to, and they looked dumbly as it sailed over their heads and into unwonted distance. Hilda started barking, her peremptory bark of command.

'You'll have to go and fetch it and have another go,' Daniel said. Theo walked off, in his loping way, and the dogs decided to follow him. There was a pause, like the gap between duellists' turns, and the Yellow Thing, thrown with not much less force than before, landed near Daniel's feet, although not so near as to suggest it was intended as a missile. When Cosmo and Hilda arrived, they were running so fast they skidded into Daniel's shins and wrestled and growled as they tugged it to and fro.

Theo approached, looking bashful – almost too bashful, drama-school bashful. 'The thing is, Dan, it would really help me out if I could just hover in the background – or not hover, exactly, more hang around – for a couple of days, I know these are extraordinary days, but Mum's squared it with Bernard, and he's fine—'

'Oh, she squared it with Bernard, did she?'

'We spoke … she spoke to Honoria, and she asked him if he minded me being here for Anthony's funeral, maybe helping out, just seeing how it all works—'

'She spoke to Honoria, who spoke to Bernard—'

'Oh you know, patron and all that, principal mourner, and he's absolutely fine with it, thinks it's a good idea—'

'—but not to me. Neither of you thought to ask me?'

Theo shrugged and looked up at Daniel with a winsome expression. 'Easier to ask for forgiveness than for permission. Well, it is with you.'

24

Later, as the shadows began to lengthen, Bob Achurch tolled the knell of parting day as Daniel and Bernard waited at the lychgate to receive what was left of Anthony in this world. A hearse appeared at the bottom of the lane, struggling, as it always did, with a corner nearly too tight for the stretched limousines in which our final journeys are made to earth or flame. In the old days the hearse was a rickety trolley pulled and pushed by the family and friends of the coffin's occupant between their cottage and the church and the grave. They still had the old hearse in one of the outhouses, unused for years, but somehow never to be thrown out or given a new function, its original purpose too solemn to be overwritten by another. The traditions and customs of death endured, even in the machine age, and the undertakers still retained something of the black crêpe and ceremonial of the Victorians, even as they undid their seat belts and clicked the automatic gearbox into park.

'My Lord. Rector.' Mr Williams bowed to both of them, formal, respectful, the grandson of the village joiner who had – because of that occupation – become the undertaker, given up joinery altogether in two generations and become

Williams Funeral Services. He had become prosperous with a fleet of black hearses and limousines with number plates WFS1 to 8, but the show of deference remained. The bearers travelling behind slid the coffin out of the back of the hearse and onto their shoulders. Daniel saw that one of them was PC Ross. 'Thank you, gentlemen,' said Mr Williams, and Daniel bowed and said, 'We receive the body of our brother Anthony, with confidence in God, the giver of life, who raised the Lord Jesus from the dead.' He and Bernard led the cortège up the path and into the church while the tenor bell tolled. In front of the chancel, with the de Floures tombs to the north, and the south transept opposite, filled with angled light, two coffin stools awaited. Theo stood, in almost comically funereal dress, watching from the south transept. Four large candles on stands were lit and the coffin placed on the stools. Daniel sprinkled it with water taken from the font and then he and Bernard took the pall, a rug-sized cloth of deep purple with an embroidered cross of black velvet, the de Floures arms at its centre, and spread it like a giant bedspread over the coffin, the cross and arms laying over the middle, its sides falling to the floor.

Daniel placed a Bible and crucifix on top and said words from Psalm 90:

> So teach us to number our days: that we may apply our
>   hearts unto wisdom.
> Turn thee again, O Lord, at the last: and be-gracious unto
>   thy servants.
> O satisfy us with thy mercy, and that soon: so shall we
>   rejoice and be glad all the days of our life.

Mr Williams and his men retreated and left, solemn to the last, and Daniel and Bernard sat vigil in the front pews, one on either side of the aisle. After a couple of minutes, when he realised nothing was going happen, Theo sidled away.

Bernard lasted half an hour and quietly left; Daniel waited another few minutes and then rose, the ritual elements satisfied. He left the candles burning – a nicety ecclesiastical insurers disapproved of lest an accident cause an untoward cremation – locked the south door and the porch gate and slipped out through the tower door, which he left open, as custom dictated, so any who wished to sit vigil with Anthony could do so until the hour of his funeral.

His mother was in the kitchen feeding the dogs, a process which even his arrival through the back door could not interrupt.

'Darling,' she said, over the clatter and slurp of Cosmo and Hilda, 'shepherd's pie for supper' – a lamb bleated distantly – 'it'll be half an hour. I'll let the dogs out.'

He went to his study. He was just writing in his diary an account of the reception of Anthony's body when there was a knock at the door.

'Dan, may I?'

Theo came in before Daniel could speak and sprawled on the Sofa of Tears.

'Question,' he said.

'Right.'

'The vigil, how long is it meant to go on for?'

'Overnight.'

'What's the point of that?'

'It's to show respect to the departed. I suppose it derives

from Christ's watch in the Garden of Gethsemane after the Last Supper.'

'Remind me?' Theo lit up a Silk Cut.

'After Jesus and the disciples had a meal together in the upper room they went to the garden so he could pray' – Daniel nodded to an ashtray on a side table – 'and the disciples kept watch with him but they kept dropping off and in the end he was alone and prayed to God that he would be spared what was coming.'

Theo looked blank.

'His arrest and trial and execution.'

'No such luck.'

'It wasn't really luck, Theo. It wasn't something he could have dodged.'

'He could have. He could have turned them all into pillars of salt or something.'

'Yes, I suppose he could have.'

'So why didn't he?'

'Because he needed to suffer and die as a man first, so that he could then make right the whole of humanity, as God. That's what it took.'

Theo grimaced. 'God, that's a bit twisted. And quite difficult to comprehend. No wonder they all fell asleep. But why aren't you there? I mean, I understand there's not a lot going on, but why aren't you keeping vigil? Aren't you supposed to be on his side?'

'I was, for a decent interval. But these are ceremonial things to be observed rather than instructions to be followed. And we all drop off in the end, for we are mortal. That's fundamental, Theo: we are imperfect people called to perfection, so get used to failure.'

'I'm an actor, that's something we have in common. A lot of sitting around doing nothing, though, which must be boring.'

'No, not at all. And if it is boring, that's a burden to shoulder rather than a drudgery to be avoided.'

'I was bored and I only lasted five minutes. How long did Bernard do?'

'Half an hour. I lasted about an hour. I'll go back later and say the Office for the Dead.'

'Is that a bit more lively?'

'I wouldn't say so, not exactly, but there's things to say. You could join in.'

The dinner gong sounded from the hall. 'Shall we?' said Daniel.

'I'll just finish my fag, Dan. See you in there.'

They had shepherd's pie with peas and carrots, perked up with Worcestershire Sauce. 'A couple of shakes is all it takes,' muttered Theo, delivering the advertising slogan as he shook it vigorously over his supper.

'You must remember, Theodore,' his mother said, 'it belongs to the days when food was either too bland to taste, or too frightful to eat, so we smothered them in sauces that either gave flavour, or masked flavour, then we got to like it. Think of Stilton cheese, think of high game. They are at the heart of English cuisine. In the war they bombed the factory, but they still made it, only it came in different bottles with plain labels. It's one of the very few things I remember tasting of anything during rationing.'

'Very Church of England, to have a nose for decay,' said Daniel, still in a funereal mood.

'Oh yes, but you always did, Dan. I never had to worry, even when you were a little boy, about you turning your nose up at kidneys or brains or pheasant. You always liked offal, things on the turn, things that presaged decay. You're made for it. And I wonder if it has made you rather the detective, sniffing out corruption like one of the dogs. You too, Theo, in your way, wanting to get to the bottom of things. Relentlessly.'

'I wonder where we got that from?'

'Not from me. I would rather leave things to decay undisturbed.'

They ate in silence. Daniel thought of Cosmo and Hilda, curled up in their basket next to the Aga; their enjoyment of scent, even the most pungently revolting, was utterly promiscuous. He watched them sometimes suddenly sniff, not a delicate savouring of a faint scent, like a parfumier, but something which involved the whole body, a great hoover that came from the depths of their long chests, sucking the smells through their flaring nostrils, and sending the data into the large part of their small brains that decoded scent. A dachshund on a scent was impossible to distract; sometimes they would shoot off like a greyhound after a hare; sometimes they would roll in it in ecstasies of abandonment, in spite of his cries of protest. The world for them was primarily a smellscape, interpreted first through odour rather than sound or sight. He wondered if that was one of the reasons he found them so fascinating.

Audrey had a yogurt from a little plastic pot for pudding. Daniel, unsweet in the tooth, had nothing. Theo finished the bottle of Côtes du Rhône he had brought and drunk two thirds of, and then they cleared up. Audrey washed, he dried and Theo put things away, a division of labour that went back to the boys' childhood.

'Your great-grandfather,' Audrey said suddenly, for no obvious reason, 'died in his forties leaving your great-grandmother with thirteen children to feed. How do you think he died?'

'Was it drink?' said Theo.

'Why do you say that?'

He shrugged. 'It usually is.'

'Yes, you're right, he was a drunk, but that's not what killed him.'

'What did?'

'It was the cure for drink. He was put into the county asylum by his father, and the treatment was a form of hydrotherapy. Patients – inmates, really – were stripped and put in a tiled room with a tilting floor and a drain, and drenched, doused, hosed with water. I don't know why. But for someone like your great-grandfather, already ruined by drink, probably having terrible withdrawal symptoms without alcohol, then to be submitted to this so-called treatment… it was too much for him and he died.'

'Why did they think that would cure alcoholism?' Daniel asked.

'Perhaps they thought it was a sin, and that it could be washed away? More your department than mine. But how cruel it was. Not just for him but for his wife and children. And how shaming. One has to understand how terribly people feared being shamed in those days.'

'Why?'

'Status, I suppose. Remember your great-great-grandfather had been born in a humble cottage, the son of silk weaver, and had made himself into a man of business and position. Like most self-made people, he had a sense that everything he had made he could lose. Your grandmother feared the workhouse all her life, long after it had closed, because when she was a child and her father died, it was what stood between them and the poverty her grandfather had only just escaped.'

'But Granny and Grandpa were as rich as stink!' said Theo.

'They were, but that did not take away her fear of poverty. A part of her was always the little girl who had lost her father and whose mother had sat in the parlour wondering how she would feed and clothe and educate thirteen fatherless children without any money of her own. You don't just leave that behind, it's with you for your entire life. It shaped your father's life, and I think it shapes yours, too.'

'How?'

'Well, you embrace it, Theo, through living the precarious life of an actor. And you recoil from it, Daniel, you fear it. The reverses of fortune. The collapse of a comfortable world. It's why you're a parson, it's why you love stationery.'

Theo, who earlier had snooped round Daniel's study, thought of the dedicated jar of panel pins on the upper-left side of his desk, between the jumbo paper clips and the hole punch reinforcers.

'And let our ordered lives confess the beauty of thy peace,' Audrey sang, all but tunelessly.

~

After the dogs had done their poo-poos, Daniel went to church to pray. The dogs followed him in through the vestry door and set off on their olfactory exploration of the darkening nave. Not entirely dark, for the four candles around the coffin standing in the chancel were lit. The candlelight flickered when a draught came and went, and Daniel was distracted almost at once from the prayers in the Office for the Dead. And then he noticed the silence of the dogs: his stomach tightened for a second as he remembered the last time they had been this quiet in church and he looked round. In the dark beyond the pools of yellow light from the vigil candles, he saw the outline of a person sitting in a pew at the back of the church. He knew who it was just from the way she sat and the place she sat in, as she did at every service, usually with her sister, but not tonight. Dora Sharman looked up at him as he turned round, and then looked down again, and continued with her prayers. He continued with his, and as he got towards the end said the Nunc dimittis out loud; the phrases, the cadences were so familiar to the dogs that they returned to the chancel and sat beside him, sensing that he was nearly done.

'May the Lord bless us, protect us from all evil, and bring us to everlasting life,' he said out loud.

'Amen,' replied Dora. She started to look for her hat, coat and bag as Daniel came down the aisle towards her.

'No Kath tonight?'

'She didn't want to come, Rector. But I can say prayers for both of us. I gave the dogs a biscuit, I hope you don't mind.'

'I wondered why they were quiet. Were you and Anthony close?'

Dora seemed surprised by the question. 'Close? No, no. But we are Champton people. In the old days when the head of the family died we would keep vigil in the old chapel. All night. Butler and housekeeper began it and ended it. We lesser creatures filled in the middle. Housemaids did the midnight shift with footmen. Many a romance began that way. Love by candlelight and a dead body.'

'I have often noticed how funerals are followed by weddings,' said Daniel. And it was true. It was not unusual to marry a couple who met at a wake.

'Keep the numbers up. But I did like Mr Bowness, as it happens. He was different. A different view of things. I suppose it was because he was not easy in himself.'

'How do you mean?'

'The drink. I think he had something that ailed him that he wanted to forget. But he was never mean, unlike some.'

The candlelight made her eyes glisten. This least sentimental of women had tears in her eyes.

'What's the matter, Dora?'

She said nothing, but reached into her bag and produced a handkerchief and held it under her eyes. Daniel sat beside her. After a minute or two she put her handkerchief away and stood, put on her coat, and gathered up her bag and her hat.

'I'm not one for weeping and wailing, Rector. But it is sad when someone dies, isn't it? Mr Bowness, Mr Thwaite. Neither should have ended up like they did.'

'Dora, why do you think they were killed?'

She did not at first reply. Then she said, 'Careless Talk Costs Lives. You're too young to remember. It was a poster in the war to get us to shut up in case of spies.'

'I've seen them.'

'And anyone who's been in service knows how dangerous loose lips can be.'

'Discretion assured, Dora. But who, or what, do you think is behind this?'

'How can we know? Mr Bowness and Mr Thwaite are dead and gone. That's what I think about. I don't speculate.' She was waiting for him to move so she could leave.

He stood and let her out and she left without saying anything more, crocheted hat bobbing out of the tower door, leaving the dogs still looking expectantly after her.

25

Daniel took the dogs out not long after dawn the next day, not only because it was a beautiful morning, but because he wanted to avoid Theo. On the day of Anthony's funeral and with Ned's yet to come, he decided not to take his usual walk round the lake. He did not want to have his eye caught by the bath house and the recollection of what happened there to cast a shadow over the day. He walked towards the house, but instead of going down the drive through the baroque fanfare of its gates, he went to its north side and there found his way onto the Holly Walk, another of Repton's ideas which the green-fingered de Floures had planted two hundred years ago. There he let the dogs off their leads and they raced along the path, flanked by old holly bushes, tangled and untidy now, and trees ragged with ivy. Holly Walk led from the garden out into the park and then, wilder with every step, down towards the stream that eventually fed the lake, with an old ornamental bridge over it; he had seen kingfishers there before, and a heron lazily feeding, and once what he hoped was an otter but was probably a mink, for nature here was not for long untouched by human enterprise and its attendant folly. He herded Cosmo and Hilda past the badger setts that riddled the banked sides of the path, past the holes that appeared between the exposed and tangled roots of the bushes on either side. He dreaded losing them down one of those holes and having to pull them out by their tails, or dig them out, or rush them to the vets with gashed snouts.

The end of Holly Walk came abruptly, terminating in a flight of crude steps which led down to fields, sometimes blue with linseed and flax, but now yellow with oilseed rape, the crop Nicholas Meldrum wanted everywhere. Daniel found it too assertive, much preferring the dusty blue of flax, even more missed when the bright yellow turned orangey as the season continued, and it began to reek of something cabbagey and rank. It was just coming now, and the fields of alternating green and yellow around Champton made Daniel think of Norwich City Football Club.

He walked along the river and although he did not see the kingfisher he heard a couple of larks as they spiralled upwards from the field. Easier to hear than to see, boringly small and brown if your eye could make them out as they ascended. Vaughan Williams' music, so much loved, had got there before them, but to him the larks sounded nothing like the yearning solo violin rising over the strings in the musical equivalent of a full English breakfast. To him they sounded like fax machines, chirruping, gossipy, and another little flutter of anxiety passed through him as he walked beside the stream.

Et in arcadia ego; if it wasn't the bath house, it was the chirping of the larks, or the dogs catching a scent, or even the jarring yellow of the oilseed rape. Even here, in the gentle glory of this English idyll, were reminders of the trouble that had come upon them – that was *still* among them, he was sure.

He paused next to the stream and watched the way the light caught the currents and eddies and made them sparkle. The branches of an alder overhung the stream from the opposite bank and they trembled and shook in the breeze, in contrary motion with the light catching the rushing water. A cross pattern which almost seemed to vibrate: it caught Daniel's attention and held it so strongly it was almost hypnotic. His sense of time and place fell away and beside the stream on that lovely morning he suddenly felt gripped by terror, and he knew it to be the same terror that both Anthony and Ned must have felt after the blow was struck and life began to leave them. It was so powerful and so unmistakable that he was conscious of nothing else. And then, as soon as it came, it passed. A feeling of intense pathos followed. The pathos of their deaths, and the loneliness and fear of their final, undeserved moments, and something else, something beyond that, a depthless sadness. And then something cold and hard and impenetrable, like stone, fell, and he was conscious again and thought, That was the murderer.

This – the last ghostly visitation, the thud of cold, hard stone and the limitless sadness behind it – was something he had felt before, something he had felt here in Champton, and he thought again that the murderer was one of them, lived among them, was intimately connected with Anthony and Ned and everyone else.

26

In The Flowers, the Staveleys were eating the profits.

'Ooh, macaroons,' said Dot, helping herself to one before the plate had actually touched down. Norman miserably declined, the GP having pronounced the sweet things he craved at elevenses no longer permissible. Millie Staniland carefully placed two cups on the table.

'Anything else, Mr Staveley?'

Norman could think of a thing or two but tried to put that from his mind. He had lately begun to look at breasts, waitresses, students, secretaries at County Hall, and once at a petrol station when, as he was filling up, a young woman in a Peugeot 205 at the neighbouring pump suddenly looked back at him and he saw in her distaste his own asymmetrical desire reflected. He was not dying to have more sex than he was having in his marriage, although that was another strictly limited diet, or different sex from the tea and biscuits that had done for him and Dot since their wedding night. It was youth, he thought: the skin, the shining eyes, the thick and lustrous hair… And now it was escape too, like falling into a pool of water, and all the anxieties of the present disappearing, washed away, in its lustration. His conscience sent another spurt of adrenalin around his system and he jerked as he recalled again that idiot Anthony Bowness praying at the back of church, and the surge of anger that he – interloper, innocent, failure of a man – could imperil everything Norman had achieved, his standing in the eyes of the world, and of Dot.

These surges of adrenalin had started coming more frequently – anxiety attacks, according to an article he had seen in Dot's magazine; male menopause, apparently, but he thought it more psychological than physiological, a troubled conscience rather than hormones.

'I've got a thumping headache,' he said as she experimented with dunking her macaroon. 'I'll just nip back home for a Panadol.'

'Your tea will get cold, Norman,' she said.

'You have it, love, I can't manage it.'

He left, his wife looking after him for a moment before reaching over for his cup.

The air on his face made him feel a little better, and then a little worse, and he tried to breathe regularly as he walked along, but the surge of adrenalin came again, and he started to walk faster, and began to break into a sweat. This, he thought, is how a heart attack happens. Then, feeling that he was being watched, he glanced up to see Anne Dollinger looking at him from outside Stella's. After a second she waved. 'Are you all right, Norman?' He waved back and made a pointing gesture as if to say, Can't stop, and carried on his way, but nearly stumbled and had to try to look like he was rushing rather than losing his balance. He made it round to the bus shelter and sat down to get his breath back. He said out loud,

'Shut up shut up shut up,' and a woman standing at the bus stop he didn't know, and hoped didn't know him, turned and snapped, 'I never said anything.'

'Not you,' he said, still struggling for breath, and then the edges of his vision grew misty grey and he thought of Anthony Bowness sitting at the back of church, indistinct in fading light.

The passing bell rang from the tower of St Mary's and as it pealed clouds appeared and brought the lovely early morning to an end. 'Funeral weather,' said Daniel, in cassock and surplice, hood and scarf, to PC Scott, white-gloved in his number ones, with medal ribbons on his breast, as they waited at the lychgate for the de Floures family to arrive. The family had walked up to church from the house: it was tradition, but perhaps not the best idea under the circumstances, for their arrival at the foot of Church Lane gave the platoon of photographers and television crews an excellent opportunity to press about them, intruding on private grief for the public's satisfaction. The family walked, rather than ran, that gauntlet, not saying a word, Bernard looking ahead with what degree of dignity he could muster, in the most formal degree of dress – a black tailcoat and black waistcoat and black tie – leading his party not of three, as Daniel expected, but of four. He was flanked by Alex and Honoria, she in a smart black dress and he in a boxy black suit, wide at the shoulder, narrow at the waist, double-breasted; and with them a man Daniel knew a little, in a bad black suit. He was tall and lanky, closer to Alex in looks than to Bernard, but with a more gentle expression. He looked like a country cousin – slightly uncomfortable, there on sufferance – but he was the son and heir, Hugh de Floures, home from the wide wheat fields of Canada.

Daniel always found these arrivals at the lychgate a little awkward, for he could not sustain the smile of sympathetic welcome suitable for mourners for the time it took them to arrive. Instead he usually pretended, in the English way, not to have seen them, admiring the Achurches' forsythia, or a gargoyle on the tower, or the cooing of a collared dove, until the funeral party was only a few steps away and he could turn to engage.

'Bernard, Alex, Honoria. And Hugh, so good to see you and so glad you were able to come.'

'For God's sake, Dan,' said Bernard, 'let's just get on with it.'

Margaret Porteous, who had temporarily and irregularly taken over Anthony's functions as churchwarden, was looking at them from the porch. Daniel turned, gave her a signal and she disappeared inside the church.

Daniel turned back to the family. 'Are we ready?' he said, and shepherded the de Floures up the path.

Mrs Buckhurst from school had taken the place of Jane at the organ console and started playing 'I Know That My Redeemer Liveth' as they entered the church. It was full, and every head turned with the de Floures' arrival and every eye stared at the prodigal returned. Daniel saw them into the family pew and stood to the side as the choir emerged from the tower, in cassocks and surplices, led by Bob Achurch, who had stilled the passing bell to be crucifer and lead in the procession. They set off, trebles first, new choristers in ruffs holding folders too big for them, the ladies of the top line in their unflattering Oxford caps, and behind them the altos, including the Staniland children upon whose voices adolescence was working its embarrassing changes. Daniel fell in behind them as they passed around the coffin, now denuded of its pall, under the chancel arch where they peeled off, left and right, into the choir stalls. Rector and choir bowed in unison to the altar, the crucifer fixed the processional cross into its bracket, and as Daniel ascended the lectern, the music stopped. Perfectly done, he thought to himself with inappropriate satisfaction, and welcomed the congregation to church.

Scattered in unwonted places were clumps of Champton people deprived of their normal seats by strangers, but not the Sharman sisters, whom he saw wedged uncomfortably into their customary pew at the back of the north side, not permitting a party of four to occupy the only space in which they could sit together. Others had gone to the back and the sides, their usual places now filled with people from Anthony's past, from the family, from Grub Street, from Oxford, from Soho, a mix of patrician faces and garret-pale faces and rosy drinkers' faces.

Daniel often thought the most reliable obituary was the one presented by the people in the pews, who told the truest tale of the life of the departed. He remembered one he had taken in London of a young man, a former parishioner who had died of AIDS, whose birth family was Yorkshire Salvation Army, and whose elected family were S&M devotees. To the left pews of men in black caps, to the right men in a different sort of black caps, leather rather than wool, and each surprised to see the other.

One face was from Anthony's present, DS Neil Vanloo, who Daniel was pleased to see; he was wearing a black tie which Daniel wondered might be the slip-on rather than the tied kind, standard police issue. He read the Bidding Prayer and they stood to sing the first hymn, 'Love Divine', to an unusual tune, 'Fairest Isle' by Purcell, one of his loveliest, but few knew it, and there was a tricky moment in the first line – on 'loves excelling' – when a semiquaver in the score was a semitone up from what the congregation, and half the choir, wanted to sing. *Et in arcadia ego*, he thought again.

The Address was given by Anthony's former editor at a literary magazine and was a masterpiece of how to say what is true but not unkind; Honoria read, beautifully, 'Fear no more the heat o' the sun' from *Cymbeline*, and flinched slightly at 'thou art past the tyrant's stroke'; Bernard followed with the lesson, from the fourteenth chapter of the Gospel of John, and people blinked at 'in my Father's house there are many mansions'; and Daniel preached a short homily about our fear of abandonment, about coming home, and at that Hugh looked up at him from the family pew.

Prayers were offered, then they stood to sing the 23rd Psalm to Crimond, a tune and words so serviceable they did for weddings and baptisms too.

> *The Lord's my Shepherd, I'll not want;*
> *he makes me down to lie*
> *in pastures green; he leadeth me*
> *the quiet waters by.*

After the commendation, Mr Williams' four stalwart men, all moonlighting police officers, were joined by Alex and – there was a murmur at this – Honoria, who hoisted the coffin onto their shoulders and walked stiffly past the gates of the de Floures chapel, closed to cousins, and out into the churchyard where Bob Achurch and Nathan Liversedge had prepared a grave in the family plot in the south-west corner. Into this earth Anthony's mortal remains were deposited, Honoria and Alex straining to control the webbing bands on which the coffin was lowered. 'Man that is born of a woman hath but a short time to live. He cometh up, and is cut down, like a flower…' Then Daniel, with a handful of earth Mr Williams had helpfully put in a little pot for him, let it fall into the grave in three goes – 'earth to earth, ashes to ashes, dust to dust' – and it rattled onto the coffin lid in a grim tattoo. For those for whom this was too chthonic, Mr Williams had provided single red roses, a gentle gesture spoiled by the surprising thud as they hit the lid.

It had begun to rain, lightly but enough for a car to be sent from the house to take the family back and to avoid the predations of the press. Daniel was in the vestry with Theo, filling in the register.

'How many do you reckon were there, Theo?'

'Oh, I dunno … a hundred and fifty?'

'I think that's right.' He wrote 144.

'Isn't that a bit dishonest?'

'It's not entirely accurate, but these things never are.'

'So why not just say "about a hundred and fifty"?'

There was a knock at the open door. It was DS Vanloo.

'Are you busy?'

'Yes,' said Daniel, 'but come in. This is my brother Theo.'

'Oh yes, I recognised you from *Appletree End*.'

Theo couldn't conceal a tiny preen. 'Oh that's very flattering, from a *real* policeman.'

Neil said nothing.

Daniel filled the silence. 'Theo, can you make sure Mum's ready? I'll be over in a minute.'

Theo shrugged. 'OK. Are you coming to the knees-up, Detective Sergeant?'

'Yes, sir. I just need to speak to the rector.'

'I'd love to speak to you later, if I may?'

'OK.'

Theo left, closing the vestry door with overdone delicacy, as if it were him granting them privacy rather than them requiring him to leave.

'What's this? A tally of sins?'

'I'm just falsifying some figures.'

'Careful.'

Daniel signed his name in the column, closed the book and screwed the cap back on the Osmiroid 75 –14K italic nib, piston-filled from a little bottle of registrar's ink, which wrote grey but turned to dense and unfading black. He took a square of blotting paper, laid it gently on what he had written and then put it away. He put the top back on the bottle of ink and then returned it, alongside the blotting paper and the pen, to its proper place.

'That was like watching a tea ceremony,' said DS Vanloo.

'I can't bear to be slapdash about these things.'

'Everything in its proper place?'

'Yes,' he said, and took off his hood and scarf and surplice and hung them up where they belonged. 'It was good of you to come,' he said. 'Do you normally?'

'I do. How are you?'

'I'm all right. A bit shaken up. You know how it is. The community I'm meant to look after is shaken up too.'

'And that can be revealing. You would notice that.'

'Oh, you're on duty.'

'Something's happened in this community that's given someone a reason to kill not one but two of their neighbours. And you are the person, I guess, who is best placed to pick all that up.'

'Perhaps. Some would say Mrs Braines at the post office.'

'I don't mean who's doing what, I mean a level up from that: changes in the way the community works, light and shade. You know what I mean. What's your hunch?'

'I would not want to overstate a hunch. But I *think* this is the work of one person, and a local.'

'Why.'

'Changes in light and shade.'

'Can you give me more than that?'

'Not exactly. It's not forensic, it's more intuitive. But I sense something coming into focus. It might help if you told me what you know, and I did the same.'

The detective paused, thought and spoke.

'What do you want to know?'

'Who was where and when.'

'We know where everyone was around the time of both murders, or where they say they were. No one saw anything suspicious, or nothing credible. We've had a few people come forward with names, but nothing that checks out.'

'Any front runners?'

'Alex de Floures. People don't like him. Bob Achurch, because he was a commando. Lord de Floures, because he has the bad blood of his ancestors. Nathan Liversedge, because of his gypsy past. Nothing to go on. But what about you?'

'I think I have seen the murderer.'

'What?'

'I think I have seen the murderer. I don't mean *witnessed* them in the act. I mean I think have seen the person who did this, but I don't know who it is yet.'

'What do you mean, "seen" them?'

'I mean that there is something about the murders – the person who committed them – that I recognise. It's very hazy at the moment, but what I am beginning to sense about the crimes points to an individual, though I cannot see their identity just yet. Does that make sense?'

'What are you sensing?'

'Someone who is full of anger. It's been held in check, but something has happened that has caused it to come to the surface. A secret revealed, something like that. I've buried murder victims before, and this is not the first time I've looked out into the pews and thought I could see the killer sitting in front of me.'

'You felt that today?'

'I don't know. Perhaps. Are you coming up to the house?'

'I am now. Shall we walk?'

'It's raining and I have to take my mother and my brother. Do you want a lift?'

Audrey was waiting in the kitchen with Theo. She looked out of place there, thought Daniel, in her best black coat and hat and gloves, wearing pearls and a diamond brooch, like a dowager on the wrong side of the green baize door.

'Oh, hello,' she said. 'You're the policeman, aren't you?'

'Detective Sergeant Vanloo, Mrs Clement. We spoke after Mr Bowness's death.'

'Yes, I remember you. How kind of you to come. Daniel, shall we get off before Stella Harper eats all the sandwiches?'

The dogs as always looked stupidly affronted when he stopped them at the door with his foot. Hilda gave a cross little yap.

'You'll find the Land Rover rather antique, Detective Sergeant, and probably not roadworthy. Theo, can you make a space?'

Theo started throwing things from the back seats onto the pile of junk behind them: plastic bags, newspapers covered in muddy paw marks, old road maps, bungees, clothes pegs, a ball of twine. To the sound of crashing gears, and a whining engine, they lumbered down the drive and out into the park, creeping along the road to the house, sending the lambs scattering before it.

'Just as bad on the queen's highway, Sergeant,' said Audrey as Daniel mismatched clutch to gear change, and lurched with too-late corrections to drift away from the desired line. 'I do hope you never meet when you're on traffic duty.'

'I don't think the sergeant does traffic duty these days, Mum.'

'Just as well, for I would hate him to have to suffer a conflict of loyalties. Mind you, I expect even your terrible driving would seem less threatening to public safety than some of the literary contingent up from town. You could practically smell the snug on them. Very convivial.'

'Some faces I half recognised, Mum,' said Theo, 'from the Grouch, the French.'

'French, darling?'

'French House, Mum, it's a pub in Soho, popular with convivial literary types. And the Groucho Club. Just round the corner.'

'I've read about it. Celebrity watering hole,' said Neil.

'It's the sort of members-only place famous people go to be with other famous people to do the things they can't do in public.'

'Like what?'

'Oh, you know, coke, affairs …' said Theo, trailing off.

But it was too late. 'Are you a member, darling?' asked Audrey.

'Yes, I am.' Silence fell over them for a moment. 'I hardly go.'

'Was Mr Bowness a member?'

'I don't think so. Younger set. He might have gone to the French House, maybe, but I don't think I've seen him there. I think he would have been more Academy Club or Gerry's.'

'Drink for Anthony, I think,' said Audrey from the front, 'not drugs and strumpets.'

Theo said, 'I just use it to get something to eat after a show. Play snooker. Have you been, Dan?'

'I'm more an Athenaeum type. I used to see Anthony there sometimes.'

'And Hugh too,' said Audrey. 'Can you remember the last time he was at Champton? Which Lady de Floures was current at the time? Terrible suit, don't you think? Looked like he'd run into Marks and Sparks and grabbed the first dark one on the rail.'

They squeaked and rattled the short distance through the park, scattering damp ruminants before them, until they saw Nathan Liversedge, wearing an unsuitably flamboyant sash, directing cars to a taped-off section of grass. He gestured at Daniel in a way which resembled semaphore and his heart sank, for he never knew what these signals were supposed to mean, having not learned to drive until he was in his thirties, and with such poor aptitude for its various operations it was all he could do to maintain the basic requirements of motion and steering. When people started gesturing at him, he rather lost his confidence and couldn't tell if they meant left or right; he had once driven into a ditch because he had begun to panic when a Rotarian had grown impatient with his indecision at a family fun day in Brighouse. He was also more than usually self-conscious because of Neil Vanloo in the back, someone who looked – and was – rather more handy, which made him feel more than usually unmanned. He stalled and crashed the gears. His mother sighed. Nathan let his guiding arms fall uselessly to his side.

'Daniel, shall I?' said Neil, already half out of the back.

Daniel got out and Neil got in and within two seconds had parked the Land Rover with a gliding inevitability in its appointed place.

'He can write a shopping list in Hebrew but he can't wire a plug,' said Audrey. 'Still, it doesn't hurt the golden boy not to be good at everything.'

Theo had found a broken umbrella and did his best to shelter Audrey from the rain that spattered on the courtyard, and guided them towards the doors to the hall, where Millie and Christian Staniland stood holding trays of a serviceable champagne, which was going faster than expected, thanks to the Soho set. Behind them in the noisy and convivial hall Daniel saw Alex in a clump of those disreputables, more at home with them than with his own, standing around an uncomfortable-looking PC Scott. It looked like he was jabbing Scott in the chest, but he was asking him about his medals, 'Ooh and what's the blue-and-white stripy one for?'

'That's the Korean War service medal, sir.'

'Is that the one Daddy calls MacArthur's Pyjamas?'

Scott gave him a look. 'It is called that, sir, yes.'

The Thwaite women were standing slightly apart, in black, reminding Daniel of the photograph of the three queens in deepest mourning for George VI. Everyone seemed to be skirting them – apart from Honoria, who swept by with refills and canapés – for there was nothing in the etiquette manuals on how to address those mourning for two instead of one. Beyond them, Hugh was the centre of intense interest. Margaret Porteous, Anne Dollinger and Stella Harper were circling like sharks, while Hugh explained, in a dutiful monotone, how the great window told the story of the de Floures family from the Norman Conquest to the twentieth century, through its rises and falls, to a man whose interest obviously dropped off before he had even got to the Civil War.

Audrey was suddenly in there too, striding towards the son and heir, with her hand outstretched, and cutting past Margaret, next in the queue. 'Hello, Hugh,' she said. 'Audrey Clement – you won't remember me, I live at the rectory. Daniel is my son.'

'Of course I remember,' he said politely, and shook her hand.

'How lovely to see you back at Champton. It must be … how long?'

'It was Alex's twenty-first.'

'Ah, of course. What a night! But Canada seems such a long way away, and I imagine farming such wide spaces, well, it must very difficult to get away much. I've never been, but I've always thought it such a *romantic* country. And Daniel adored a book when he was boy about Canada and a fur trapper – Dan, what was it called?' She beckoned him to come over. 'I was telling Hugh about the book you loved when you were a boy about a fur trapper in Canada.'

'*Hank Le Trappeur*,' said Daniel. It had been a school assignment – to help them with their French – and they had renamed it 'Wank Le Crappeur', which was the only thing he could remember about it.

'Hello,' he said to Hugh, 'I'm so pleased to see you. My condolences.'

'Thank you, Padre.' He looked enquiringly at Neil.

'This is Neil Vanloo,' said Daniel.

'I'm Hugh.' They shook hands.

'It's Detective Sergeant Vanloo, Hugh, and he's part of the investigation,' Audrey got in quickly.

'Oh. Thank you for coming. Why did you come?'

There was an awkward silence.

'It's not unusual, sir,' said Neil, suddenly formal. 'You get involved.'

'Oh, I see, I didn't mean to be rude, you're most welcome, but I wondered if it's like in films: the cops come to the funeral because they think the murderer won't be able to stay away. Funny to think he might be here now, eating our canapés and drinking our wine.'

'Who could say, sir.'

'You're not going to.'

'No, sir. I must pay my respects to Lord de Floures.' Neil smiled and went.

'I hope I didn't offend him.'

Hugh was often a bit punchy, Daniel had noticed, when he was back at Champton. His visits were few and he kept them short, concerned with family matters, as custom dictated, and estate matters, which he undertook diligently, for one day it would be his responsibility; but to Daniel he always looked like someone returning to his old school where he had been unhappy and feeling once again the fears and miseries of childhood. Bernard had confided in him that he was not sure that Hugh could hack it, but his hands were tied, the estate entailed and they would have to make it work, because one day Hugh would be recalled from the wheaty plains of wherever he was in Canada to put on his black suit once again and sit in the family pew – only this time for good.

'Daniel, could I come and see you about something?'

'Yes, of course.'

'When's convenient?'

'I'm free tomorrow for coffee, say at eleven? At the rectory?'

'Thank you.'

Margaret Porteous was suddenly there, leaning in and looking up, like a space-invading supplicant. 'Hugh, Margaret Porteous, we met at Alex's twenty-first, you were kind enough to explain … aspects of arable farming … in Canada.'

'Hello, Mrs Porteous.'

'Margaret, please. I'm sorry that today is a sad day rather than a happy occasion. Were you close to Anthony?'

'He was my godfather.'

'Oh, I *am* sorry,' Stella Harper cut in. 'Such an important relationship, I think, godparent to godchild. My own were very dear to me.'

'We weren't really that close. He was just always … there.' Hugh looked around the saloon and the portraits of his ancestors looked back at him. 'Like them. Like here.'

'How lovely to feel so very strongly rooted. To know that Champton will always be here, no matter how far we roam. You must miss it.'

Hugh shrugged. 'Like I said, it's always here.'

Audrey got in again. 'So big, so wild. And the *bears*. I understand in winter they come into town and go through your rubbish?'

Alex approached, with a disreputable in tow, wearing a shapeless dark suit with trainers.

'I want you to all to meet Will. He has a gallery in the Docklands.'

Will mumbled a hello and they shook hands.

'We have some *very* exciting ideas for the bath house,' said Alex, 'an event that will be talked about for years and years, like a Tudor masque.'

'Didn't someone just get murdered there?' Hugh said.

'That's going to be part of it,' Alex's eyes gleamed. 'A blood ritual and a sort of *tableau vivant* of the mural.'

'Are you sure that's wise?' asked Daniel, looking around to see if the Thwaites were in earshot. 'It was, after all, a murder?'

'Not the first, nor the last on these blood-soaked acres, Dan.'

'But rather a recent one.'

Hugh said, 'I remember the last time I was back was for one of your "spectacles", I think you called it. The one with the nude dancing in the orangery.'

'Oh yes. And then the dancers covered each other in paint and rolled around on big pieces of paper on the floor and we hung them up.'

There had been some comment about this in the local and national press. It was, Alex said, his calling card.

'Do you know what that reminded me of, Alex? The League of Pity Parties we used to do when we were kids. Do you remember? Teas in the orangery and then we played games in the garden – Splat the Rat, that kind of thing. And one year there was a painting competition. You had to squeeze some paint from tubes onto one side of a piece of paper and then fold it in half and make a butterfly. Do you remember that?'

'I do. I won first prize.'

'That's going in the catalogue,' said Will.

'Yes, you did, but you entered fifteen butterflies and Grandpa was the judge, so of course one of yours won and everyone said it was a fix.'

Alex crumpled a little at that. 'Maybe not for the catalogue after all.'

Daniel wondered if Hugh knew that what he said could hurt his brother. Then he saw his own brother and Neil standing in an alcove at the edge of the saloon between two busts on plinths, which made them look like they had brought ghost companions. Neil smiled at him, but with urgency, so he went over.

'Dan, Dan,' said Theo, in his master of ceremonies voice, 'I've been swapping cop stories with the DS.' He liked the jargon of others, a shortcut to the necessary impersonations of his job. 'Lot of overlap, his life and yours, no wonder the vicar detective is such a familiar figure.'

'I've often wondered,' said Daniel, 'how Father Brown got away with it.'

'I never liked those stories much,' said Neil. 'Cops don't read much crime fiction.'

Theo said, 'Robbers do. I did a play once in Wandsworth nick and got involved with the reading group at the library. All they really wanted were stories about crime. Come to think of it, it was books about criminals as heroes. The Krays and *Papillon*, true crime.'

'I don't read much vicar fiction,' said Daniel, 'apart from Trollope, who I've always found exceptionally sympathetic. And I liked William de Baskerville in *The Name of the Rose*. Have you read it?'

'Saw the film,' said Neil.

'*Loved* the film,' said Theo. 'Maybe I should watch it again for research?'

'You'll find parish life very different from that of a Benedictine monastery in the fourteenth century.'

'I don't know. Both murder mysteries, aren't they?'

Daniel was silent for a moment. 'I must talk to the Thwaites,' he said, 'no one else is.'

He breached the cordon of embarrassment around them and Angela immediately leaned in to him. 'Thank God for vicars. We were feeling like Typhoid Marys.'

'Oh dear.'

'Are we trespassing, bringing our bereavement to someone else's wake?' asked Jane.

'You knew Anthony, Jane. Of course you would want to come. I think people perhaps don't know what to say.'

'It's funny what they do say to the freshly bereaved. One of the partners at my firm said he'd prefer not to talk about it, as if it were his problem and not mine,' said Angela.

'I was once on a funeral visit and someone said to me they did not want to talk about their bereavement because it was a bit personal.'

Angela laughed. 'The English way.'

'But not this sort of English,' said Jane, 'the nobs don't seem embarrassed.'

'I think,' said Gillian, 'that sort of social embarrassment is really a middle-class phenomenon. Think of the slum funerals in Leeds, like a tragic day out.'

'But the nobs don't show their feelings, do they? Assuming they even have any.'

'I think most of them do, only sangfroid is considered such a virtue they don't display them,' said Daniel.

'They do display them,' said Angela. 'Look around, dead ancestors staring at you from every angle.'

'Gone, but not forgotten,' said Gillian, 'unlike our dead. We disappear, don't we? We only last as long as memory.'

Jane winced. 'That's what I was so frightened of with your dad's mind going. Being forgotten while you're still there.'

'Erasure,' said Daniel, a thought, but out loud.

'The band? What a trendy vicar you are, Daniel,' said Angela.

'Is it a band? No, it's an idea in philosophy. Heidegger, I think: something is both cancelled and yet still there, like a crossed-out word.'

27

The next day after breakfast Audrey opened the heritage biscuit tin and declared that the selection therein was of insufficient grandeur for the guest invited for elevenses – the 'Honourable Hugh', as she had started to call him, pronouncing the initial H in both words – and her resolve to go to the shop to obtain fresh supplies. This was not strictly true. The selection was underpowered, but the village shop would not have anything on its few shelves of higher distinction. This did not matter, for Audrey did, in fact, have better biscuits hidden in the pantry, and what she really needed was a pretext to catch the morning parliament at the post-office counter, always busy the day after a funeral, but especially so today with the appearance of the heir to the de Floures at Champton.

She rushed down Main Street, pushed open the post office's creaky door, the bell dinged, and there at the counter were Mrs Braines, Dora Sharman, Anne Dollinger and Stella Harper, who immediately fell silent. Normally Audrey would have picked up the warning, but she was too excited by this morning's news and too pleased to have cornered her foes.

'Morning, ladies,' she said, in a business-like voice, and tucked herself in behind Dora Sharman. No one said anything for a moment.

Then Mrs Braines said, 'Anything for you at the back, Mrs Clement?'

'Is it my turn. I wouldn't want to push in …?'

'Go ahead, Audrey,' said Stella, 'we're just catching up … with the news.'

'The first shall be last and the last shall be first, then.' She made rather a show of edging past the other ladies to the counter. 'Mrs Braines, what do you have in the way of biscuits? Not everyday, but best biscuits.'

'What you see, Mrs Clement,' said Mrs Braines, nodding at the shelf of cash and carry packets of Rich Tea, Bourbons, Digestives, Garibaldis and the new milk-chocolate Hob Nobs that Anne Dollinger had introduced at Knit and Natter.

'Packet of Hob Nobs, please,' said Audrey. 'Better have something special to offer for elevenses.'

'Elevenses?' asked Stella.

'Yes, Hugh's coming. Wasn't it lovely to see him yesterday, even though it was a sad day.'

'Yes, lovely to see him,' said Stella, 'and what an honour for you to have him to yourself.'

'Ourselves, dear,' said Audrey, 'he's coming to see Daniel.'

'Yes, we know,' said Anne, an unusual note of daring in her voice, her eyes immediately shifting to the floor.

'Yes, and with such exciting news,' said Stella.

Audrey's heart missed a beat. 'Yes, isn't it? Well, I mustn't keep you any longer …'

'I wonder what it will be? Simple or splendid?'

'Who knows? Anyway I must—'

'What's the normal routine for such things, Audrey?'

Audrey realised it was she who had been cornered. But she was not going to go down without a fight.

'Such things?'

'Yes. What can we look forward to?'

'I couldn't possibly say, Stella. As I'm sure you will appreciate, there are confidences involved.'

'Not confidential. Alex told Jean Shorely and Jean told us. So feel free.'

There was a silence.

'I can't remember, Audrey, if you were here for the last one.'

Audrey, between wariness and curiosity, finally said, 'I quite forget. Which one?'

'Wedding, dear. The last Lady de Floures. You'd think number three would have been a quiet affair, but no it was all bells and whistles. You would have remembered. But perhaps I'm confusing you? Hugh is getting married. That's what he's going to see … the rector … about.'

Anne gave a muffled squeak of triumph.

'As I say, Stella, there are confidences involved.'

'Funeral weeds today, wedding veils tomorrow,' said Dora Sharman, in a way that suggested this was a piece of established lore rather than a line she had just thought of.

'So often the way,' said Audrey. 'I think all Champton could do with a great occasion, something to celebrate. Church full with rejoicing rather than lamentation.'

'"For I will turn their mourning into joy, and will comfort them, and make them rejoice from their sorrow." The prophet Jeremiah,' said Dora.

'A full church, with full facilities,' said Audrey, in her deadliest sing-song voice, 'isn't that so, Stella? A new loo for a new era.'

'You mean having a toilet? In church? I thought we had put the kibosh on that,' huffed Dora.

'Oh, haven't you heard?' said Audrey, all innocence. 'Stella changed her mind. Reason prevailed!'

Stella, through gritted teeth, said, 'I hear they put in a very nice one at Lower Badsaddle.'

'Wasn't there a terrible row there about taking pews out?' said Jane.

'Pews, pews, pews,' said Stella. 'There's more to church than pews.' She gave a tight little smile. 'Goodbye, Audrey. Do give our best to Hugh.'

Audrey took the Hob Nobs and left.

Stella turned to Anne. 'She's like a gambler who cashes in her chips when she wins and never gives you a chance to win them back.'

'Never mind that,' said Dora, 'what's this about a toilet? You said we wasn't going to get one.'

Stella said, 'Compromise, Dora, compromise – sometimes we must stand firm and sometimes we must bend.'

'Doesn't sound like you. How did she get to you?'

'It isn't about... *getting* to one, Dora, it's about resolving one's differences, should they occur, amicably and generously. Anyway, I have a thousand things to do, good morning!'

And she sailed out into the street, not waiting for Anne, leaving the little bell over the door tinkling on its coiled spring.

28

Daniel and Theo were sitting in the study.

'Not this one, Theo.'

'It's not much good to me if you won't let me observe the things you actually do. How am I supposed to get it right?'

'If it were up to me, you wouldn't be seeing anything at all,' said his brother. 'This is a private interview. It has to be, it's confidential.'

'Hardly, everyone knows Hugh's getting married.'

'That may be so, but I have to ask personal questions to satisfy the legalities, and intimate questions about possible previous marriages—'

'That's *exactly* what I need to hear.'

'How would you like to discuss such things in front of a third party making notes?'

'Wouldn't care.'

'Well, you need to do a bit more homework on what clergy actually do. So, in the nicest possible way, go away.'

Theo looked out of the window. 'I might go into the village. Knock on some doors. See what they make of you?'

'Do that,' said Daniel, and then immediately regretted

it, feeling it was like letting a ferret loose in a coop of jittery hens.

'See you later,' said Theo, unfurling himself from the sofa. 'Can I take the dogs?'

Daniel thought for a moment. 'I'd rather you didn't.'

'Spoilsport.'

As Theo left, a shaft of sunlight fell across the coffee table, making a bowl of peonies, which his mother had put there, look even more wonderful. Daniel loved peonies, the tightly furled balls beginning to break open, like amazing news you are bursting to tell. The door had barely closed when it opened again, and Audrey came bustling in, the *Daily Mail* in hand, folded to a column of print. 'Darling, you must see this!'

There, under a picture of the de Floures family at the lychgate with Daniel's surpliced arm just visible, a column was headlined CURSED DE FLOURES DYNASTY: MURDER AND MARRIAGE?

Yesterday the de Floures family buried their cousin at the church on their historic 15,000-acre estate at Champton. Anthony Bowness, the estate archivist, who was stabbed by an unknown assailant last month, was laid to rest in its once tranquil churchyard, where generations of the family, going back to the Norman Conquest, are buried. Police enquiries continue. But what of future generations? Eldest son and heir of the present Lord de Floures, the Hon. Hugh de Floures, who farms 2,000 acres in the prairies of Canada, attended and it is rumoured he will next return with a fiancée. A Canadian chatelaine for Champton House? She would not be the first to be drawn from outside the English aristocracy. The present Lady de Floures, Carla Petrucci, is Italian. She is the third wife of the present Lord de Floures, rarely seen and thought to be living at her family estate near Siena. But will the maple leaf one day be flying over Champton House? Sources close to the family reveal that Hugh de Floures is due to have a powwow with the vicar today. Nuptial smoke signals are predicted.

Daniel sighed. 'How did they know? And I haven't even begun to talk to Hugh about his intentions, if he has any. This is most embarrassing.'

'I *know*,' said Audrey, her eyes shining. 'Did Alex say something to one of his literary friends? It looks as if they've cropped you out, darling, what a shame. And they've said vicar, not rector.'

All parishes leak, thought Daniel, but a parish like this – so powerful a generator of gossip – was leakier than most. Partly it was because of the prestige of the de Floures, whose doings were of interest to newspaper editors and gossip columnists as well as Champtonians, but partly because it was a small community and small communities tend to disseminate information more swiftly than large. There was the post-office counter, there were established lines of communication between the house, Main Street and, he was embarrassed to admit, the rectory, its telephone among the first to alert the wider world when news broke. He had been obliged to have an awkward conversation with his mother, once or twice, when her understanding of the necessary discretion of his dealings had not been fully in accord with his own. But she had then accused him of being too punctilious, too protective of the over-sensitive – worse, too restrictive with information that the community deserved and sometimes needed to know. How, he had asked, could one be too punctilious with matters that were told him in confidence? She snorted and said people could be unreasonably insistent on protecting their privacy. 'Hoarding it like a treasure that is owed to the world. It is a kind of vanity.' Daniel asked her how she would feel if he were to share with others the details of her life, but that, of course, was quite different and not what she meant at all.

'Daniel, he's here!' said Audrey, as a Land Rover in far better shape than his turned in the drive and came to a halt. 'Front door!' she said. 'It's as I thought! Wedding bells!'

Hugh stood on the doorstep looking more relaxed in his normal daily dress of jeans, a jumper and Tricker's Derby boots, as common an accoutrement for graduates of the smarter agricultural colleges as a school tie for Old Etonians. He looked more himself than in the enforced formality of yesterday's funeral weeds.

'Welcome, welcome, Daniel's expecting you!' Audrey ushered him in and tapped on Daniel's door.

'Come in,' said Daniel, rising to meet him, having sat down a minute ago only for this purpose. He gestured to the Sofa of Tears and winced to see the copy of the *Daily Mail*, open at the gossip column.

'I'll make coffee,' said Audrey.

'You've seen the news, then?' said Hugh.

'Oh yes. How awkward. My mother brought it from the post-office parliament this morning for me to see.'

'Tomorrow's fish and chips,' said Hugh.

Daniel took the paper from the coffee table, put it on his desk and settled into the armchair opposite. 'But is it right? Are you intending to marry?'

'I am. Michelle. She's a vet. I met her inseminating cattle.'

'Oh, I see. The birds and the bees.'

'Surely we're not going to have that kind of conversation?'

'Lord no, I don't do sex.' Daniel could not remember the last time he had advised a courting couple about a sex life they'd been happily getting on with for years. 'First, congratulations, at your wonderful news.'

'Thank you.'

'But we do need to deal with some formalities.'

Daniel went through the checklist, the Church of England obliging its clergy to take on the role of bureaucrats thanks to its hybrid identity as a sort of religious branch of the civil service. Had either been married before? No. Was she a Canadian citizen? Yes. Did they qualify to get married at St Mary's? That was a bit more complicated, for although neither were resident in the parish, Hugo was heir to the title and the estate, and that, in the eyes of the community, meant he belonged.

'I'll have to apply for a licence to satisfy the legalities. I can't think it will be a problem. And then, in due course, we need to discuss what you would like in the service,' Daniel said. He wondered, for a moment, if there would be some traditional Canadian wedding customs, like dancing on logs or hallooing into an echoing valley.

'There's another matter, Daniel,' said Hugh, looking like a man about to broach a sensitive subject. 'My mother. And my step-mothers.'

The present Lady de Floures, Carla, 'lived abroad', an arrangement which suited both partners in the marriage; and then there were two more: the first, Hugh's mother Pamela Lady de Floures, now lived in a vegetarian commune in Argyll where she ran the owl sanctuary, and the second, Wendy Lady de Floures, who had remarried an obscenely rich property developer in Atlanta and continued to use the title for its useful cachet. She was mother to both Honoria and Alex, whom she had not 'stifled with maternal affection', as Bernard once put it to Daniel.

'Are we to … field a full team?' asked Daniel.

'I don't know. It's the first time it's come up, the marriage of the son and heir with more than one Lady de Floures in play.'

'What does your father think?

'He'd rather none of them came, but … *toujours la politesse*. What is the correct form, and can it be managed?'

'Your mother must, of course, be invited and treated to all the dignity the mother of the groom enjoys. Carla should perhaps be invited, in the hope she will not accept. Wendy … well, there's a case for inviting Wendy too.'

'Do you think they'll behave? They've never been in the same place at the same time before.'

'I don't know, but ideally invite everyone in the confident expectation that they will all behave.'

'Ideally …'

A knock at the door, and Audrey, without waiting to be invited, came in backwards holding a tray. 'Coffee!' she cried brightly as Cosmo and Hilda ran in, squirming with excitement, and threw themselves onto the vacant lap of the visitor.

'Cosmo! Hilda! Get down!' said Daniel in his ineffective way. Hugh, who treated dogs like he treated people – with an even coolness – was less interested in them than they in him: when their presented bellies did not receive a rub, they left for a vacant armchair.

Audrey handed out cups and saucers and plates, shortbread from the biscuit tin and United biscuits which she had cut in half as a nod to daintiness. She then hovered and Daniel thought she might be expecting to be invited to join them. 'Thanks, Mum,' he said, and gestured to the door. But Audrey would not be so easily dismissed.

'*So* thrilled at the news,' she said. 'All Champton is behind you.'

Daniel winced, twice.

'I'm not sure it's official yet,' said Hugh, raising an eyebrow. 'But thank you.'

'We're just delighted that you've found someone.' Daniel winced again. 'And someone who will bring something so wonderfully different to our sleepy world.'

'That's a long way off, Mrs Clement,' said Hugh.

'Audrey, please.'

'And we have more pressing matters to deal with, like what to do with the existing Lady de Floures, or ladies de Floures.'

'I see,' said Audrey, and shooed the dogs from the armchair so she could settle in it. She was good at these things. 'You must, of course, invite your mother, but you should invite the others in a way that would discourage them, nicely, from coming.'

Daniel wondered if his mother had gone too far and not got away with it. But Hugh, after a pause, said, 'Any ideas?'

'Well, I think your mother is in the bag – do check there's not a clash with the timetable for owl nesting, if there is such a thing? As for Carla, perhaps if the wedding were to clash with a previous engagement which would be difficult to break. Where does she live?'

'She lives in Italy, I think. Siena?'

'What's the horse race thing they have there?'

'The Palio.'

'When is it?'

'July and August. She's on the committee, or whatever passes for a committee. They always have horses in the race, so she won't leave town.'

'Easy. Arrange it then, can't be helped. Wendy, however… that's more difficult, don't you think?'

Daniel had already tuned out of the conversation and was going over in his mind not the permutations of the guest list but the permutations of the liturgy. What would she come in to, and to what would they leave? It would have to acknowledge her origins, but he could only think of the lumberjack song from Monty Python, and a number from an operetta about military cadets in Victorian Ontario called 'Farewell O Fragrant Pumpkin Pie' which a master at school with a taste for such arcana used to sing as a party piece. Neither would really go with the Book of Common Prayer service of Holy Matrimony, which he felt sure Bernard would insist on, even though Daniel had used – had always used – the 1928 revision of it, which was lovely and less embarrassing (foregoing, for example, the mention of fornication). It was also, strictly speaking, illegal, since the House of Lords had refused to pass the legislation that would have made it so, a casualty of an era when church matters were the subject of hot disputes in parliament.

'Brilliant!' said Hugh, as Audrey suggested that the wedding take place on a red-letter day in Atlanta's social calendar, clashing with an event for which no apology could be countenanced. 'If they are as socially ambitious as you say they are,' said Audrey, 'I should think there'll be a least a month of days when they're spoken for. How could we find out?'

'Honoria,' said Hugh. 'She'll know someone who'll know.' He looked pleased. 'Good double act, Daniel; you and your mother seem to have it all sorted.'

Daniel had never thought of himself and his mother as a double act when it came to solving matrimonial problems, but he had to admit she was good at it. How much easier would he have found the brides of Belgravia, and their mothers, with his own at hand to help?

And then Cosmo, having eaten four halved United bars while everyone's attention was elsewhere, was sick next to the photocopier.

29

Dora and Kath were having coffee too, not at The Flowers but at the kitchen table in their little cottage overlooking the stream that went through the middle of the village. Theo was sitting there, scratching Scamper's tummy; he had rolled over, unable to resist the fuss Theo bestowed on him like flattery on a Tudor king.

'That's one difference,' said Kath. 'Scamper hates the rector.'

'Hates the dogs, Kath, not the rector.'

'Does he? Who's a naughty boy, a *naughty* boy,' said Theo, and rubbed his tummy some more. 'Good job I didn't bring them.'

'You wouldn't have got in if you had.'

On the slightly rusty, rickety stove the coffee maker boiled and seethed, and the strong and bitter coffee the sisters preferred sprung like a geyser into the pot.

'Daniel must like your coffee, though?'

'He's more likely at the congregational in town. It's a caff now, they do cappuccino with a machine, how he likes it.'

'Do you see much of him?'

'Yes, all the time,' said Kath, 'we're church people. And in a place like Champton, you couldn't hide away if you wanted to.'

'No, I meant does he come to call. Pastorally?'

'Yes, he'll knock on the door – unlike Canon Gill, who used to walk in without knocking, until I told him not to. Your brother is the ... what's the word ... courteous type.'

'My mother thinks he's courteous to a fault. She thinks he's too diffident, avoids a fight.'

Dora looked at him. 'He doesn't really need to fight now your mother's here. She can do that for him.'

'I had noticed.'

Dora poured the coffee into little cups. 'How did she get Stella Harper to give up the fight to save the pews?'

Kath turned to her. 'I didn't know she had.'

'Yes, I was in the post office with Mrs Harper t'other day, and your mother came in, and the pews came up and Mrs Harper gave one of her frosty smiles and said she weren't bothered if the rector moved them after all. Your mother smiled back, but it was not a kind smile. I thought she were rubbing it in. How did she do it?'

Theo shrugged. 'I've no idea, but it sounds like her.'

Kath was still looking at Dora. 'Why didn't you tell me?'

'Oh I don't know, I didn't think of it until now,' she shrugged. 'But that's often the way, I find, with rectors, they need someone on their side to do their fighting for them when they're turning the other cheek, as they have to do, I suppose. Canon Dolben were the same. He was here for years. Do you think your brother will stay long?'

'How could he possibly want to leave Champton?' said Theo, taking the coffee Dora offered. The cottage was not so much little as tiny, one of a terrace that had been built in the 1700s for those who worked on the estate. They were still mostly occupied by former servants and tenants; they had been once thatched but were now tiled, an example of one of the infrequent upgrades the estate provided.

There was a knock, followed by the sound of the back door opening and a voice shouting, 'Dora? Kath?'

'We're here, duck.'

It was Nathan and Alex. Both were surprised to see Theo at the kitchen table; Alex because someone he associated with seamy Soho looked unusually incongruous in the Sharmans' kitchen, and Nathan because he was carrying a sack, and in it something was moving around. Scamper raced to sit at his feet, his little tail wagging so violently it looked like a rudimentary propellor.

'Hullo, Theo, how are you?'

'All good, just researching my new part – helped enormously by these ladies.'

Nathan glanced at Theo, then looked away.

'Don't worry about him, lad,' said Dora, indicating Theo. 'He's not a telltale.'

'I've got you that rabbit, a big one, Dora. Do you want to keep it or et it?'

'Let's have a look at him, then.'

Nathan opened the sack and produced a rabbit the size of a badger, holding it by the scruff of its neck. Scamper barked and the rabbit squirmed.

'Oh, isn't he handsome?' said Alex.

'Et it,' said Kath.

'Do you want me to sort it for you, Kath?'

'No, duck, give it here.'

She took the rabbit and walked down the passage to the back.

'Bap said you'd been round to see him to talk about films,' said Nathan, turning to address Theo.

'Sort of. It's for a part I'm playing – a parson, like my brother. I've been trying to get a feel for parish life.'

'You'll certainly get a feel for it at the Liversedges,' said Dora. 'If you're lucky, you'll leave with a rabbit or a pheasant or a pigeon or two. Muntjac if you're lucky.'

'Muntjac?'

'Little deer, you must have seen them, running around,' said Alex.

'Oh yes, I thought they were ornamental.'

'Eating, not ornament. Champton was one the first places to have them; the Duke of Bedford gave them to my great-grandfather so we'd have the full set. We had every kind of deer in the park in those days, from reds to muntjacs – we ate them all. The only thing we don't eat now are the swans and the peacocks, and we used to eat them too, once.'

'We have to keep the deer down,' said Nathan, 'or there would be more than we can manage. Bap can dress you one, if you want?'

Theo looked out of the window, just in time to see Kath, outside the little barn, whack the fat rabbit's neck with a rolling pin in one expert blow. It stiffened and then went limp in her hand.

30

Daniel had just cleared up the half-digested Uniteds from his study carpet when he saw Anne Dollinger coming up the path with a look of determination, like a Jehovah's Witness on the attack.

'Daniel,' she said, 'may I see you about something?'

'Of course.' Business or social? Daniel wondered for a moment, but her demeanour told him the former, so he invited her into the study, where she sat awkwardly on cushions still bearing the indentation of Hugh.

'What can I do for you?'

'How are you, Daniel? These are dreadful times indeed, and we wondered how you are coping?'

'Thank you, that's very kind and thoughtful of you. I'm OK, I think. How are you?'

'Very shaken, it's an awful time,' said Anne, and faltered. 'There's something I need to tell you.'

'Please do.'

'Something I remembered,' said Anne, 'about the day of the murder. It just came into my mind today, and I don't know if it is relevant and I wanted to ask what you think.'

'Go on.'

'I saw Norman Staveley walking along the brook, in a hurry, on the far side, walking from the direction of the church, and it must have been about the same time as the murder because *Stop the Week* was on the wireless, about half past seven. Nothing unusual, except he was in a hurry and something about that stuck in my mind.'

'Why now? Weren't you questioned by the police?'

'Yes, of course, but I didn't think of it *then*. It was only today, when I saw him walk past the shop, stagger past more like, that I remembered. He's normally a sedate sort of man and it looked peculiar, and I said so to Stella, and then I remembered. But what should we do? I don't want to get Norman into trouble, and it's probably nothing...'

'You must tell the police. At once.'

'We wondered if you would, seeing as you know that nice sergeant...'

Later that day another visitor came to call, expected this time for tea, but with very little notice. Parked on the drive was the unmistakable conveyance of the bishop, his glossy black Rover Sterling looking like Queen Victoria in widowhood next to Theo's compact Golf. It had a dividing glass between driver and passenger, due to the distinction and antiquity of the Diocese of Stowe, so that the holder of the See might be spared the conversation of his driver, on this occasion his chaplain. For Daniel an episcopal visit usually meant trouble, and the news of his eminent and imminent arrival had sent Audrey into a frenzy of faux-casual hospitality. A walnut cake was bought from The Flowers, at an inflated price, the silver coffee pot was cleaned, and some of her best tulipa 'Ballerina', fiery and late flowering, that she'd been saving for the flower festival were cut and arranged in pentecostal displays around the house.

But the bishop had asked Daniel to show him the church, scene of the crime, privately, leaving Audrey and Theo to entertain his chaplain in the kitchen. The Reverend Gareth Nuttall, who held that post, was slender and sleek and groomed, unlike his superior. He needed the loo, which he pronounced with verbal quotation marks, and as the dogs followed him curiously out into the hall, Theo said, 'Jesus Christ, Mr Slope is living still.'

Audrey had thought the same – Slope, the oleaginous chaplain to the Bishop of Barchester in the novels of Anthony Trollope, still reliable as a guide to clergy types more than a century later. 'That "loo" that "call me Gareth" – not very Trollope, is it?'

'I noticed you didn't give him your Christian name in return.'

'Certainly not. You know they filmed *Barchester* at Stowe? When the producer telephoned the dean to ask what they would need to do to make it look like the 1860s, the dean said, "Nothing."'

As the sound of the clanking flush, like a broken bell, echoed, Gareth reappeared in the kitchen, the dogs still following at his heels. He pushed them away, not too subtly, with his foot, shod in a black Oxford that looked over smart. Theo began to interrogate him.

'Bishop's chaplain? Is that like a batman?'

'No, not a batman. More an aide-de-camp.'

'And do you know where all the bodies are buried?'

Gareth pulled at a double cuff. 'Discretion is necessary, as I'm sure you will understand.'

'Will you one day be a bishop yourself?'

He pulled at the other double cuff.

Daniel and the bishop stood in the chancel looking down the nave to where Anthony's body had been found.

'Such a battle you're having, I'm sorry.'

'Thank you, Bishop. I'm not sure which is more difficult: the fact of the deed itself, or what it sets off in others.'

'How do you mean?'

'The fact of murder – twice – or what it brings up to the surface.'

'Oh, that. I didn't mean that. I meant your reordering.'

Daniel had almost forgotten about the plans to take out pews and put in loos. It seemed an age since that blew up and upset everyone.

'It's so much better, don't you think, to open up the space, *ad majorem dei gloriam*?'

'It had rather slipped from my mind. But how did you know about that?' said Daniel.

'I know about everything. I also know it will be harder for you than for the dean to take out the cathedral pews. We only had to convince the canons – notoriously unbiddable, but of unusually like mind in this matter. The Victorian Society moaned, but they would, wouldn't they? You have to take the congregation with you. Bring them to the cathedral. Show them what we've done. It may help?'

'I don't know if it would. After what's happened, perhaps we should do nothing, absolutely nothing, for a while. Business as usual.'

'There is no standing still.'

'That's what I said to a parishioner who was moaning about it. She thought exactly the opposite, and I'm beginning to wonder if she was right.'

'Of course you would think that now, having to deal with all the unpleasantness. But it will pass.'

'It will. It would help if we could catch the murderer.'

'Indeed so. They nearly always find them in the end. Perhaps I might have that cup of tea now?'

Gareth seemed relieved when the bishop returned, through the back door this time and into the kitchen where Audrey had put him instead of the drawing room. He followed Daniel and the bishop to Daniel's study and was looking for a chair when the bishop said, 'Thank you Gareth, that will be all.'

'My Lord.' He slid from the room.

'I wish he wouldn't call me that. When he started, it took a day to two before I realised he meant me.'

'Can't you tell him not to?'

'I suppose so, but he is so very punctilious. I feel rather judged by him.'

The bishop almost sprawled on the Sofa of Tears and Daniel felt he should have offered him his own chair, partly for his comfort, but partly because that is what is done in church when the bishop comes, the best chair for the *sacerdos magnus*. In spite of his dislike of being milorded by his chaplain – and

Daniel wondered if he really minded that much – he was to the manner born: the son of a bishop, ordained at the earliest opportunity, right after theological college at Cuddesdon, 'the Sandhurst of the C of E', as it had been described. He had been a bishop's chaplain himself, dean of a Cambridge college and principal of his old theological college, from where he was appointed to the See of Stowe, as effortless a rise through the ranks as any. He was, however, more complex than his entry in *Crockford's Clerical Directory* revealed, a scholar at Cambridge and at Oxford, the world's leading authority on a highly technical problem in the transmission of New Testament text-types in the second century – but also a Blue: a rower and a rugby player. Bookishness prevailed and the rangy athleticism of his youth had become heaviness in age.

He heaved himself into a slightly less uncomfortable position on the sofa.

'So. How *are* you?'

'Quite well, thank you, Bishop.'

'Your mother seems in excellent form.'

'She is.'

'It must be very difficult for her with everything that's happened.'

Daniel thought. 'Not really, she seems to be rather enjoying it.' He smiled.

'And what about *you*? It's a heavy burden you are carrying.'

'You deal with it. What else can you do?'

'And how is the parish?'

'Unsettled, volatile, anxious. Losing two of our number to murder is … tectonic. And I think we all know, whether consciously or unconsciously, that the murderer is one of us.'

'Are you sure?'

'I think so. On the evidence, as I understand it, it could be anyone, a passing psychopath – that scenario suits some – but my feeling, my conviction, is that it is one of us.'

'Why?'

'I know there's a story that I cannot yet see which will explain everything. It's a bit like reading Isaiah before the birth of Christ: it's pointing in a certain direction, but you can't see where yet.'

The door swung open and Audrey appeared carrying a tray of tea things; Gareth followed, carrying the cake.

'Thank you,' said the bishop. 'What splendid-looking cake, Mrs Clement.'

'May I slice and pass this round, Mrs Clement?'

'Don't worry about that, Gareth,' said the bishop, 'we'll manage.'

After a beat Gareth retreated, encouraged, gently, by Audrey.

'Tea, Bishop?' Daniel poured.

'Scripture is such a puzzle. Jews reading Isaiah might interpret it in quite a different way, of course. We've had all those years of Nine Lessons and Carols, so our narrative is rather imprinted on us. Are you a Hebraist?'

'No.'

Daniel cut the cake. It was sticky and luscious and light all at the same time.

'Not really my thing, either. We had to do Greek and Hebrew when I was a student, and read all the Fathers in Greek and Latin. But it was Greek that I enjoyed most – and it taught me how to solve puzzles.'

Daniel nodded in what he hoped was an attentive way and sipped his coffee.

'Detail, always, but don't forget to step back too. I remember spending hours of study, puddles of ink, looking at a rather mysterious textual problem in Ephesians, trying to work out which version – it was a tiny difference – was older and why it had changed. As I sat in the library poring over the text, a chap next to me, a biblical theologian, was looking at Colossians, which, as you know' – how donnish he is, thought Daniel – 'is closely related, and we started going to the pub and talking, and I realised that he wanted Colossians to say certain things in certain ways and I wanted Ephesians to say different things in different ways. He tried to build great structures on the foundation of the Epistle and I kept saying, but you can't do that, the text is not secure, and he kept saying my absorption in minute detail was like trying to interpret the *Ring* cycle by looking at the second bassoonist's music stand. Are you following?'

Daniel nodded, and wondered if he should properly wait for the bishop to take a bite of his slice of cake rather than go in for one first.

'And then came an epiphany. I stood back, and rather than look at the details I looked at the landscape and I realised that the question was not which variant was older – because in a way that was not important. Important if you wish to establish an original text, but what *is* an original text? What the author – who wasn't Paul, by the way – wrote down? The first draft? The final draft? The version that went out to the churches along the Aegean coast? The version that went into the canon? Once I had stopped looking for the original version, the whole thing opened up for me like a flower, and I started asking more interesting questions. Why did this matter to the people who read it and cherished it and preserved it?'

He finally took a bite out of the slice of cake.

'Archilocus said we are either foxes or hedgehogs,' said Daniel, 'knowing lots of things or one big thing, not both.'

'Perhaps hedgehogs should be more foxy, and foxes more like hedgehogs. Step back, Daniel, step back… I say, this cake is absolutely scrumptious.'

Daniel wondered where this was going.

And then it came.

'We've been stepping back and looking at the diocese, our resources and the challenges we face, and I wanted to speak to you about the possibility of parish reorganisation.'

Daniel's coffee turned cold in its cup.

'Parish reorganisation?'

'Yes.'

'Champton in with another parish?'

'Parishes.'

This was unexpected. This was unthinkable. But – stand back and think about it – the amalgamation of parishes had become the norm, with smaller congregations and the clergy spread thin and the money even thinner. Why should Champton be any different? But it *was* different. How could Champton St Mary amalgamate with anywhere else? It was a case apart, bound into the life of the estate, not the neighbours, and to yoke it together with anywhere else would be like marrying a walrus to a pyramid. And then there was Bernard; it would be a brave bishop who got to tell Lord de Floures that his rector was in future to be shared.

'Parishes?'

'Yes. You know Maurice Legge is retiring? And that means the Badsaddles will fall vacant.'

Upper Badsaddle and Lower Badsaddle, on the northern edge of the estate. It might as well be Ulan Bator.

'There are some legalities we would need to straighten out,' the bishop put on his magnanimous face, 'but would you consider becoming rector of Champton St Mary with St Thomas the Martyr Upper Badsaddle and St Catherine Lower Badsaddle?'

The music of that appealed to him for a moment, but only for a moment. 'I'm very honoured that you should think of me, Bishop. You mentioned legalities?'

'Yes, lay patrons and all that. Lord de Floures is yours – oh, it rhymes – and Upper Badsaddle is mine, Lower Badsaddle is St Alphege Cambridge's, which happens to be my old college and I am sure they will be reasonable. So the question is, do you think Lord de Floures will be reasonable?'

'I'm sure he will think he is being reasonable, Bishop. Only you might not think it so.'

'Ah.'

'The de Floures have been patrons for centuries. Bernard takes it very seriously.'

'Does he?'

'I would say he does.'

'The thrice-married Lord de Floures?'

'To err is human.'

'Oh, quite so, but if I may be frank with you, Daniel, the old days when the patron paid for the chancel roof and expected his bastards to be baptised in return are gone.'

I don't remember you hesitating to take Bernard's money when the cathedral wanted the organ fixing, thought Daniel. He said nothing.

'I think it may be time for Lord de Floures – for *all* of us – to face reality. I appreciate that he will find it a difficult reality to face, which is why I wanted to talk to you Daniel, to see if you could, like John the Baptist, prepare the way.'

How little you know me, thought Daniel. 'Would that not more properly come from you, Bishop? Or the Archdeacon?'

'Eventually, yes, But I would be very glad if you could deploy your diplomatic skills as you have so successfully in the past, and for which we were – and continue to be – so grateful. Make straight in the desert a highway, and all that?'

'Then I shall of course speak to Lord de Floures, Bishop.'

'Good, good. Now, how are you bearing up under the stress of the past few weeks? You and your people have been constantly in my prayers. If you need anything, you only have to ask.'

Inspiration came.

'Well, there is perhaps something, Bishop.'

'Anything!'

'The second victim, Ned Thwaite. His death has been not overlooked exactly, but Anthony Bowness's, for obvious reasons, got a lot more attention, which has been – I think – a mixed blessing for his family. No one wants the sort of media interest Anthony's death caused, but I think Ned's widow and daughters have felt rather pushed to one side and his loss not adequately acknowledged. The coroner has released the body, so we are arranging his funeral, and it occurs to me that it would do a lot to help them – and the parish, I think, at

this very difficult time – if you were to conduct his funeral?'
The bishop's smile stiffened slightly. 'If, of course, you are able
to fit it in? I know you're so busy.'

'I am, Daniel, a pastor before I'm anything else. If you
need me ...'

'Oh yes, we *do* need you.'

'... then, of course, I will. You can perhaps make
arrangements with Gareth?'

'That's very kind, Bishop. And you'll stay for lunch
afterwards? Lord de Floures has very kindly offered to host.
He does rather a good buffet.'

31

Daniel did not rush to the big house after they waved the bishop and his chaplain goodbye, the glass divider beginning to rise before Gareth's foot was even off the clutch. He made some phone calls, he had an exhausting conversation with his brother about what the lower clergy thought of the higher clergy and then declared he was going to write a sermon. Only when he heard Theo drive off did he walk out to the house through the park and went in through the kitchen, where Mrs Shorely looked up at him from the desk.

'Are you after his lordship?'

'I am, Mrs Shorely.'

'He's in his study. Shall I tell him you're here? He's with someone. That policeman you like.'

What was Neil Vanloo doing with Bernard?

'If you would.'

As she picked up the handset from the businesslike phone, bristling with buttons, through which the kitchen communicated with even the furthest corners of the house and estate, he noticed that her desk was positioned in front of a shallow cupboard; the cupboard was open and Daniel could see dozens, if not hundreds, of keys, hanging on dozens of hooks, so many that you would need a key to the keys if you wished to unlock the cricket pavilion, the bath house, the lawnmower shed, the church, the front door...

'Rector's here to see you, m'lord... very good, m'lord.' She replaced the receiver. 'He says you're to join them. Do you know the way?'

Daniel went a little uncertainly through the dark corridor that connected the kitchen end of the house to its residential parts – plain doors that opened on to splendid rooms, others that opened onto different corridors, too confusing to navigate there directly. He found his way first to the saloon and thence to Bernard's study. Bernard and Neil Vanloo were looking at a pile of papers on the desk.

'Come in, Dan. Drink? The detective sergeant here has declined to join me.'

It was not an invitation Daniel felt he should decline, so he took a whisky and soda, which gave Bernard a reason to finish his first and pour a second.

'DS Vanloo's returning Anthony's papers. What he was working on the day he was killed.'

Daniel looked to Neil. 'Anything illuminating?'

'Not that I can see. It's mostly inventories from the works department a hundred years ago or so. Lists of jobs.'

'Anthony was looking at our golden age, the age of Victoria, queen and empress,' said Bernard. 'Fleets of servants, vast shooting parties, gardeners and under gardeners and grooms. We could do a display for Open Days.'

Daniel thought there was some distance to go between the ledgers and inventories and lists and the stories of the lives of the people who created them, most of them unknown and leaving no trace, apart from a wage bill or a description of work, a faint trace in the memory of their great-grandchildren.

'What did you want to see me about, Daniel?'

'The bishop came for tea.'

Bernard looked puzzled. 'Which one?'

'Ours. I have news.'

Neil Vanloo straightened up. 'I must be off. Would appreciate a word later, Daniel, if you can spare a moment?'

'Yes, of course. Do you want to wait at the rectory? Mum will let you in.'

'Thanks.'

Bernard looked peeved. 'Let me see you out, Detective Sergeant.'

As Bernard walked him to the door, Daniel leafed through the books on Bernard's desk, cloth-bound, the name of the department stamped in black on the cover: *Stables, Carpentry Shop, Butler, Housekeeper.* The writing was lovely, a steady but flowing copperplate, a dying art in the dawn of the computer age. Daniel thought of the machine he had seen in Rymans, in which you typed on a keyboard and the words appeared on a screen, so that you could correct them before everything was printed as neatly as a typewriter. It was wildly expensive, prohibitively so, but soon, he thought, everybody would type and no one would write and the manuscript – with its individuality, its character, its quirks, its marginalia – would fade away.

Stalls, house stables: made good.

Church furnishings: made, installed.

Desks, for her Ladyship's Reading Room: made, installed.

Her ladyship's reading room, built by a pious de Floures for the edification of the villagers after she closed the pub lest the navvies building the railway spent all their wages on dinners and mayhem. Liquor quickly beat literature, the pub was reopened and the reading room turned into a house.

Bernard was back. 'What does he want to see you about? I tried to get it out of him, but he turned into a clam.'

'I really couldn't say, Bernard.'

'No, but I could. Norman Staveley summoned to the police station, want to know why?'

'Not especially.'

'Last person to see Anthony alive. In church on the night he died. There was a row. Then he left, according to him; next thing he knew, Anthony's body was discovered by you. The upstanding councillor thought this information irrelevant to the police inquiry. He always was a shifty fellow.'

Daniel said nothing.

'Shifty family, too – his father and his grandfather before him. They used to work here, and his wife and her people too. They moved on. Something not right about it, though my papa never said why. Mama couldn't stand him.'

As Bernard spoke, he poured himself another drink – his third? 'What news from Stowe?'

'You're not going to like it.'

And indeed he didn't. Daniel could see he did not like it at all, so he left no gap in the narrative for a protest to be launched, until he got to the bishop's gently extorted offer to take Ned Thwaite's funeral. 'So he will be rather at your mercy, Bernard, or beholden at least. And everyone will be here.'

'Bloody idiot! What right has *he* to deny me *my* right? We've been patrons here since, I don't know, the Wars of the Roses! I bloody gave him ten grand for the bloody organ or whatever it was! How *dare* he? I'm going to write him a very shirty letter indeed.'

'Hold your fire, Bernard. Let's think this through. He wants, for obvious reasons, to amalgamate Champton with the Badsaddles—'

'*Badsaddles!* What has Champton to do with the Badsaddles? They were for PARLIAMENT.'

'I don't think this will get very far without your consent, Bernard. So he has a long way to go and, if I know him at all, once we make it awkward, he will move on to something else.'

'Well, awkward we will be.'

'Yes. Starting with Ned's funeral. It would be only proper for you to say a few words to mark the occasion, to thank the bishop for his continuing and sensitive pastoral care.'

Bernard considered this and saw its merit.

'Oh, good plan. When is Ned's funeral, by the way?'

'I thought a decent interval between Ned's and Anthony's was better for Jane and the girls. The coroner's done with his body so we can start getting it arranged.'

'A week decent enough?'

'I'll find out. It all revolves around availability at the crematorium. He's going to be scattered over the dale he came from.'

Neil Vanloo was waiting in the study when Daniel got back. Audrey, like a predator circling its prey, was hovering. But

Neil was the questioner, not the questioned. Pleasantries were batted back with pleasantries, until Daniel's arrival obliged his mother's reluctant retreat to the kitchen. 'Just shout if I can get you anything!' she said to the closing door.

'What's happened?' said Daniel.

'We've had Councillor Staveley down at the station. He's talked.'

'Was it him in church?'

'Yes. He went to see Anthony. He saw him arrive to lock up after he'd left the pub and followed him. Didn't think anyone saw him. Anthony was saying his prayers, but Staveley interrupted him. Confronted him.'

'Confronted him with what?'

'Anthony had been going through the archives and found something that Norman didn't want found. Accounts, which showed that the estate had paid a substantial sum, at the time, to his grandfather, who was a chauffeur when he left their employment.'

'A pay-off?'

'Yes, a large one. Turns out his grandfather had put Lord de Floures' aunt in an extremely compromising situation. They bought his silence, enough to make him go away, but instead he started a garage in Braunstonbury, a garage that somehow managed to get all the work on the estate and eventually provided for Norman and Dot to move back to Champton and – even better – for Norman to become a stalwart of the Conservative Association and a county councillor. The chairman was Lord de Floures: a constant reminder.'

'And a constant reminder to Norman too that his success through hard work, bootstraps, good Thatcherite narrative,

MBE assured, was actually a bit murky.'

'Exactly. It just couldn't get out. So he confronted Anthony, offered him money, only Anthony wasn't interested.'

'And then?'

'Left him there, according to him. Came home. Next thing he knew, blue lights were flashing and someone phoned Dot and told her the news. He's been sweating ever since. What do you think?'

'Motive, opportunity... but I don't think so. Norman's pompous, not murderous. And what about Ned?'

'My thoughts too. But he's not the only one helping us with our enquiries. Nathan Liversedge is in too.'

'Nathan? Why?'

'We got word from the Hampshire force about him. Robbery with violence. Someone took an old lady's pension, she put up a fight, he punched her lights out. A name came up, Joe Blewett, and he took off. The Blewetts and the Liversedges are related, gypsy family tree, goes back generations. Joe Blewett is Nathan Liversedge, we think. When did he arrive at Champton?'

'I'm not sure. Not long after me. Six or seven years ago?'

'It fits. And then there's the grandfather. He's had quite a life.'

'So I've heard.'

'What had you heard?'

'I think he was a prize fighter when he was young.'

'He was, at the fairs and illegal bare-knuckle fights probably. He became a debt collector. There's talk, pub talk, he did more than collect debts.'

Daniel did not react. Neil noted him not reacting, and said, 'Do you think it's possible that Anthony and Ned found out about Nathan, and Edgy killed them to protect him?'

'I think it is possible Anthony and Ned found out something about Nathan. I don't think Edgy killed them.'

'Why not?'

'Doesn't fit.'

'Doesn't fit your mental picture?'

'It doesn't.'

Neil looked like he was about to ask another question, but stopped. He thought. And then he said, 'I'm not sure I'm getting the full story here, Daniel.'

'No one ever gets the full story.'

'You know what I mean.'

Daniel had hoped this could be avoided, but it could not. 'I need to speak to someone,' he said. 'Can you wait?'

'Don't be daft.'

'Do you trust me, Neil?'

Neil looked at him. 'Yes. But that's not the point in a murder inquiry.'

'On the basis of that trust, can we resume this conversation later? I need half an hour – it will make no difference.'

'That's a lot to ask, Daniel.'

'I know.'

The detective sighed. 'You have half an hour.'

'Thank you.'

Daniel left Neil in his study. He tried not to rattle his keys and alert his mother, but the dogs heard him and summoned her.

'Daniel?'

'Mum?'

'I know about Norman. It's all over Champton. Did he do it?'

'You know I can't say anything.'

'Well, if Norman Staveley is a murderer I shall eat my hat. But let's eat kidneys in sherry instead, your favourite. I sent Theo to Dennis's.'

The post-mortem promise of Dennis's kidneys and the luscious richness of sherry, his comfort food since childhood, dispelled the thought of porridge and tea, a diet he may have to get used to if what he was about to do turned out to obstruct a murder inquiry. 'Can it wait a few minutes?'

'I suppose so. Your brother's still in the pub.' She looked out of the window and saw a car parked next to the Golf. 'Is that detective still here?'

'He's in the study, but I really won't be long.' Daniel pulled his coat off the hook.

As he closed the front door behind him, he heard Audrey's voice rising. 'Detective Sergeant, I hear congratulations are in order!'

32

Daniel fastened his coat against the evening chill and set off down the lane. How much did Edgy know about Alex and his grandson? How much would he be able to bear when it came out? A man with a man. Unforgivable in Edgy's tradition, even if the world outside was changing. And he did not think that Alex and the gypsy boy would be something Bernard would enjoy either. Maybe Anthony knew. Takes one to know one? Maybe there was more to it than met the eye?

He did not want to think about that. He thought instead of Edgy suddenly telling him one day, when he was round at the cottage, about his old life, and how what he had done in his work – discharged without any twinge of conscience at the time – in age had come back to vex him. A story about a man he had dispatched in a town in the south of Italy. He had come up behind him, left hand round his forehead, gently bent his head back and drawn the blade across his throat – and with a hiss and a gurgle the life had gone out of him. But he was not a man, he was a boy, a teenager, and since Nathan had come to him, the look of surprise on the victim's face had reared up in his memory, and in Edgy's dreams sometimes it was not his face but Nathan's.

'You must report this,' Daniel had said, and Edgy had laughed.

'No, I won't. I want ease for my conscience, not people prying into my business. And it was a long time ago, but not so long that my clients wouldn't think it their business too.'

'I cannot offer you the peace you seek if you do not.'

'Then I will have to go without, Rector.'

'So why are you telling me?'

The road ended and the drive to the house began. Separating the two were the gates, magnificent confections of wrought iron and gilt, the de Floures arms worked into them between circlets of flowers in two rows. How they liked to stamp their marks of ownership on everything, from bookplates to monograms on a hanky, if not the arms then the circlet of flowers. A rebus, it occurred to Daniel, a pictorial representation of the name, if you allowed for Norman French.

The gates hung between two massive pillars surmounted by eagles and a keypad on a jarringly unsympathetic post stood at Land Rover-window height on the right. Daniel bent and squinted and put in the code – 1066; the motor whirred and the gates swung slowly open. But Daniel did not walk up the drive; he stood at the north lodge, where Alex lived by day (he lived by night in the south, where his bathroom and bedroom were located) and knocked on the door.

Honoria opened it. 'Hello, Dan. He's inside.'

Alex was lying on the sofa in his living room cum studio, looking half Isadora Duncan half Siouxsie and the Banshees.

He was picking at a plate of what looked like shrivelled testes balanced on his stomach.

'Alex, are you all right?'

'No.'

'I need to talk to you.'

'What about?'

Daniel turned to Honoria, who had followed him in.

'Honoria, would you mind leaving us?'

'Yes, I would.'

This was awkward. 'I need to speak to Alex about something confidential.'

Alex said, 'Nothing is confidential from my sister. Would you like a sun-dried tomato?' He held up the plate.

'No thanks.' He thought for a moment. 'Alex, this involves someone whose confidence I have to respect.'

Honoria said, 'They're lovers, Dan. Didn't you know?'

Daniel was silent for a moment. 'I thought that perhaps there was something sexual happening. That's what I need to see you about, Alex. I promise you I will be as discreet as I possibly can be, but it is a murder inquiry and it will come out.'

'Come out,' said Alex, 'yes, exactly that.'

'It is not illegal, Alex' – he made a mental calculation – 'you are both of age, and lapses happen.'

'Lapses?'

'Yes. I have found people are much more forgiving of such things than we think they will be.'

'What do you do when you lapse, Daniel? Fuck a gypsy boy?'

'No, not my weakness, but I want to reassure—'

'We're not lapses, Daniel, we're *lovers*.'

Honoria said, almost snapped, 'Oh Daniel, they've been lovers for years.'

Alex stifled a laugh and Daniel felt again that he must seem ridiculous to him. And then he saw he wasn't laughing but crying.

Honoria went to his side and took his hand and then enveloped him in a hug as the tears began to flow and his body shook with sobs. 'Darling boy, darling boy…'

Daniel was silent, embarrassed at having only half understood what was between Alex and Nathan. Not a transgressive liaison, a knee-trembler in the woods, but a love affair.

Alex stopped crying and Honoria gave him her hanky and he dried his eyes and said, 'God, I must look awful.' Then he turned to face Daniel and said, 'You thought, didn't you, that he was my bit of rough?'

'No,' said Daniel, '… actually, yes.'

'Me preying on him, exploiting him for my wicked gratification?'

'I didn't understand that you were in love. I just saw people being secretive, as if it were something they were ashamed of.'

'Not ashamed, Dan, careful. Imagine how this will go down with Daddy? And with Edgy? No wedding bells and the de Floures tiara for me. Or for him. Oh, and how the village will love it. We'll have to elope to Sitges.'

Daniel wondered where that was.

Alex said, 'But why would you know? And it did begin with a quick one behind a tree and I did initiate it. And yes, I was excited by the gypsy boy… And it continued, just sex, and then one day I realised it wasn't just sex.'

'What changed?'

Alex shrugged and said simply, 'I realised he was a person.'

'Who caught you?'

Alex was silent, and then said, 'Ned Thwaite, down at the bath house. We were lying together and there was a face at the window. Ned, with his camera and his notebook and his endless curiosity.'

33

In the study Neil stood at the window, looking out as the shadows grew suddenly longer across the rectory lawn and beyond lay the park, orderly, managed, made beautiful. Inside, however, all was back to front. He turned to face Daniel, sitting uncomfortably, a supplicant on his own Sofa of Tears.

'Edgy's confessed,' said Neil. 'He walked into the station an hour ago.'

'Oh no no no … It can't be.'

There was a pause and a sigh. 'Dan, he's confessed. There's motive, there's opportunity, there's everything.'

'Except he did not do it.'

'Alex starts coming on to Nathan. Nathan obliges, scared for his job, money, maybe he's a gay gypsy, maybe just bored stiff. Anthony discovers them, threatens them, blackmail or something. Edgy finds out. Edgy has form.'

Daniel shrugged.

'Nathan tells him about Anthony, about Alex. It's a threat to his grandson, a threat to him – reputation, face, family status, all important. After Open Day he sees Anthony going into church …'

'But what about Norman Staveley?'

'He saw Councillor Staveley come and go. It made him more anxious. Maybe he knew about Nathan too? So he made up his mind. Went into church. Confronted Anthony. Frightened him. Didn't take much. Found out what he wanted to know. He had said nothing to Norman Staveley, which is why he is still alive, I think. But Anthony… Edgy found the secateurs, killed him – a professional job we've always said – and got away.'

'What about Ned?'

'Ned saw Alex and Nathan at the bath house. Nathan tells Edgy, Edgy deals with it. He brought in Ned's camera…'

'The Canon AE-1?'

'Yes, a Canon AE-1. No film in it, but it's definitely Ned's. It's got his name on it. Dynotape.'

'What does Nathan say?'

'He's not saying anything.'

Daniel picked up a yellow plastic pencil, not because he wanted to write, but because he just needed to do something. It was, he noticed, Neil's preferred model, a Pentel SP 0.9 mm.

'Enough, Dan. I think we need to talk formally. I need you to come with me to the station.'

Daniel exhaled. 'Yes, of course. I'll just tell my mother.'

In the kitchen Audrey was tossing some bloody kidneys in flour, a job she rather liked because they reminded her of damsons with a bloom on them.

She raised an eyebrow. 'Don't tell me you're a suspect.'

'Not exactly.'

'What on earth do you mean?'

'I suppose I'm helping them with their enquiries.'

Audrey wiped her hands on her apron. 'Theo had to go to Dennis the butcher to get kidneys. I had to go to the pub for a bottle of sherry. To make *you* your favourite supper. Let me talk to him.'

'I'd much prefer it if you didn't.'

But she was halfway out of the door, Cosmo and Hilda falling in behind her, like seconds.

'Detective Sergeant, I don't understand why you seem so determined to ruin our supper. You're not a Mountie, and my son is not your man.'

Neil replied, 'It's a murder inquiry, Mrs Clement.'

The dogs looked from him to Daniel.

'Let's go, shall we?' said Daniel. The dachshunds wagged their tails, ever hopeful that every departure would be for their benefit.

It was not. Daniel closed the door on them and noticed that his mother shared the same expression of anxious frustration.

'I'll drive,' said Neil.

Daniel went to get in the back.

'Don't be silly, Daniel,' said Neil. They both sat in the front and immediately felt awkward to be so close together in the new *froideur*.

And then Theo appeared in front of them, walking up the drive. 'Hello,' he said, and indicated for Daniel to wind down his window. 'Have I missed supper?'

'No, but I must. I'm going to the station to make another statement.'

Theo breathed out beer and cigarettes as he said, 'Why now?'

Neil leaned over, 'New developments, sir.'

'You mean Norman Staveley? Everyone was talking about it in the pub. Did he do it?'

'Not Norman,' said Daniel, 'someone else.'

'Not *you*?'

'No, of course not me.'

'Who then?'

Neil said, 'If you don't mind, sir, we must be going.' But Theo didn't move.

Then he said, 'Not Edgy?'

Daniel and Neil said nothing.

Theo laughed. 'Don't be ridiculous! It can't be Edgy.'

It was Neil's turn to look puzzled.

Theo said, 'His hands.'

The phone rang. Daniel – at that moment quietly digesting kidneys in a rich sherry sauce – answered.

'You were right. He didn't do it.'

'Beyond question?'

'Beyond question. He could hardly open his fingers, let alone stab someone to death with a pair of secateurs. But why didn't you just say?'

There was nothing he could say about Edgy confessing his sins to him or about his murderous employment, which he had abandoned not on account of conscience, but arthritis.

34

'My dear people, I am so very glad to be with you today as we say farewell to Ned, and to stand among you as your pastor in this time of darkness and to proclaim again that we live in the light of Christ, a light which all the darkness of the world cannot extinguish.'

A week had passed since the excitement of that extraordinary day, when Champton's heir, Stowe's bishop and Braunstonbury's detective sergeant had all called at the rectory. That was how Audrey would remember it, rather than as the day her son was nearly taken by the detective sergeant to answer questions relating to a murder inquiry. That inglorious hour had faded to dimness, and today everyone's attention turned to the chancel arch, under which the episcopal throne (actually the old town clerk's chair from Braunstonbury) had been placed to accommodate the bishop.

Gareth, his chaplain – vested in cassock, surplice and purple stole – stood awkwardly behind and to his side, handing things and holding things: a mitre, a crozier, his text. The bishop was usually far less fussy about what he was wearing than his chaplain, but Gareth had rather forced him to put on the cope Daniel used for weddings and the mitre that matched it, which had belonged to a previous incumbent whose great uncle had been the Bishop of the Arctic. He must have had an unusually large head because whenever it was used it required a little padding to keep it stable on the visitor, and that made it fiddly when it came off and came on again at the relevant moments in the service.

With the bishop presiding, and his chaplain there too, it was a little crowded in the clerical stalls, so Daniel was sitting on the opposite side, next to the de Floures pew. Bernard and Hugh and Honoria and Alex – in a determined show of family piety at Bernard's insistence – were all sitting in exactly what they wore for Anthony's funeral only ten days before. There was rather a clash of precedence as a result, with not one but two lordships to contend with, the bishop and the patron, and the widow and daughters, who sat in a tearful trio in the front pew. Daniel recalled conducting a funeral in Belgravia, attended by a minor royal representing the Queen, which meant there was a complicated order of precedence dictated by the Lord Chamberlain's office, which required the family to be seated not last, but second from last, that being reserved for the 'Royal Rep' lest lèse-majesté ensue. Daniel had had to bustle up and down the aisle to get the family in before the minor royal arrived, but when she did he did not recognise her because he got her mixed up with her cousin, and there was a terrible moment in the narthex when she kept smiling at him while he kept looking over her shoulder for someone else.

The bishop, typical of his kind, enjoyed his role as chief pastor, partly because it returned a more flattering reflection than most of the things he had to do, and partly because it was easier to please people. He was also good at it, good with a crowd, his personality large and outward-facing, and what was sometimes overbearing at the dinner table or in the office was well-fitted to churches, cathedrals, the House of Lords. He radiated confidence and the parish responded to that, like flowers to sunlight; he was an outsider but with the best of intentions and that too served to convert into excitement some of the anxiety that had fallen over the parish since the day Anthony had died in the pew where today Kath and Dora Sharman, in their unchanging configuration, sat in Sunday best.

They sang hymns which belonged to Ned's Yorkshire chapel background, 'How Great Thou Art', 'To God Be the Glory', which always made Daniel think of rugby songs, and then Katrina Gauchet, his successor as head teacher, gave the address, praising him for his lifelong commitment to the education of the young, his stewardship of the village school, and for his tactful and helpful support in his retirement and her headship.

'Ned was an invaluable friend, always ready, but only when asked, to give advice. He was generous with his time and knowledge too: with the school, as we explore our wartime history, and with me personally. I was very touched by his help trying to track down Hervé's French family. His death has only confirmed our desire to continue "the disinterested pursuit of knowledge", as he liked to say, and to which he dedicated his life.' She turned to Jane and the girls. 'But before any of that, he was a family man, devoted to Jane and his daughters, and our hearts go out to them in their loss.'

Angela read from Ecclesiastes. '*To everything there is a season, and a time to every purpose under the heaven: A time to be born, and a time to die…*'

She faltered, very slightly on 'die' but recovered.

'*A time to plant, and a time to pluck up that which is planted. A time to kill. And a time to heal…*'

Daniel would not have chosen this reading with its patterned insistence that everything in life and death fits to the patterned action of God. It was all very well with a ninety-year-old great-grandmother, with a life well-lived and ready to go, but a man killed at a time which seemed so randomly, cruelly, early was a different matter. But still the parallel cadences sounded and soothed.

'*A time to weep, and a time to laugh; a time to mourn and a time to dance…*'

Please, God, thought Daniel, and prayed for the healing of this community, for the return of its balance and pattern, for justice for Ned and for Anthony, for the person, or persons, unknown who had visited this terrible thing on Champton and its people.

Angela's voice slowed as she approached the end of the passage.

'*That which hath been is now; and that which is to be hath already been; and God requireth that which is past.*'

She went back to the pew at the front and took Jane's hand.

Daniel left his stall, bowed to the cross on the altar, bowed to the bishop and went up into the pulpit. He looked out into the congregation: the Thwaites at the front, the Sharmans at the back, the de Floures in the family pew, Champtonians in their usual clumps, a little displaced here and there by strangers, DS Vanloo, dutiful policeman, Mr Williams and his black-jacketed men, impassive.

'I went to see the bishop last week,' Daniel began, and sensed behind him a rustle of episcopal robes. 'We spoke about what happened to us here at Champton over the past few weeks and I am very grateful for his counsel and his presence with us today.' He half-turned and half-bowed. 'What stayed with me – and has stayed with me all week – was something he said about perception. And it's this: sometimes we have to step back to see what's obvious. Sometimes our preoccupation with what is in front of us means we miss the big picture. Step back, look at the landscape, see how the matter that absorbs all our attention fits into it.'

By now the congregation was settling into the quiet inattention which the faithful of the Church of England bestows on preachers.

'A few weeks ago we met to celebrate Easter. As dawn rose, the darkness of Good Friday was banished, finally, decisively, by the light of the resurrected Christ. Like Mary and the apostles, who went into a graveyard to find a body, did not find it, left it, baffled, we too acclimatise ourselves to living in a world that looks exactly the same but is transformed.'

One of the undertaker's men looked at his watch.

'This miracle of the unexpected provision of life where we expected death is anticipated in the story of God's people, from the Israelites at Meribah, restive, complaining, anxious, thirsty – and then Moses strikes the unyielding rock with his staff and it yields a spring of water and everyone drinks.

'To speak of life-saving refreshment, and life beyond death may seem especially difficult at a time when we are only too aware of the reality of loss.'

Jane Thwaite began to weep. Her daughters held her hand more tightly. Angela gave him a look.

'We know that Ned goes into the mystery of God's eternity, as Anthony did before him, and as we all will; but what we *want* is for him to walk through the door, as if nothing had happened. So what use are trite sentiments about the dead living again in a place we cannot see or hear or visit?' He looked around the congregation. 'We must … we must …'

He faltered. Rather, he stopped speaking, and looked. Silence. After a few seconds people who were looking down looked up. Silence. One of the undertaker's men stood up, thinking they had got to the end and it was time to collect the coffin. Silence. The seconds became twenty, then half a minute, and those who hadn't been listening at all began to think they had been asked to keep a minute's silence for Ned, but had missed it, and gently composed themselves into attitudes of greater solemnity. Two minutes? Rustling behind him, then footsteps.

'Daniel, are you all right?' whispered the bishop's chaplain.

But Daniel was not listening. He was thinking of the moment beside the stream on the morning of Anthony's funeral, when the movement of the alders and the movement of the water thrummed, and he felt that ghost moment, when the membrane between this world and another world was thin.

'Daniel, what's wrong?'

And it was like now, looking into the congregation and seeing for the first time the meaning that lay beyond. And he knew why the murders had happened. And he knew who had done them. And in the thrumming composition sitting in front of him, he picked out one detail, the face of DS Neil Vanloo.

35

Bob Achurch led out the bishop, followed by Daniel and Gareth, two abreast, and then the coffin, with Jane and her daughters bringing up the rear. Once they were outside, the bishop said, 'Are you all right, Daniel? What happened then?'

'I'm sorry, I'm not going to be able to do the committal.'

'Well, I'm not doing it. Gareth, you'll have to. Daniel, do you want to sit down?'

'No, I want to speak to the detective sergeant, the man following my mother down the path.'

Audrey, as near to rushing as could decently be done at a funeral, overtook the Thwaites, followed by Neil Vanloo.

'Daniel, what happened? You looked like you were having a petit mal.'

'Not a petit mal, Mum, a revelation.'

'Well, you must come and drink something. Cup of tea? Whisky?'

'Actually, I need to speak to you,' he said to Neil.

'I thought so. Is there somewhere private?'

'Let's go to the rectory, we can dodge the crowd that way. Mum, will you look after the bishop?'

Audrey's eyes narrowed. 'Yes, of course. But what am I to tell Bernard?'

'Tell him I'll get to the house as soon as I can. And get him to keep people there until I do.'

Jane and her daughters arrived. 'Are you all right, Daniel?'

'Jane, I'm sorry, I can't go with you to the crematorium. The bishop's chaplain will officiate.'

'Yes, of course, but what about you?'

'I'll be fine in a minute. I'll see you back at the house.'

Before any more questions could be asked, and to beat the crowd beginning to pour out of church, he and Neil left and went the long way round to the rectory.

They sat at the kitchen table. The dogs made a fuss of Neil, but quietened more quickly than usual, which made Daniel wonder if he had the mystical powers of a Crocodile Dundee.

'Are you OK, Dan? You look like you could use that drink.'

'I know who did it. I know why. And I think you should send officers to Stella Harper's house.'

36

Bernard stood in the saloon, once more the dispenser of champagne and sandwiches. Only this time his mind was not so much on the cost of his hospitality as the irritating purple prelate, who was not only avoiding him but doing so by trespassing on his rightful role of host. The bishop was at this moment in conversation with Alex, who was feeling the quality of the bands of purple tasselled silk which hung from a sort of cummerbund straining to contain the episcopal circumference. Audrey Clement had ordered Bernard to keep the wine and sandwiches coming until Daniel and Neil Vanloo arrived, and that was especially irritating because the Sharman sisters were nowhere to be found, leaving the waitressing to Mrs Shorely, who brought to customer service the skills of a Mrs Danvers, and Honoria, who appeared to be rather enjoying it. He would not have admitted it, but a part of him did not want his daughter to serve drinks alongside his housekeeper, for it threatened a distinction he wished to preserve. Anne Dollinger was circling the bishop too, and the longer they did that, the longer he would have to wait before he could raise one or two pertinent matters which, as patron of the living, fell to him.

Hugh was talking to Katrina and Hervé Gauchet about complicated genes, which in Canada was nothing unusual: half the population had French and Scottish and native and Métis, for in a frontier country things are apt to get mixed up.

Nathan Liversedge, in his version of Sunday best, was eating a pile of sandwiches and looking uncomfortable as Nicolas Meldrum asked him if he knew what had happened to the colony of bats, an inconveniently protected species from his point of view, that had been discovered in the old stables but seemed now to have gone.

Dot and Norman Staveley were there, facing down Norman's disgrace, which turned out not to be as bad as suspected. Audrey tried to stifle her disappointment when Dot cornered her about the Open Gardens Scheme, trying to convince her to get Theo to come as an added attraction to the rectory's normal offer of jams and chutneys and marmalade. 'I'll ask, Dot, but he's filming a new programme and I don't know if he'll be able to.' Cutting off any further discussion with, 'By the way, I think you're being *so* brave.'

'All Champton is here, all life is here,' thought Bernard. But the mood changed as Jane Thwaite and her daughters arrived back from the crematorium. Jane looked tired, braced herself when she came in and took without hesitation a glass of champagne as soon as it came within reach. Angela and Gillian, the former steely, the latter looking crumpled, stood on either side as people came up to say how sorry they were, and hadn't Angela read beautifully, and how *fond* …

The bishop, retreating backwards to escape Anne Dollinger, had, without realising it, arrived in Bernard's corner of the saloon. 'Bishop, how good of you to come!' The bishop turned to face him. 'May I have a minute with you?'

'Of course, Bernard. I was just discussing your most interesting plans for reordering the church…'

'Plans, plans, plans; just what I wanted to talk to you about…' and taking him by the elbow, he steered him away.

But not all of Champton was there.

Alex was the first to notice the thin column of smoke rising above the lake.

Neil noticed it too as they waited for the patrol car to meet them at the rectory.

'Where's that coming from, Dan?'

The smoke rose in a straight line on that windless afternoon.

'It's from the park. They're burning larch, I think. Nicolas said they were going to clear it from round the lake.'

'That's the wrong kind of smoke.'

Daniel frowned at him, thinking, How do you know the difference between the right and the wrong kind of smoke? And then he realised what it was.

'Neil, the bath house!'

At that moment the squad car turned into the drive, no lights, no sirens, but crunching the gravel as it braked and came to a halt.

Neil rushed outside, and from the kitchen Dan heard the dogs start to bark and scratch.

He followed Neil out to the squad car. He was talking in police-speak to two uniformed officers and saw them off with a slap on the car roof. It lit up with blue light.

'Daniel, we need to get to the bath house – can we take the Land Rover?'

He rushed to get the keys. The dogs were going frantic, mistaking the coming and going as a cue for a walk. Neil was waiting at the Land Rover.

'I'll drive,' he said firmly. Daniel handed over the keys and moments later they creaked and rattled out of the rectory drive and into the park.

'Fire Brigade on its way. And you were right about Mrs Harper.'

'Oh no, no!'

'Dead in a chair, telly still on, curtains drawn. Nobody noticed?'

'It's a tradition here to keep the curtains drawn on the day of a funeral, for when the hearse passes. Out of respect. How did she die?'

'We're not sure. She was in her dressing gown, a mug, a plate and a cake fork on the side table. And a cake on the counter in the kitchen.'

'Walnut?'

'Yes, it was. How did you know?'

'It was her favourite.'

The smoke was rising more thickly now, and as they rounded the trees and turned towards the lake, Daniel saw not only smoke but orange flames leaping from the bath house's windows. From here he could hear a roaring and crackling, the flames reflected in the surface of the lake and also, like a spark, in the windows of the house on the other side of the park. And then another spark of blue that blinked on and off as the squad car arrived. Tiny figures were standing on the terrace watching. As the Land Rover got nearer, Daniel looked at the edge of the lake directly opposite and saw two figures silhouetted by the fire, the uniformed officers, and between them a third who barely came up to their shoulders.

Daniel could tell even from the silhouette that it was Dora Sharman. He ran to her. 'Dora, where's your sister?'

Dora pointed to the bath house, now barely recognisable in a veil of orange fire, the heat so intense they all took half a step backwards as it rolled across the lake. 'She's in there.'

Daniel thought of the priests of Baal, consumed by divine fire. 'Lord, have mercy...' he said out loud.

'She took off after the funeral. She must have seen you and him. Was it in the sermon when you got it?'

'Yes.'

'I thought so. So did she, I reckon. I wondered when you would. What was it?'

'It was seeing you and her, sitting where you always sit, like you always do. Head to one side, hands crossed in your lap.'

'That's how we were taught at Sunday school. But how did you work it out from that?'

'I saw it in the mural. One of the figures, sitting exactly like that, same pose exactly. I see it every Sunday, you and Kath at the back of the church. And there it was in the mural. I realised it had to be one of you, and you told me that you were in Norfolk during the war and Kath stayed. And then it all became clear.'

'What became clear?' asked Neil.

'What happened to Kath. But Dora, did you know?'

'Of course I knew.'

'No, did you know what Kath had done?'

Dora thought for a moment. 'There's knowing and there's knowing.' She glanced at Neil. 'I'm not saying any more about it for now.'

With a terrible crash, the roof of the bath house fell in, a column of sparks spiralling upwards into the smoky air and a hiss of steam where the red-hot timbers spilled into the lake.

On the terrace in front of the house, half a mile away, Alex de Floures thought of the end of *Götterdämmerung*, when Valhalla, ablaze, sank into the waters of the Rhine. 'Fantastic...' he said out loud, but only Honoria heard him.

37

Bernard poured the drinks. Daniel and Neil, Alex, Hugh and Honoria, and Audrey and Theo sat in the library. Through the windows, on the far side of the lake, a fire engine was spraying water from the lake over what was left of the bath house. A crew had been in and found a body. Female, they thought, about five foot three.

Daniel and Neil had brought into the house a faint smell of smoke, like the smell of clothes the day after Bonfire Night, and when anyone caught a whiff of it a sombre feeling fell on them.

Everyone but Audrey. 'Kath Sharman!' she exclaimed. 'How on earth could a woman of her size, and age – a tiny little *bird* – stab and bludgeon two men twice her size to death?'

'Because she knew what she was doing,' said Bernard.

'Yes,' said Daniel, 'I think she did. This place was not only a convalescent hospital in the war.'

'No,' said Bernard. 'It was a training centre for the SOE.'

'SOE?' asked Honoria.

'Special Operations Executive,' said Bernard. 'Men – and women – who were recruited to be dropped behind enemy lines in France and work with the Resistance. They came here to acclimatise themselves to Frenchness, I suppose, and so there were French intelligence officers here too. The painter, he was one. And Kath Sharman, who had been a parlour maid or a kitchen maid, I can't remember which, was one of the staff who stayed on to run the house when the French came. And I suppose events took their course.'

'A love affair!' said Audrey. 'Between a scullery maid and a dashing French officer.'

'It was a love affair, I think, and in the chaos of war and displacement, the scullery maid – I don't think she was a scullery maid, but never mind that for now – crossed the line. I don't mean between above stairs and below stairs, that distinction had already faded, or between proper and improper – what did that mean once the world was on fire? It was the distinction between soldier and civilian, which the French, especially the artistic types, like you, Alex, never seemed to find important, as we did.'

Honoria looked puzzled. 'Are you saying Kath Sharman was in the SOE, Daddy?'

'No, of course not. Or could she have been?'

Audrey spoke up. 'She need not have been. She was intelligent, she was resourceful – perhaps you did not see that in her, being only a housemaid? Perhaps none of us did; they were just the spinster sisters who lived in a little cottage in a place where people still point at planes. But lots of women whom no one thought much of did extraordinary things in the war.'

'And up at the house,' Bernard said, 'they were a band of brothers, and sisters, and Kath was one of them.'

'Bit more than a sister, Dad,' said Alex. 'I do find it extraordinary that they trained her to be a killer.'

'She was in love, I suppose.'

'And so was he,' said Daniel, 'which is why he painted her in the bath house mural.'

'Which one is she?'

'The lover.'

'That was Kath Sharman?'

'Yes, it was. I didn't see it at first, because, like you, it didn't occur to me that Kath could be a subject for a painter. I did not see her as he did.'

'That's becoming rather a theme,' said Honoria.

Daniel went on. 'So – a love affair, formed in the turmoil of war, everything was uncertain, the world shook.'

'And her lover, the painter chap,' said Bernard, 'was on the plane that crashed in the park. She must have heard it. Perhaps she saw it? We weren't here when it happened. I was very sorry to hear he had died, but he was not the only one. We did not dwell on such things. Better to let them fade away.'

'But he left a record in the mural, unseen, or seen by hardly any, in the bath house. It was only when I stood back and stopped looking that I recognised her in it. From her shape, her outline, the pose. That's how she sits in church, her head at exactly that angle. I noticed it because she was one of the few who really listened when I preached.'

A twinge of embarrassment passed over them, but not Bernard, who did not notice.

'And so you realised that Kath had a past, a connection to the French. An intimate connection,' he said.

'And a child,' said Neil.

Bernard nodded. 'Yes, she could have. I remember her appearing at Rudnam, it must have been 1943, or thereabouts, and Dora, who was already there looking after my mama, rather fussing over her.'

'She'd had the baby?'

'I suppose she must have. It was how they dealt with things in those days, my papa and the rector. Unmarried pregnant servants were sent away to Norfolk or up to Argyll to have the baby quietly, and then the child was taken in.'

Audrey nodded. 'And then she had to come back and everyone would have known, and no one would have said anything, and there she was, grieving a lover she couldn't talk about, and the loss of a child she couldn't talk about. So she buried them both, in memory, in feeling, in her heart. How terribly sad.'

'Canon Dolben told me something about that—' Daniel began to say, but Neil interrupted.

'Hervé Gauchet?'

'I think so, don't you? So he was near to her. But I don't think he knows that Kath is his mother.'

'Was his mother,' Honoria corrected. 'But none of this explains why she killed Anthony and Ned.'

Daniel said, 'I think I know. Where did Kath and Dora always sit?'

'At the back, on the left,' said Audrey.

'At the back. Why?'

'Because it's Champton, and everything fills up from the back,' said Alex.

Daniel shook his head, 'Because you won't be observed.'

'Doing what?'

'Crying. Flinty Kath, who never shed a tear and looked at the world with an unblinking eye. How could she share, or even show, her grief? So she sat at the back, and it became her place, and only Dora could see her tears, springing like water from the rock.'

'What set it all off?' asked Bernard.

'Something I said. I announced plans to reorder the church. The back pew, *her* pew, was going to be removed – remember how much had been taken away from her? So the thought of losing what little she had, her place in church, her place of private grief, was unbearable. The thought of that was too much, and something broke within her. I had no idea.'

Audrey spoke. 'But why kill Anthony? She came to church and saw him praying at the back – in her place, was that it?'

'He wasn't praying.'

'He was kneeling on a hassock in a pew. What else was he doing?'

'Do you remember there was talk of a reprieve for the back pews?' said Daniel. 'If they were medieval, as someone said, then removing them would be much more difficult. But when Bernard and I looked through Anthony's papers the other day – Neil, you returned them – I found a carpenters' workbook from the 1880s. There was an entry for church fittings. I can't think of any woodwork that went in then apart from – possibly – pews. If they were made by an estate carpenter in the 1880s, he would have left his mark on them. I think that's what Anthony was doing, looking for the maker's mark to see if the pews were Victorian, good diligent churchwarden that he was. If they were, then they could come out, and Kath would lose her place.'

Audrey still looked puzzled. 'But how did she know that's what he was doing?'

'It was Open Day. Anthony was in his office, by the old kitchen. Kath and Dora were on duty, showing people how the servants had lived, in the kitchen and in the attics. I remember her grumbling about the stairs. Alex drove Anthony away, and he left the carpenter's workbook open on his desk. Kath must have seen it and understood what it meant. And she went up to the church to check the pews. So did Anthony. I'm afraid she couldn't let him tell anyone what he'd found.'

'So she killed him. My God!'

'Yes. She took a pair of secateurs – not a very efficient murder weapon, as it happens. But she knew how to kill someone. Pulled his head back and stabbed the point of the blade into the carotid. He would have lost consciousness in seconds. And then she just went home, unobserved. Only Dora would have noticed her absence.'

'And Ned?

'Ned trespassed on her past. He was helping Katrina Gauchet with the school project for the Second World War anniversary next year. They were going to recreate what it was like in Champton during the war. He was interviewing people who'd lived through it, asking questions about the Free French. He tracked down old Gilbert Drage in his garden, hardening off his dahlias, or whatever it was. Gilbert remembered them, in fact he rather ranted about them – mercenaries, cut-throats and rapists – and next door sitting at her window was Kath Sharman, I suppose. And the thought that old Gilbert might have unknowingly given her secret away was ... too much.'

'And having murdered once, she could murder again,' said Audrey.

'Yes,' said Daniel, 'that did it for Ned, I'm afraid. That and the mural. It fascinated him and, being Ned, he decided to make a photographic record. I don't know if Kath saw him hanging around or if she was already there. I think she was the regular visitor, by the way. Vagrants don't often wash up behind them. And she took the anchor… what did Nathan call it?'

'Grapnel.'

'And she must have crept up behind him and hit him with it and rolled his body into the lake.'

'But she would have been covered in blood,' said Alex. 'And surely stabbing someone in the carotid artery would mean gallons of blood too?'

'She was standing behind Anthony, remember, and the blood would have sprayed out in front of him. And with Ned? She was in the bath house, she could have cleaned herself up there. Besides, she always wore that dark coat and hat, so the blood wouldn't have shown up, and in any case who would have seen her, or noticed her if they had?'

'Sometimes a dam bursts when there's a murder,' said Neil, 'and there's another, and another.'

'Thank God only two,' said Honoria.

'Not only two,' said Daniel. 'I'm sorry to tell you all that Stella Harper was found dead at home a little while ago.'

A cry of surprise went round the room. 'I wondered why she wasn't at the funeral,' said Audrey.

Neil intervened. 'We can't say anything about that at the moment.'

'Pews!' Theo exclaimed. 'Pews. When I was round at the Sharmans', Dora said Stella had given up the fight to save the pews. Kath looked startled by it; I thought it was an odd reaction. But that's why. Stella was the pews' main defender. And then she wasn't.'

'What happened?' asked Daniel. 'Stella was never one to give up the fight...' And then, 'Mum, was it you?'

Audrey sat up straighter. 'I spoke to her about it. I made my case. Reason prevailed.'

'Would that be enough to make Kath want to kill her, though?' asked Honoria.

'Betrayal,' said Bernard, 'unbearable for her by then. And she was not a forgiving woman.'

Audrey said, 'Walnut cake.'

'Walnut cake?'

'When I came back from the pub yesterday' – she looked round the room – 'to get the sherry for your kidneys – we'd run out thanks to the bishop coming to call – on the way home I saw Kath on Stella Harper's doorstep with a cake tin. She adored Kath's walnut cake. Was that what it was?'

'Like I said, Mrs Clement, we can't say anything about—'

'But how did Kath know about poisons?' Theo asked.

'Her father was a gamekeeper here,' said Bernard. 'They kept arsenic and strychnine, and all kinds of things. Edgy's probably got some in his shed.'

'And don't forget there was a laboratory here in the war,' said Daniel. 'I don't imagine they were messing around with bicarbonate of soda and copper sulphate. But wasn't it disposed of after the war?'

'No,' said Bernard, 'when we came back it was as if they'd done a moonlight flit. They just left everything.'

Alex nodded. 'One of the outhouses was full of test tubes and condensers and jar after jar of God knows what. I used a load of them in my degree show.'

'She must have been so desperate,' said Honoria. 'A lifelong hurt, a secret, the shame, all about to be discovered. And her son. Jesus, what will Hervé think when this comes out?'

'I don't know. I wonder if that's why she decided to end it? She couldn't face Hervé finding out who she was and what she'd done.'

38

St Mary's Champton, flower of the English Perpendicular, had become yet more floral now the weekend of the flower festival had arrived.

There had been rather a sharp debate about whether it should go ahead at all. Anne Dollinger thought it should be cancelled, as a mark of respect for Stella Harper, 'without whom our flower festival would be a sorry thing indeed'. Others thought the mood of festival at odds with a Champton still in mourning for four of its own, for it was indeed Kath Sharman's body that the firemen recovered from the charred timbers and sooty plaster festoons of the bath house.

But Audrey best caught the mood when she remarked that nature and faith both proclaim that life goes on, and no matter how heavy the loss, green shoots will come, and with them a new mood of hope. 'Just the ticket, for *all* of us!'

'Hear hear,' said Norman Staveley, who with a dented reputation and a reminder to all that his prestige was an expression of neither nature nor virtue, was experiencing a surprising renewal himself, in his life and in his marriage. Dot smiled.

Margaret Porteous protested, in an effort to intrude her authority into the gap left by Stella, and suggested the theme might be changed to something more solemn. 'Remembrance', perhaps, something with rosemary and lilies? But Audrey countered with the inarguable point that 'The Final Frontier', the theme chosen long before the events of the past few weeks, could not be more apt for those who had gone beyond the bourn from which no traveller returns.

Green shoots were not so much in evidence; rather, it looked like a series of small explosions had been frozen in time, with several ladies settling on bursts of flaming colour to suggest the excitement of what Mrs Braines' display called 'Cape Carnival'.

Others had gone for the spacious firmament on high, none with more enthusiasm than Alex and Honoria, who made heavenly bodies from globes of oasis, studded them with flowers, hung them on rods and string, and set them in orbital motion overhead, from where, freshly watered, they dripped onto the visitors below.

Eppur si muove, thought Daniel, but they nearly did not, for since the disappearance of Edgy and Nathan, gone in the night from Champton to another demesne, there were fewer hands able and willing to undertake the infrastructure the display required. Theo, who unlike his brother was actually quite handy, helped, and helped too when Alex's first-time broken heart wrecked his composure. Daniel reproached himself for this – for having failed to understand the nature of Nathan's and Alex's relationship and for that reason being unavailable, as his brother was, to be comfort, health and strength to one so wounded. A good lesson in the rudiments of ministry and pastoral care for Theo to take with him into *Clerical and Medical*, or whatever the show was called.

Eppur si muove, Daniel thought again, watching from the organ bench in the narrow gallery at the west end of the nave, where once musicians had accompanied, in tuneless ensemble, the worshippers beneath. Today that space was occupied by the organ, its dapper pipework facing front, and beneath it the console, three manuals, on which Daniel had been playing simple English eighteenth-century pieces that suited both instrument and player. He had from time to time, for his own amusement, interpolated phrases from every flower song he could think of, 'The Honeysuckle and the Bee', 'Red Roses for a Blue Lady', and the flower duet from *Lakmé*, which did cause a ripple of notice because everyone recognised it from the British Airways advert.

The iron gates to the de Floures tombs were open and Margaret Porteous, upon whom the mantles of both Anthony and Ned had fallen, was recounting the histories of its occupants with the indulgent tone of someone telling family stories rather than the salient points of the Glorious Revolution. What stories would be told of the present generation and the dark and narrow shadow that fell across the incumbency of Bernard? The present Lord de Floures was untroubled by the opinion of posterity, but much exercised by the matter of loss adjusters and buildings insurance and how the tragic loss of the bath house might be turned to profit, a matter he was at that moment discussing with Nicolas Meldrum in the library.

Jane Thwaite was in church, with Angela and Gillian, her daughters taking it in turns to spend the weekend with their mother as she adjusted to the widowhood so brutally forced upon her. And then Daniel saw the Gauchets, inspecting the school's display on the theme of Space Exploration; and with them was Dora Sharman, for the first time in public since her sister's terrible death, and the revelations about her terrible deeds. Hervé, finally together with the auntie he did not know he had, would have been the headline, had not the revelation of that heritage come in so ghastly a way.

Daniel frowned. There were the Thwaites and there was Dora, and no one knew yet what she had known of Kath's murderous enterprise. He did not think Angela would tolerate Dora's presence, on parade, in public, as if justice had been served and equilibrium restored. As he watched, the Thwaites turned one corner and the Gauchets and Dora another, and the two groups were suddenly standing in front of each other, with nowhere to go. He could not tell if anyone else had noticed this happen. The slow, fluid dynamics of people moving and stopping and moving again obscured the drama of the encounter, the daughter of the victim meeting the sister of his murderer.

It occurred to Daniel that his vantage point, at height and at distance, was apt, for only from height and distance were the dynamics of the crowd discernible. Neil Vanloo was the same, he thought, at a different angle and different height, but seeing, as he saw, the patterns that cannot be seen by those close to the action. He had called round one afternoon in the days after the revelations, when their official business was done, and asked to see the church properly. He turned out to be better informed about ecclesiastical buildings than he had appeared to be, knowing his aumbry from his sedilia, and the tour had lengthened, the conversation too, and as evening came they stood at the top of the tower, looking across the rectory towards the house. In the shadows cast by the dropping sun, an old pattern was revealed, of strips of land cultivated in the Middle Ages, the outline of a huddle of buildings and earthworks that must have been older even than the de Floures.

And then Angela nodded at Dora, Dora nodded back, the Gauchets broke to the right and the Thwaites to the opposite side. And as they passed and merged once again into the slow currents of the crowd, Daniel turned back to the organ, pushed in one stop, pulled out another, and began to play a neat little voluntary by Maurice Greene, into which he skilfully interpolated the 'Flower Song' from *Carmen*.

ACKNOWLEDGEMENTS

I would like to thank Alan Samson, Federico Andornino, Lucinda McNeile, Virginia Woolstencroft and all at Orion.

Tim Bates and all at PFD

The Margaret Thatcher Funeral Lunch Club

The Deanery Chapter of Higham

The Revd Michael Thompson

The Revd Canon Dr Robin Ward

The Earl and Countess Spencer

Baroness Professor Sue Black

Dr Frank Salmon

Cllr Andy Coles

The Efficient Baxter

... and all the people who stop to talk to vicars.

ABOUT THE AUTHOR

The Reverend Richard Coles is the presenter of Saturday Live on BBC Radio 4. He is also the only vicar in Britain to have had a number-one hit single and appeared on Strictly Come Dancing. He read Theology at King's College London and after ordination worked as a curate in Lincolnshire, London and Northamptonshire. He is the author of many works of non-fiction – including the *Sunday Times* bestseller *The Madness of Grief* – and the Canon Clement mystery series. @RevRichardColes.